Species Unknown

A novel of The Watch

By

Dan Carlson

Acknowledgements

Becoming a novelist has been a lifelong dream and I couldn't have done it without the help of wonderful people who believed in me along the way. Heartfelt thanks to Henry, Rebekah, Alex, Roy, Roxanne and Dan for reading the first drafts and making suggestions. A shout out to Tommy for telling me to keep at it and always giving great input. Thanks to Ted, Kevin, Erin and the team at The Creative Way for the ideas, critiques and advice along the journey. I thank all my friends and family in the Black Hills and Nebraska Panhandle who've been rooting for me eager to see how this project turned out. To my wife, Karen, whose love, encouragement and faith in me helped me through the valleys and over the peaks. I love you. Thank you Yeshua, without whom my life would be pointless. And my thanks to you, my readers, for taking a chance on this first novel by an unknown author. I sincerely hope you enjoy it.

Table of Contents

Species Unknown

Chapter One

The gentle patter of the rain on the tent had a soothing, almost hypnotic effect that made it difficult to stay awake. Nonetheless, Dr. Jake Sanders lay with his eyes open, watching small droplets silhouetted by the light of the dying campfire outside as they rolled down the sides of the small dome-shaped tent and merged to form larger ones. He loved camping, especially this part of it. Listening to the night sounds of the forest coming alive in a great concert of bizarre music involving bugs, birds, beasts and whatever weather nature decided to serve up.

Jake looked down as he stroked his wife's hair, her head resting on his shoulder as slow, heavy breathing signaled her surrender to sleep. Despite a long day of hiking through rugged country, her hair still smelled nice to him. Ten years had passed since they met in grad school and his love for her had grown stronger with each passing day. His mind wandered to reflect on what had been the best decade of his life.

Doctors Jacob and Abigail Sanders had the good fortune of choosing the right fields at the right time in a world where more people and political interests were showing greater concern about humanity's interaction with nature and its resources. Gail was a preeminent botanist specializing in North American plant ecosystems. Jake, a zoologist, was renowned for his research and writings about the roles and impacts of predatory species on their ecologies. The cycle of life involving the predator, the prey, and natural reclamation of the leftovers fascinated him. He was one of few scientists highly regarded both by environmental preservationists and multiuse conservationists, making his solid, science-based conclusions in high demand at the lecture halls of academia. One of his few faults made him prefer field research over public settings. Dr. Jake Sanders was not an outgoing conversationalist, preferring podiums over people in close proximity because he was prone to verbal and physical clumsiness during initial personal interactions.

That socially awkward personality quirk was the trigger that had initially attracted Gail to him, though his athletic build, square jaw, piercing blue eyes and longer-than-stylish sandy hair did not go unnoticed. They were both doing field research in Yellowstone National Park in preparation for their respective doctoral dissertations and happened to be staying at the same campground. Jake would sit alone in a fold-up camp chair beside a small fire outside his tent each evening, staring into the flames as one searches for an artist's hidden expressions in a gallery masterpiece.

Gail was vivacious, smart and outgoing with a contagious laugh and stunning beauty, never lacking male suitors wherever she went. But eventually they'd all revealed their motivations by pressuring her for exclusive commitment or sexual intimacy, both of which she'd decided as a teen to preserve for her life's one true love. She did, however, enjoy the attention and Jake's lack of it after two weeks of exchanging pleasantries in passing at the campground presented her with a rare challenge.

She was camped two sites down from Jake and decided to make the first move late one evening as he stared into his campfire again. Slipping from the darkness into the fire's flickering circle of light opposite Jake, uncharacteristic nervousness made her speak more abruptly than she'd intended.

"Hi, I'm Gail. I was going ..."

Startled by an unexpected voice and sudden angelic apparition before him, Jake attempted to stand, caught a foot on a leg of his chair, flipped over backwards and hit his head on something hard. When he came to his senses, his head was cradled in the lap of a lovely young woman applying gentle pressure to something soft on the back of his skull. A first-aid kit lay open beside him.

"I am soooo sorry!" Gail said with a sincere look of concern in her soft, brown eyes. "Are you okay? There's just a small cut on the back of your head and you'll have a bump, but I don't think it's too bad. Do you want me to call the ranger station?"

Jake experienced a flood of conflicting emotion. Anger over someone sneaking up on him flipped to embarrassment over allowing that to happen, and staring into Gail's perfect face framed by flawless, straight, shoulder-length brown hair caused him to blurt out, "You're real!"

Gail smiled as she let out a short laugh, "Well I'm glad we established that. How bad does it hurt?"

"Does what hurt?" asked Jake before turning beet red.

"You're head, silly. You feel good enough to sit up back in your chair?"

"What chair? Oh that chair. No, I think we'd better keep me like this a bit longer," replied Jake.

"C'mon, up you go mister," Gail smiled as she helped Jake sit up, taking his own hand to replace hers on his head. "You'll be fine. How about we start over? My name is Abigail, but my friends call me Gail."

"Jake Sanders," came the reply. "What brought you to my campfire?"

"I'm going on a hike tomorrow, a day trip around Lewis Lake. Care to join me?"

Some would call it fate, others Divine Providence. Jake had himself planned to hike near Lewis Lake the following day to look for evidence of a small pack of wolves reported in that area. Gail was hoping to collect fungus samples off the remains of trees felled by forest fires. Their conversation over the next few minutes, and during the following day's activity, sparked mutual admiration and affection that soon after led to deeper friendship, falling in love, and a life together the couple could have only dreamed of.

A flash of lightning lit up the tent and Gail stirred. They'd spent the day scouting in preparation for an environmental impact statement for the U.S. Forest Service concerning prospects for sustainable commercial logging around the area in which they were camped. At five-feet, four and a perfectly proportioned 120 pounds, Gail was a foot shorter and almost 90 pounds lighter than her husband, and she had to work hard to match his stride as they covered several miles through the forested hills. It had been a tiring but enjoyable day, and when the sun went down that evening with thunder rumbling in the distance, she'd asked to delay their usual nightly fireside banter and retire to their tent early.

The Bearlodge Mountains of northeast Wyoming are an extension of the Black Hills formation straddling the state's border with South Dakota. More than 90 percent of the land in the Black Hills is covered with ponderosa pine, giving them a dark appearance when viewed from a distance, hence the name. Timber was a big industry in the region, but had come under increasing scrutiny by environmental organizations seeking to have more land set aside as designated wilderness and a lot less logging. Jake and Gail had earned the respect of both industry and environment advocates when they'd worked on similar projects in Pacific Northwest because their conclusions were known for objectivity. As a result, the couple was frequently called upon to evaluate the impact a timber harvest might have within a certain environment, which, in this case, was a remote section of the Black Hills National Forest north of the town of Sundance, Wyoming.

A clap of thunder brought Jake back from his thoughts of the past to the present as the rain came down a bit harder. Gail snuggled even closer in their sleeping bag as he breathed deep through his nose to experience the fresh scent of rain in a pine forest. He was nearly asleep when an odd odor hit his nostrils, interrupting his journey into a rather pleasant dream.

Jake was jolted back to wakefulness by the scent of what he knew had to be an animal. The odor was bad, but not like that of a skunk, and the sound of wind in the pines outside meant whatever it was could still be a ways off. It was not the scent of an elk, which can be strong in September, nor was it that of a large barnyard animal such as a cow or horse. It was more like a combination of a rotting carcass and sewage. Lightning flashed again, and as quickly as he had noticed its arrival, the scent was gone. It didn't take long for Dr. Jake Sanders to fall into restless sleep.

♦ ♦ ♦

Five miles away and three hours later, Ralph Masters was a rancher with a problem. Six times in the last three weeks, while checking his herd on land he leased east of Devil's Tower, he'd come across the remains of one of his calves. What troubled him nearly as much as the hit each kill made to his wallet was the puzzling way each calf had been killed. All had broken necks or spines and their tongues, livers, hearts and, in two cases, kidneys were torn out.

Masters, a third-generation rancher in the Black Hills, had lost livestock to predators before but never like this. Coyotes favored young animals such as lambs and newborn calves. They often hunted in small packs or pairs during calving season, cut an animal off from the herd, and literally tore it to shreds. The result was bones and pieces of the victim scattered over a fairly large area. Recently cougars had become the apex predator in the area, but they also killed differently. A cougar would ambush its prey, usually from above, and sink its fangs into the victim's throat or neck while the hind claws disemboweled the animal. The cat would then eat, drag the carcass to a hiding place, cover it with brush, grass or twigs, and return over the next several days to feed on one kill. Lately a few black bears had been sighted in the Black Hills, likely ousted from the Big Horn Mountains to the west in search of a territory of their own, but attacks on livestock by them were unheard of in the area.

The recent kills were like nothing Masters had encountered in 35 years of ranching. The carcasses were left uncovered. There were no claw marks anywhere on the bodies, and the abdominal cavities had been ripped open as though something incredibly powerful had grabbed the calves on either side and pulled them open like plastic food-storage bags. The jaws of the dead calves were broken and pulled apart with the tongues forcibly ripped out. And then there were the tracks…or, more accurately, the lack of them. It had been dry the last month and the ground was hard, which was part of the problem. But in two of the cases where calves were killed in green pasture, the grass was stomped down by whatever was doing the killing and it was big. Very, very big.

It took Masters two long strides to move between the depressed areas on the grass, and, at a lean six-foot two, Masters had a pretty long stride himself. The evening's rain had been hard and left the ground wet enough for Masters to hope he could get a track going on his calf killer. He checked his watch. It read 1 a.m. His old scoped Winchester Model 70 .30-06 bolt-action rifle lay next to him on the bench seat of his 1997 Ford pickup as he pulled out of the driveway and headed up the road toward the pasture. Ralph Masters was loaded for bear. The calf killer was not a bear.

Chapter Two

Simon Standing Elk and his companions had been in the sweat lodge since shortly after sunset. Each of the eight men present, all Lakota in their mid-thirties and forties, was hoping to take something back from the experience to enrich their lives. Though not a full-fledged vision quest, the lodge and its attendant ceremonies were an opportunity for the sharing of stories, focusing on heritage, meditation, and what some believed to be a glimpse into the spiritual realm.

Simon rocked gently forward and backward as he inhaled the steam from the hot rocks before him. His life had not been an easy one. Like so many of his people, he had wrestled with alcoholism but overcame the addiction with the help of his father, a man determined to pass on to his son the ways of the ancient ones. Though sober nearly four years, Simon looked older than his 42 years. Sweat dripped from his deep brown brow and onto his thighs, a traditional lion cloth his only attire. Whether the heat of the lodge summoned the visions or induced some psycho-physiological state that fostered the imagination, Simon did not know or care. He was only aware that these sessions in the sweat lodge provided him with an escape from reality he'd once only found in a bottle. Sweat poured from his body, but he was unaware of it. He had left the lodge nearly a half-hour earlier as steamy vapors ushered him into a familiar alternate realm where he hoped his spirit guide would meet him.

Simon was walking through a forest, even as his physical body sat in the sweat lodge at the foot of Bear Butte, the sacred mountain near Sturgis, South Dakota, where many of his people came to seek enlightenment, commune with nature and pray. He was on a spiritual journey, encountering the usual creatures he saw in this forest. There were the birds, the deer, the elk and fox but no sign yet of his spirit guide. He turned a corner in the path and saw him. The old black bear was seated on a granite boulder, weeping.

"Why does my old friend shed tears?" he asked.

"I cry not for myself," replied the bear. "For the time of my kind in these woods came to an end long ago. I cry not for what has happened, but for what is about to happen."

"And what, old bear, is it that you foresee?"

"The fabric of what is, what was, and what will be is fragile," replied the bear. "And this night it shall be rent with great violence."

"I do not understand, wise one," said Simon.

"Nor do I," the black bear replied turning to look directly into the Native American's eyes. "For these are matters known and understood only by The Great Spirit whom we all serve, and it is He who must guide you through what is to come."

"But I have always come to you for guidance, old friend."

"And in doing so you have received only a vision of Truth as if veiled by the lake mists of morning," answered the bear. "Those who do not know the Way seek after it by whatever means are available to them. When the True Way becomes known, then the old passes away. This will be our last meeting Simon Standing Elk, for soon the Way and Truth will reveal themselves in things you do not now understand. You must now return to the sweat lodge, but take care. What you encounter as you travel back will test the measure of man you have become."

With that the black bear lurched forward onto all four feet and ambled away down the forest path, never looking back. Simon watched the bear disappear into the brush with a heavy heart. He was contemplating the strange words the animal had spoken when he sensed a presence behind him and turned.

There is a terror so deep, so intense, that it can only be understood by those who have experienced it. It disables the body, causes the mind to go blank and tears at the heart of one's soul. Such was the terror Simon understood when he looked upward into the face of evil itself.

"Simon! Simon! Snap out of it!" shouted Gary Yellow Hawk as he and his two companions dragged Simon from the sweat lodge.

"What has happened to him?" asked Tim Tall Oaks. "Should we go up to the Visitor's Center and call an ambulance?"

A small crowd of Native American campers, summoned by the commotion outside the sweat lodge, was beginning to gather around the men who had been inside.

"Wait a minute," said Yellow Hawk. "He's coming around! But what is he saying? I can't make it out."

"Yakwawi," whispered Simon Standing Elk between gasps of terror as if wakening from a hellish nightmare. "Yakwawi!"

A hush fell over the two-dozen or so people gathered in a loose semicircle around the men. Yellow Hawk was kneeling beside Simon, helping him up to a sitting position while Tall Oaks offered him a drink from the jug of cold water kept near the sweat lodge door for emergencies. The crowd let out a collective gasp as Simon was raised into the light cast by the campfire. His once jet-black hair was now as white as fresh fallen snow. He took a deep drink of water and began to shake, entering a state of shock.

"Yakwawi," Simon said again and again with rising volume, his voice trembling as his body shook. "Yakwawi has returned!"

◆ ◆ ◆

The kill was a fresh one. No more than an hour old, this one was a heifer that had been carrying a calf. Ralph Masters cussed under his breath. The same organs were missing, and now the unborn future of his herd was apparently also on the menu. Unlike the previous kills, this time there were tracks everywhere. At least they looked like tracks. Masters worked the bolt-action of his rifle to chamber a round and started off toward the tree line in the direction the large depressions in the pasture grass led. Every few steps the man's flashlight beam revealed splotches of blood on the ground, a trail that could be followed. The wind shifted slightly and the rancher caught a whiff of the rankest smell he had ever experienced. His adrenaline kicked in and the hunt was on.

It remained motionless, peering at the rancher from behind a large pine tree. It had watched the human arrive at the kill even as it finished its meal in the shadows. It was not afraid. It was not curious. It had no inclination to flee the man with the rifle. It really was capable of only one expression of emotion or, more accurately, a fomenting of the worst of them into one.

Hate, anger, rage, and a lust for blood began to well up in its massive frame for the second time that night.

The stench grew stronger, on the verge of being overpowering. Nonetheless, Masters pressed on. His own anger at whatever had been eating his livelihood had overtaken any sense of caution his years as a hunter had taught him. He had a gun powerful enough to handle any animal the region's forests could send into his sights, and he had a major desire to use it.

The rancher switched off the flashlight he was carrying in his left hand and stuffed it butt-end first into the back pocket of his Wrangler denims. He switched on the Streamlight ProTac tactical light he'd taped to the forward stock of his rifle and turned the magnification setting on his riflescope down to 2.5X. It was going to be close-in work. Now less than 30 yards from the trees, the powerful beam cast by his light glided slowly back and forth, up and down. He knew his cattle killer was close and probably watching him as he clicked the safety into the fire position.

The creature watched the brilliant flashlight beam sweeping the tree line and edging closer. It did not move, knowing the crunch of forest debris beneath its enormous feet would betray its position to the closing rancher. The human had no idea of the strength and power it possessed and it sensed the kill was going to be almost too easy. Then the beam of light crept upward across the massive form until it centered on two large glowing red orbs nearly 12 feet above the forest floor.

It happened so quickly Masters had no time to experience terror at the moment of his death. His final thought of total bewilderment was, *"Nothing that big can move that fast."* The beast had closed the 15 yards between them before the rancher could properly shoulder his rifle and was abruptly airborne, his gun sailing off into the night. It had grabbed him by the head and belt, lifting him into the air in one fast movement. Four great fangs crushed the rancher's neck and throat on the way up. He was already dead when it thrust him downward with incredible force, snapping his spine in two like a dried stick.

Rage became mixed with curiosity as the flavor of a new blood trickled down the beast's throat. The taste was different and pleasing. The kill had been easy. It sank down on its haunches over the dead man and began to feed, experiencing sadistic pleasure as it understood it soon would enjoy feasting on more of these creatures so easily killed and ripped open. They were plentiful, and it knew where to find more.

Chapter Three

The nice thing about early fall camping in the Black Hills is that most of the designated camping areas are pretty much deserted, or so thought Jake Sanders as he watched Gail preparing breakfast on the Coleman camp stove. He had risen early and caught a couple of fat trout in a stream that ran by the campsite at the base of a short incline. The smell of fresh fish, eggs and toast enhanced his hunger. Gail had volunteered to cook, not out of any allegiance to a traditionally prescribed female role, but because she was better at it. The Sanders made a point of eating a hearty breakfast because lunch was usually a light snack from a daypack when they were on assignment.

Jake sat on a log near the tent and allowed his eyes to move across the form of the woman he loved. Gail was wearing her long brown hair in a single ponytail that brushed the back of her gray sweatshirt as she scrambled eggs on the griddle. Her navy blue leggings reached downward into a pair light blue wool socks emerging from her Danner hiking boots. To Jake Sanders, his wife was as beautiful on this morning as she had ever been.

Gail could feel Jake's eyes on her and she smiled at the toast she was making on the second burner. It seemed more like nine weeks than nine years since Jake had popped the question. Ruggedly handsome, tall, strong, kind and intelligent, he was everything she'd hoped for in a man. What's more, she knew they could talk about anything under the sun. They both communicated their feelings, ideas and needs without reservation and that is why, nearly a decade after their first hike, they still had not had anything that could be called a real fight.

There's nothing quite like a sunny and mild fall morning in the Black Hills. The fresh smell of the pines mingled with the previous night's rain, the breakfast and fresh coffee to create ideal atmosphere in the camp. Gail walked over to Jake with a plate of food and large mug of black coffee.

"I was reviewing the last couple of days in my mind, Jake," Gail began, "And I think I have the data I need to form an opinion. How about you?"

"My opinion is that we ought to limit additional exploration this morning to our tent," replied Jake with a grin as he accepted the hot tin plate.

"We'll have ample time for that once we get this report filed. Not that I don't think your suggestion has merit Doctor Sanders," Gail added with a smile of her own. "But didn't you want to walk that ridge about a mile southwest of here to look for cat sign?"

Jake took a sip of coffee before he answered. "I've been mulling that over in my mind. We've been out here nearly a week and seen only one set of cougar tracks. Since those were several days old and made by a young male on the outside eastern edge of the proposed cut, I'm inclined to let them go ahead with this one."

"Me too," said Gail. She was seated on the log next to Jake and picking a pine needle out of her eggs. "But we ought to walk the southwest ridge again anyway to be sure… don't you think?"

Jake didn't answer right away. He had just looked southwest and noticed a group of vultures circling in the distance beyond the ridge they were discussing. Something had died, or was in the process. Nature was good about cleaning up her own messes and the birds would probably have whatever it was picked to the bone by sundown. Nevertheless, it could be a mountain lion kill. They were far more common than bears in the Black Hills and, unlike their heavier counterpart at the top of the forest food chain, they were exclusively carnivorous.

Gail had also noticed the birds as their tightening circle slowly descended. She glanced sideways at Jake as he rose and brushed toast crumbs from his jeans and the front of his khaki shirt. Her attention returned to the birds as Jake headed for the camp stove with coffee mug in hand.

Jake had just finished refilling it when he sensed something was wrong. He looked up and into the forest beyond the campsite. What was it? He was asking himself when it hit him. Total silence. Not a bird, not an insect, not a squirrel…none of the sounds that had been there moments before. The silence was complete. Then came the odor.

"Gail, honey, do you….?" Jake turned toward his wife and froze. It was immense, 12 feet tall if it was an inch. The massive shoulders were more than five feet across. Covered with short, coarse fur so black it seemed to suck light in, almost giving the illusion of being a hole in the forest, but this was no illusion. It was a hideous nightmare that defied physics by being able to sneak up on the camp so silently. Even in the brightening daylight, intense red eyes glared at Jake as it stood perfectly still behind the log Gail was seated on. All of the fears Dr. Jake Sanders had ever experienced in his life combined into one intense burst of terror would not have come close to what he experienced at that instant.

◆ ◆ ◆

Julie Reed was the newest addition to the Crook County Sheriff's Office. A recent graduate from law enforcement school, the 27-year-old blonde was not having a good morning as she raced down the gravel road in one of the department's upgraded Dodge Durango SUVs.

A bowhunter that Ralph Masters had given permission to hunt on his leased land had come across the rancher's truck and remains shortly before sunrise. In spite of the fact that Reed was the first deputy on the scene, she was relegated to errand girl as soon as more senior deputies showed up. She was the lone woman on the department payroll, with the exception of the dispatcher, Nancy, and was having a difficult time getting some on the force to take her seriously as a cop. Now, while others got to investigate what was obviously a suspicious death, she'd been sent to find two nature scientists supposedly camped northeast of the crime scene to see if they could come and help determine what had killed Masters.

Julie suspected her looks were part of the problem. In addition to being a fitness fanatic, a former regional title-winning women's rodeo calf roper and a barrel racer, Julie Reed was as deadly as she was beautiful. She'd traveled to China when she was 19 to study martial arts, thanks to financial help from her supportive father, and became the youngest American woman to earn the Wing Chun fighting style's coveted gold sash. From China she traveled to South Korea and was working on a second dan black belt in taekwondo when news came that her father had been murdered. He'd stumbled upon a meth lab while hunting in a remote section of Thunder Basin National Grassland south of Upton, Wyoming, and surprised the crooks operating it. They gunned her dad down in cold blood. That's when she decided she would use her formidable physical skills and mental discipline training to bring criminals to justice.

The only child of a single parent, Julie was left with a sizeable estate and used the funds to enroll at the Wyoming Law Enforcement Academy in Douglas where she aced every test, mental and physical, in near-record time. She worked the family ranch between Sundance and Moorcroft for a while as she waited for the right job to open up in law enforcement. Then she learned Crook County had budgeted for two new deputy recruits and jumped on the opportunity. Being a local gal remembered as a hard worker, exemplary student and exceptional athlete likely helped her get one of the jobs, but she'd kept her martial arts skills under wraps, preferring to tell people she'd been doing cultural studies in the Far East in hopes of improving U.S. beef exports to the region before her dad was killed.

She hadn't been a deputy long before it became very apparent she wasn't just a pretty woman in a uniform. Drunks, druggies and any other morons on the wrong side of the law who chose to test her abilities quickly regretted the error. Two nights earlier she'd single-handedly broken up a bar fight in Beulah and had four male suspects on the ground outside before her backup arrived. Two were still hospitalized. She was wondering if she'd ever win the respect of her peers as she turned right onto an old logging trail that led to the area where the scientists were reportedly camped.

◆ ◆ ◆

Jake Sanders could not move. The coffee mug slipped from his hand and smashed on the ground. Gail, unaware of what was behind her as the light wind was in her face, peered curiously over the rim of her mug at Jake as she took her final sip.

"Look out! Behind...!" Jake yelled. But it was too late. In one swift motion the beast reached down to grasp Gail's entire right shoulder and hurled the woman upward to the left...sending her smashing full force into the trunk of a large pine. The impact knocked the wind out of Gail, but she remained conscious. The monster leered down at her, exposing huge canine fangs in a jaw that jutted prominently from the lower portion of the huge football-shaped skull.

"No!" screamed Jake as he picked up the biggest rock he could find and threw it as hard as he could at the beast's head.

15

In an almost instantaneous and fluid response, the monster's right upper limb came up, caught the rock in mid-flight, and flung it underhand back at Jake with incredible force. Jake's last thought before the softball-sized piece of granite struck him in the torso was, *"It has intelligence?!"*

The force of impact picked Jake physically off the ground and toppled him backward over the camp stove. Pain shot through his torso as he tried to catch his breath and stand up, but couldn't. The creature took a step toward Jake but stopped abruptly, looking down to its left. It was Gail, on her knees beside a huge hairy leg. She had managed to pick up a three-foot stick of pine about as thick as a baseball bat, swung it with all her might, and broke it across one of monster's ankles where she thought something like an Achilles' tendon might be. There was one, but it didn't matter. The tendon was nearly as big around as the stick.

Gail tried to stand and run but only made it as far as a squat before the creature grabbed her hair, lifted her up by it, and swung her forcefully into the trunk of another large ponderosa pine. The loud snap of her spine was like a knife through Jake's heart as he struggled to his feet screaming at the monster in rage, fear, agonizing sorrow and frustration. Gail's limp body hung on the tree, impaled, a section of broken branch protruding from her torso below her breasts.

The creature pulled her off the tree and again lifted her, this time to its gaping jaws. The fangs sank into her neck and throat with an audible crunch and grunt of guttural satisfaction from the massive beast. It decided it would feed on the female more after it killed the male and again took a stride toward the screaming, sobbing, shell of a man that had fallen to his knees. Jake hoped he'd die as quickly and bravely as the love of his life had a moment earlier.

Weighing in at more than 1,200 pounds, the creature was more than a match for an unarmed man. It was not, however, for a five-foot-seven angry blonde with an armored sport utility vehicle and an attitude. The Durango was nearly airborne when it rocketed into the camp and its grill guard slammed into the big beast's lower limbs at 40 mph. Deputy Julie Reed had seen all she needed to when her patrol vehicle had crested a rise a quarter mile up the trail as the creature killed Gail. She had just enough time to switch off the airbag before the SUV's impact sent the beast into the air. Its

16

huge right shoulder partially caved in the Durango's rear roof as it fell over the top of the vehicle, which continued forward to a position between the beast and Jake.

Julie didn't hesitate for a second, grabbing the 12-gauge Remington 870 tactical shotgun from its mount as she bailed out of the now stopped vehicle.

"Can you move?" she screamed at Jake who was kneeling near the front right fender. She knew she had to use the few seconds of advantage her initiative had bought them well. "Get in the truck!"

"My wife!" screamed Sanders.

"Later! Now MOVE!"

The blow had temporarily stunned the creature, and it took a moment for it to reorient itself. It was about six feet behind the Durango on its side. Uncontrollable rage began to sweep through its body. Who was this that dared interrupt its kill? The monster started to rise.

Julie aimed the shotgun at the center of the creature's massive chest and let a blast of buckshot fly before she rolled across the hood of the Durango and grabbed Jake by the shoulder, pulling him toward the passenger door. The creature took the small spread of buckshot in the upper right chest; the impact spun it a bit back to the right. It momentarily lost footing and fell back onto a hip. This was no ordinary beast, however. Its chest was nearly four feet across and about as thick, protected on all sides by short, thick hair and layers of dense muscle and bone. The shotgun pellets didn't penetrate even an inch, though the force of the impact and the noise were enough to get the beast's attention. It had never experienced what a firearm could do until that moment.

"C'mon mister, work with me!" shouted Julie as she pulled the Durango's passenger door open for Sanders and worked the pump action on the Remington with her other arm to chamber a fresh round.

The beast, mostly obscured from the deputy's view on the opposite side of the Durango, reached over and took hold of the log the couple had been eating breakfast on. It rose and hoisted the huge timber over its head with both front limbs, the diameter of which were more than half that of the log. It brought the log back over its head, intending to smash the two humans on the other side of the vehicle.

Julie was not about to let that happen. Her next three shots struck the creature's chest in rapid succession, timed perfectly just as it was bringing the log back. The combination of the shotgun blasts and the weight of the log behind its head were enough to knock the beast off balance again. This time it fell over backward, log and all. She noticed Sanders was having trouble getting into the vehicle so she kicked him in the butt, depositing the bulk of his weight onto the front passenger seat, and started around the front of the vehicle toward the driver's seat. The creature was just getting up but still wobbly when two more shotgun blasts hit its lower legs, knocking it back down. Julie was at the driver's door with one shell left in the shotgun. The creature deftly swung the top half of its body forward and legs back, landing in a crouch. The lack of breasts on the bloodied chest caused Julie to guess it was male. Blazing red eyes locked on the face of the uniformed woman aiming the gun…a face that was…smirking?

Officer Julie Reed's last shotgun blast hit between the tree-trunk-like thighs of the crouching monster before it could spring. Her hunch was right, it was male. A deep, thunderous roar of pain erupted from the creature as it rolled for a moment into a fetal position with its back to the deputy. Julie tossed the shotgun into the Durango, turning her back on the beast for a moment as she reached in and pulled Jake the rest of the way onto the passenger seat. Then she turned her attention back to the creature as she drew her Sig Sauer P320 semiautomatic service pistol. In that moment the beast had started to roll downhill toward the stream below the camp. Julie was able to put six .45-caliber bullets into it before the creature rolled through some dense brush on the bank and into the cold water, which had an immediate reviving effect. It rose to its full height and glared back over its shoulder at the woman on the hill above. Then, with amazing speed and surprising silence, it ran into the forest on two straight legs with what appeared to be arms swinging like those of a great ape occasionally touching the ground for support like a gorilla. Julie jumped into the Durango, swung it around and drove back down the logging trail away from the campsite, also with a good deal of speed. The fight had ended in a draw but neither participant would be content with anything less than complete victory the next time they met.

Chapter Four

Simon Standing Elk lay sedated in a hospital bed at Rapid City Regional Hospital. Dr. Lance Cook stood outside his room looking at Simon's medical charts. He was the ER physician who had initially admitted Simon and was trying to determine what kind of additional treatment might be needed when Simon's father and another Lakota man arrived.

"Good morning doctor. I am Peter Standing Elk and I was told my son is in this room. Can you please tell me what has happened?"

Dr. Cook regarded the man for a moment. The Native American was wearing cowboy boots, old faded jeans, and a worn plaid shirt with long gray braids of hair hanging over both shoulders. He was a stark contrast to the physician's clean-cut male model look.

"Your son has had quite a shock to his system," the doctor began. "And to be honest, the situation has us a bit confused. He is not technically in shock any longer and his vital signs are strong. But he remains in a trance-like state. We have had to keep him mildly sedated because he gets very excited if we do not."

"In other words, doctor," observed Peter, "There is nothing physically wrong with my son that you have been able to determine."

"That is correct, sir," replied Dr. Cook. "However, I was about to recommend a few more tests as a precaution to be sure. I noticed on his driver's license that Simon had long dark hair as of a few months ago. Can you tell me when his hair turned white?"

Peter glanced at the silent companion who'd accompanied him to the hospital. The man had a mysterious quality about him. He appeared to be about the same age as the senior Standing Elk, in his late sixties, and was similarly dressed. The second Lakota was wearing a leather pouch about the size of a laptop bag over his right shoulder. Peter turned back and looked into the doctor's eyes.

"Perhaps your tests will prove unnecessary, doctor. The man with me is one of my people's spiritual leaders. He has experience in these matters.

Since you have determined there is nothing physically wrong with my son, will you permit us to see if we can bring him out of this condition?"

"I don't know about that," replied Dr. Cook skeptically. "I mean no disrespect to your people or your ways, but this hospital does things in accordance with certain rules, regulations and medically proven techniques. What is it that you propose to do?"

"Nothing that will threaten the health of my son or anyone else," Peter responded. "I invite you to join us if you're uncomfortable."

Curiosity now had the better of Dr. Cook. He ran his hand through his thick brown hair and sighed heavily, looking down at the shorter and older men in front of him. "Okay, but I reserve the right to intervene at any time."

The two Native Americans exchanged a look and entered the room with the doctor in tow. Peter Standing Elk stopped short when he saw his son. The thick black mane of hair he had seen on Simon two nights before at dinner was white as snow.

"Doctor, has my son said anything since he was brought here?" asked Peter.

"We've had him since around one this morning. Since that time, he's been muttering about a yak-a-wee coming or something like that," said Dr. Cook. "What's a...."

The previously silent Lakota shaman moved quickly forward, put a hand on each of the doctor's shoulders and locked eyes with the man, their faces inches apart. Dr. Cook was momentarily alarmed and noticed for the first time how extremely bright and intense the old man's eyes were. He could sense urgency and deep concern on the face of the shaman.

"Listen to me carefully," the shaman spoke evenly and softly, but with intensity that equaled his expression. "Is it possible the word this man used was Yakwawi?"

The answer came from Simon Standing Elk on the bed beside them as he slowly turned and spoke hoarsely for the first time since the men had entered the room, "Yakwawi has come."

"Son, do you know where you are? Do you know me?" asked Peter Standing Elk as he rushed forward and took his son's hand.

"I...am...afraid, father," came the reply.

The shaman moved to the opposite side of the bed and regarded his patient. He reached into the leather pouch and removed a tiny plastic bag, the contents of which he began to stir into a Styrofoam cup of water on the bedside stand.

"Now wait just a minute," objected Dr. Cook. "I can't let you administer anything to this patient before I know exactly what it is."

"Don't be concerned, doctor," said the shaman. His gaze moved up to meet the doctor's. "This is an herbal remedy my people have used for many years to clear the mind. It contains nothing illegal or regulated. This man's father and I will take full responsibility for the result. If you resist us, we will simply check the man out of your facility and treat him elsewhere in the same way I plan to here. This way, however, you may supervise the process of recovery and might even learn a thing or two. My hope is that we can do this quickly, quietly, and without causing a racial incident."

Tensions between the Native American and non-Indian communities had been high in western South Dakota. Dr. Cook had always thought himself open-minded on alternative treatments and was not eager to do anything that could brand him a racist. He was also not eager to lose his job. Dr. Cook walked to the door of the room. He glanced up and down the hallway, quietly closed the door, turned to the shaman and nodded.

The greenish concoction had a pleasant taste and Simon Standing Elk finished the drink. The shaman then took a small container of pungent yellowish paste from his pouch and began to chant quietly as he moved it back and forth under Simon's nose. This went on for a couple of minutes and Dr. Cook became increasingly nervous. The shaman put the container back in the pouch and clapped his hands loudly above Simon's face twice.

Simon Standing Elk shot upright in bed, looked intently at each of the men around him for a moment, and then spoke.

"Father," he began excitedly. "I was in the sweat lodge at Bear Butte with my friends last night. I had a powerful vision, one that upset me greatly."

"I know, my son," said Peter. "Try to relax, and tell us exactly what you saw."

"Before we do that," interrupted Dr. Cook, "I have a couple of things that I must do."

The doctor moved to the bedside with his stethoscope at the ready. He checked Simon's heart rate and respiration before taking the man's blood pressure. All appeared slightly elevated, but in the normal range and much better than before the two guests had arrived.

"Okay, he checks out fine," said Dr. Cook. "But I want to keep him here another night for observation just in case." The doctor turned to the shaman and said, "Can I have a word with you outside, sir?"

"No, thank you," replied the shaman as he reached into his pouch once again, this time to flip a hidden switch. With his other hand, the older man dropped something into the doctor's lab coat pocket.

Dr. Cook was a bit startled by the shaman's answer and action, but didn't know how to respond. The important thing was that his patient was better, and for all anyone knew, he would get the credit. The doctor turned abruptly and left the room.

Simon Standing Elk began to recount his story to the two elders now seated next to his bed. He told them of the sweat lodge, the fellowship, the stories and then the encounter with the spirit bear in the woods. He had just finished the part where he saw the horrible beast when the door to his hospital room burst open and two suit-clad men stepped smartly in. Both were more than six feet tall. One was blonde. The other older and dark. Both had close-cropped hair. Except for crisply pressed white dress shirts, each was dressed completely in black and wearing dark sunglasses. Seven in the morning was a bit early for visitors, and slight bulges under their suit coats meant they weren't there to deliver flowers.

Peter Standing Elk stared at the two men who had just entered the room, and rose to confront them. As he did, however, the shaman's right hand fell on his shoulder.

"It's alright," the medicine man explained, "They are here because I summoned them."

"Who are these men?" asked Peter. "And when did you call for them? You've been with me since we left the Reservation this morning and spoken to no one else but the doctor and my son."

"The time for questions and answers will come soon enough, old friend," the shaman said calmly, but with strength of authority in his voice. "For now, we must check your son out of this facility and go with these new friends."

"We are not going anywhere until I understand what is happening here," protested Peter as he glanced first at his son lying on the bed, and then at the two silent intruders blocking the door.

"Events are unfolding that transcend you, your son, me, and these men," explained the shaman. "We have known one another for many seasons, Peter. We have endured much together. In that time I have never asked you for anything, but I ask you now to trust me. No harm will come to anyone in this room if we do as I say. We must leave this place and go with these men at once. Please."

Peter regarded the two men closely. There was no hint of emotion in their expression. They stood still and ramrod straight, arms at their sides, the bulges under the sides of their now unbuttoned coats strongly communicated they were to be taken most seriously. Relenting, Peter turned to the shaman and nodded.

The younger of the two men at the door swiftly moved into the hall for a moment and returned with a wheelchair. The older man moved to the bed of Simon Standing Elk and, bending down, took the younger Lakota's arm over his shoulder and helped him into the wheelchair. The shaman poked his head into the hallway and motioned everyone to follow as he stepped out of the room.

A nurse at the station down the hall noticed the men were leaving the patient's room. "Wait a moment gentlemen," she called as she rose to go to them.

"We're checking out," explained Peter Standing Elk.

The nurse approached the group of men as the elder of the two strangers slipped some papers into the shaman's hand from behind.

"The doctor has not informed us yet of your discharge," explained the nurse. "Please return to the room until I can get Dr. Cook to approve this man's release."

"It has already been taken care of," explained the shaman as he handed the papers to the nurse, along with an envelope addressed to the hospital billing department. "You will find that all is in order on the release forms. You will also find a bill for the hospital's services and payment in full for those services."

It was not proper checkout procedure. The nurse eyed the documents with a look of suspicion, yet they seemed to be in perfect order. There was the release paperwork signed by Dr. Cook, an up-to-date bill for services rendered, and the envelope contained a cashier's check for the exact amount signed by a tribal official. Still, the nurse knew something wasn't right. Normally a patient would be discharged and the payment arrangements taken care of at the administration window downstairs if the patient was uninsured. Then there was the look of the two men in black. She suspected they were law enforcement or government agents of some kind. She faced a crisis of decision. Just at that moment, Dr. Cook came around the corner and saw the gathering in the hallway.

"Dr. Cook!" called the nurse, "These men..."

"It's okay Kathy," the doctor waived as he turned to go into another room, "Let them go." Dr. Cook smiled slightly as he fingered the 1901 P Morgan Silver Dollar in his lab coat. Whoever his patient's benefactors were, they'd certainly done their homework and somehow knew of his passion for collecting rare coins. To any casual observer, the item in his possession was just an old silver-colored coin. The doctor knew its value as a collector's piece was more than $400,000. It had been a very strange, but very profitable night shift.

"I'm sorry for the delay, gentlemen," the nurse said apologetically. "I was merely..."

"We understand completely and commend your diligence," said the shaman. "Thank you for your concern."

With that, the five men disappeared into an elevator down the hall. It descended into a basement parking garage normally reserved for ambulances. The men climbed into a waiting dark blue van with a wheelchair lift and darkly tinted windows before speeding away.

Chapter Five

The ride was bone-jarring, but Deputy Julie Reed was not about to slow down as the Durango bounced down the logging trail she had taken to the Sanders' camp. The man in the passenger seat beside her was a basket case, alternating between uncontrollable sobbing and screams of terror, obviously in shock. She wasn't sure if the screams were the result of the experience they had just been through or her driving, not that it mattered. All she cared about was getting him the medical help he needed, and getting herself the backup she needed to track down and destroy the thing she'd seen kill the woman. She had never encountered such a monstrosity and really didn't care what it was. It committed a gruesome murder in front of her and she was certain it was responsible for the rancher's death as well. It had to be stopped before it killed again. The tree line was just ahead, then a half-mile of open range before the blacktop. That's where Deputy Reed planned to rally the troops. She'd radio for the sheriff and an ambulance, and also planned to alert the Wyoming Game and Fish Department. The clock on the dash read 7:57 a.m. With any luck they'd have this matter wrapped up by lunch. The Durango shot out of the trees.

"What the...?!" Julie shouted as she slammed on the brakes, skidding the Durango to a stop a scant few yards from a dark navy blue Black Hawk helicopter parked across the trail; its rotor blade idling.

Julie had seen enough weird stuff for one morning, and nearly hitting a helicopter straddling the only semblance of a road leading out of the forest within a two miles of her did not improve her disposition. The side door of the Black Hawk opened. Six men wearing black business suits and dark glasses leapt from the doorway. They approached the Crook County law enforcement SUV, three heading toward each side of the vehicle. Deputy Reed had had enough. She flung open the door, drew her pistol and leveled it at the nearest man.

"Sheriff's office!" she shouted. "Stop where you are and raise your hands above your heads...all of you!" To her surprise, all the men stopped and complied.

"Gentlemen, I have had a very bad morning and am not in the mood to be messed with. I don't know who you are, but I have a man here who needs medical attention and you are in my way. Now get back into your whirlybird, close the door, and fly away. You can keep playing whatever government game I presume you're playing while I go do my job."

Julie Reed's entire body jerked, shook and went rigid. She couldn't move her arms or legs and felt consciousness slipping away. She had not seen nor heard three additional men and a woman emerge from the trees behind her, nor had she heard their stun units charging over the whine of the chopper's engine. The newcomers had correctly suspected the deputy was wearing a bulletproof vest, so small darts from one of the stunners were fired into her upper buttocks near the spine just below her body armor. Each dart was connected to the charged unit by a hair-thin length of wire. Enough voltage was sent into the young woman to render her physically incapable and mentally incoherent. As she fell to the ground, the woman moved quickly forward with a syringe in hand. Seconds later, the deputy was in a very deep sleep.

Dr. Jake Sanders was still rubbing his head where it had hit the dashboard during the Durango's sudden stop. The passenger door swung open and he looked up to see a dark-suited man leaning over him. Jake was in no condition to offer resistance and soon joined his female rescuer in dreamless sleep. The team quickly, but gently, loaded their two captives into the Black Hawk and it lifted into the sky.

As the helicopter rose above the treetops, a large dark blue semi pulled off the blacktop road onto the logging trail. One of the mysterious men had remained behind to drive the deputy's SUV up a ramp into the back of the truck. After it was loaded the big rig disappeared down the blacktop toward Interstate 90.

Meanwhile, a second team clad in hazmat suits was at the Sanders' campsite. Every piece of evidence was meticulously collected and catalogued. Hair and blood samples, shell casings, plaster casts of footprints and tire tracks, along with both conventional and infrared photography were part of a well-choreographed routine. All of the Sanders' camping and research equipment was loaded into plastic boxes, and Gail's body was placed in a coffin-sized refrigeration unit.

When all had been completed, the helicopter that had dropped the site sanitation team off returned and lowered a large wire basket. Team members were retrieved along with their evidence and cargo. As the last man prepared to leave, he took a wooden box about the size of a loaf of bread from the basket and set it on the ground in the center of the camp. He then climbed into the basket and was winched up to the hovering aircraft. The chopper's nose tilted down slightly as it headed north toward the old military radar installation just across the Montana border minutes away. The noise of the rotors had just faded from the campsite when the wooden box vanished in a white-hot, but nearly silent incendiary explosion that engulfed an area a hundred yards across in searing flames. The chopper pilot radioed the U.S. Forest Service to report seeing smoke while on a National Guard training flight. It would be at least a half-hour before the first firefighters arrived at the scene and by then every trace of the morning's events would be gone. In one sense Julie Reed had been correct after all. The matter had been resolved by lunchtime.

Chapter Six

Dr. Jake Sanders awoke to the sound of calling gulls and the salty scent of fresh sea air. He lay still for a moment, trying to decide if he was dead, dreaming or insane. Memories filtered back into his head slowly. Recollections of an assignment in the Wyoming Black Hills with his wife, and an environmental impact project he was working on with her. There was a horrible monster, a lady cop, gunshots and a helicopter. It had to have been a dream, a terrible nightmare. He was, after all, in a very comfortable bed with fine silk linens.

The doctor sat up and took note of his surroundings. The room was luxurious by any standard. Exquisite paintings hung on the walls. There was a small writing desk crafted of polished hardwood in one corner. To his right, a breeze gently blew into the room through the screens of sliding glass doors that opened onto a small patio equipped with a round table and two chairs. The patio merged with magnificent white sand that formed a gently sloped beach to the ocean's edge about a quarter-mile away. To his left was a closet with double sliding mirrored doors. Next to it, an open door showed a bathroom with elaborate fixtures. On the wall, eight feet from the foot of the bed, was a combination bookcase/entertainment center complete with video and music players. A dresser was to its left, and the desk was to the right of the unit. A large oak door to the left of the dresser was closed. Jake decided it was time to separate truth from reality.

Step one in his mind was to find Gail and get some answers. He rose and went into the bathroom. While he did not find Gail soaking in the tub as he had hoped, he did conclude he was not dead. The pressure on his bladder made it clear it had been some time, so he relieved himself and washed his face. Harsh realities began to sink in when he saw his face in the mirror over the vanity. He had what looked like several days of beard growth on his face. Gail would never have tolerated such stubble. He looked to check the date on his watch. It was gone. Jake realized he was wearing silk pajamas. He had never owned a set in his life, preferring boxer shorts and a T-shirt. Panic started to set in.

Jake stepped back into the room and went right to the large oak door. It was locked. He knocked on it. No response. With increased urgency, he pounded on the door.

"Gail?" he shouted, "Is anybody there?"

There was no reply. Jake went to the glass door by the patio, which was open, and tried the screen door behind it to access the beach. The screen door was locked. He tried to force it but could not. Exasperated, he decided to break through the screen. To his amazement, it was as solid as a steel cage with no give whatsoever.

"This can't be real," he said aloud. "This can't be happening. I must still be dreaming."

At that precise moment, the ringing of a telephone shattered the atmosphere in the room. Jake, startled at first, turned to the phone on the bedside stand. He hurried over and lifted the receiver to his ear.

"Gail?" Jake asked.

"Good morning, Dr. Sanders," a male voice said at the other end of the line in what Jake identified as an Australian accent. "Please get dressed. We will send for you in thirty minutes."

"Where's my wife?" Jake asked. He still refused to accept the reality of what he recalled having seen in the woods.

"Thirty minutes, doctor," the voice said just before the line went dead.

For the first time since Gail Sanders death, her husband was beginning to get hold of himself. The terror of the truth still stabbed at his heart, but his formidable brain was starting to kick in. Jake went to the closet. There was an assortment of clothing, all of it in his size. He selected a pair of tan Dockers and a green short-sleeved pullover from the rack, pulled some clean underwear from the dresser drawer and re-entered the bathroom. As he removed the pajamas the question of who had undressed him and put them on entered his mind.

Jake showered longer than usual, but experience in the field at night had taught him how to estimate time without using a luminescent watch that might have given his position away to whatever animals he was watching. After what he figured was about fifteen minutes, Jake dried off and tackled the stubble with a shaving kit that was in the top drawer of the vanity. He finished drying his hair and dressing just as there was a knock on the door.

"Come in," Jake called, "As it is painfully obvious that you don't want me to come out."

The door swung inward and two people, a man and a woman entered. The man was shorter than Jake, but powerfully built and younger. About twenty-five Jake guessed, with long sandy blonde hair and brown eyes. In spite of his imposing physique, a broad and apparently genuine smile seemed to engulf the lower portion of the young man's head.

"Dr. Sanders, you may call me Jeff," said the man with a thick Australian accent.

The fact that the man had said "you may call me" instead of "my name is" did not go unnoticed by Jake, but it did not stop him from taking the outstretched right hand and confirming the fellow had a powerful grip.

"And I am Dr. Sora Wu," said the woman, an attractive middle-aged oriental with straight, black, shoulder-length hair. "You have been through a great deal, Dr. Sanders. I have been responsible for your medical care since your arrival here and I need to check your vital signs before we proceed. May I?"

"You haven't asked my permission for anything yet," noted Jake dryly. "So why start now."

The woman checked Jake's pulse, respiration and blood pressure as he sat on the edge of the bed. Then she gentle prodded his left abdominal area and chest.

"Looking for something?" asked Jake.

"Does this give you any discomfort?" asked Dr. Wu as her prodding continued.

"None at all. Why do you ask?"

"Considering you arrived here a few days ago with a bruised spleen and two broken ribs I'd say you're doing nicely," the woman replied with a slight smile Jake found patronizing.

"C'mon, I don't recall…" Jake halted as the flash of the beast intercepting his rock and hurling it back raced across his mind. All color drained from his face. He stood up, grabbed the woman by the lapels of her lab coat and thrust his face inches from hers. "Where is my wife?!"

The young man quickly placed his right hand on Jake's shoulder and pushed him back onto the bed.

"Dr. Sanders, we mean you no harm, but will not tolerate abuse," said Jeff. "Please calm down and come with us so that your many questions can be addressed."

Jake composed himself, apologized to Dr. Wu and rose, motioning for the pair to lead the way. Dr. Wu did so, but Jeff remained behind Jake as they left the room and entered a long and lavishly decorated hallway.

Chapter Seven

Deputy Julie Reed was doing her best to figure out what was going on. Four days earlier she'd awakened to find herself in the nicest beachfront hotel room she had ever seen. Or so she thought. While she had not yet forgiven whoever was responsible for the abduction that landed her there, she certainly couldn't complain about her treatment. The food was exotic and exceptional. The workout facilities were the finest she'd ever used. The limited number of people she'd interacted with had been polite and even somewhat respectful. Though she had not be given free reign of the luxurious compound, she was permitted to do whatever she pleased as long as she phoned for an escort before leaving her room. She'd tried breaking out the first two nights, but her room was apparently escape-proof.

She was walking down a hallway with a very tall and muscular black man who'd said his name was Ibutho. They had worked out together a few times in a well-equipped gym. Unknown to Ibutho, Julie was carefully taking stock of his strengths and weaknesses. She guessed from his accent that he was from some African country, but had no idea which one. She also had no idea where she was or why they had taken her, but was about to do something about it.

On entering the gym, Julie waved Ibutho over to an area surrounded by mirrors with a padded floor. Both were clad in high-performance athletic wear. "Tell me, Ibutho," Julie began, "Do you have any hand-to-hand fighting skills?"

"I have sparred on occasion, Miss Julie."

"You up for a few rounds? I used to spar regularly as part of my workout routine and think I might be getting a bit rusty."

"I do not wish to harm you, Miss Julie," Ibutho replied opening his arms and extending them palms upward.

It was just the gesture Julie was waiting for. The woman looked at Ibutho over her left shoulder and with lightning speed swung her right leg completely around in an attempt to land a high kick on the left side of

Ibutho's head. Instead, she found herself hanging upside down with the man's left hand firmly gripping the ankle of her kicking leg.

"I do not wish to harm you, Miss Julie," Ibutho said again with a wide white toothy grin on his deep brown face. But he'd underestimated Julie's flexibility.

With a fast, strong motion Julie brought the heel of her free foot crashing into the wrist of Ibutho's extended left arm, which reflexively released his hold and allowed the woman to fall toward the mat. Before her shoulder even hit the pad, Julie was executing a scissor kick bringing her right foot hard into Ibutho's left ankle as her left heel, moving hard the opposite way, struck behind the man's left knee.

Feeling himself falling to his left, Ibutho pushed off and away with his right leg and landed upright six feet away facing Julie in a modified boxing stance. But combat wasn't the woman's objective. She sprinted to the free weights and grabbed a 10-lb. dumbbell in each hand. The one in her left she hurled hard at Ibutho's head with a fast underhand. But her right arm was her pitching arm, and she launched the second weight lower and faster. Ibutho's initial reflex to protect his head brought both his hands up to catch the first weight and he realized his mistake a split-second later when the other slammed into his groin.

Julie didn't even wait to see if Ibutho went down. She grabbed a 25-lb. weight and ran to the nearest mirrored wall. With all her strength, she slammed the weight into the mirror in hopes of breaking out of the room for some unescorted recon and a possible means of escape. But the weight bounced back with the same amount of speed and energy Julie had applied to her blow.

She felt herself backpedaling with the weight over her head when it was lifted from her hands as her back hit something solid.

"I do not wish to harm you, Miss Julie," Ibutho's deep voice said quietly behind her. "We have finished exercising now. You must dress for an important meeting."

Exasperated, Julie resigned herself to the reality her plan had failed. "Meeting with whom?"

"Someone you know and someone you do not yet know," replied Ibutho. Behind the unscathed one-way mirror of the gym, a tall man in a very expensive suit turned to a woman in battle dress uniform (BDU) camo and asked, "How long has it been since we saw someone actually fight on par with Ibutho?"

"About four decades sir. But in his defense, Ibu isn't getting any younger," the woman replied.

"Nor are any of us," the man commented. "I think it's time I introduce myself to our guests."

◆ ◆ ◆

Dr. Jake Sanders and his escorts arrived at the end of a hallway where two massive oak doors began to swing inward as soon as they arrived. Dr. Wu, Jake and Jeff entered. The room was huge, about 100 feet square guessed Jake, with what had to be a 20-foot ceiling. In the center of the room was a large hardwood coffee table atop a magnificent Persian rug spread on a marble floor. The wall opposite the doors was a handsome wood bookcase that spanned its length from floor to ceiling. Sliding ladders offered access to the higher shelves. The wall to the right was covered with tall glass windows and a pair of French doors that opened onto a spacious marble terrace overlooking the sea. Between the doors and the table was a large modern desk with a flat-screen computer monitor, a keyboard, a telephone, a penholder and a legal pad. No more, no less. The wall to the left of the entryway housed the largest big-screen TV Jake had ever seen along with banks of smaller, but still large, video monitors on either side.

"You're looking much better than the last time I saw ya. I am very sorry about your wife."

Jake turned. He had not heard Julie and her escort arrive behind him. He almost didn't recognize her. She wore a tank top and casual hiking shorts in place of a police uniform. It was the last half of her statement that cut his heart deeply. He was coming to accept that the horrible memories haunting him since he'd regained consciousness were, in fact, true. Before he could respond, a new voice echoed across the room.

"Good day Dr. Sanders, and to you as well Miss Reed. Please do come in, and the rest of you may leave with my thanks."

Jake and Julie turned to see a tall, impeccably dressed man standing next to the desk. It was as if he'd instantly materialized there. As the others turned to leave, the man motioned toward the coffee table bounded by two large dark-leather armchairs near each end with matching sofas on either side.

"I am certain there are many questions you wish to have answered," the man said with a clipped British accent. "I shall do my best to do so. But we may as well be comfortable as we converse."

The man strode to the armchair nearest him and motioned Jake and Julie to one of the sofas.

They both sat on the one nearest the door; their gazes transfixed on the imposing figure as he unbuttoned his suit coat, tugged gently on the thighs of his trousers and sat down in the armchair nearest his desk before turning to face them. He pressed a small button on the chair and the center of the coffee table depressed slightly before sliding to one side. From below rose three cups, a tea kettle and a coffee carafe. The cup nearest Julie contained sweet chai tea, her favorite. The man took the carafe and poured coffee into the cups nearest Jake and himself, its robust aroma prompted Jake to eagerly accept the cup handed him by their host.

"Let me begin by offering my sincere apologies to you both for the means employed to bring you here. As we proceed it will become evident to you why this was done. And to you, Dr. Sanders, may I offer my deepest sympathies on the passing of your wife, Gail. While your memory may be a bit foggy for the next day or so, I am sorry to tell you that your recollections do, in fact, bear witness to reality. She was killed, and you were injured, by a horrible creature."

Jake opened his mouth to speak, but the man held up a hand and said, "Let's begin with the basics first. Who am I, what is this place, and why are you here?"

Chapter Eight

The creature scanned the valley below from its hiding place in the rimrock cliffs overlooking the Belle Fourche River as the sun crept lower behind the hills. Daylight was grudgingly surrendering its last hold on the sky to the coming night. The beast gnawed on the lower leg bone of a mule deer that had been careless enough to walk beneath a ledge that had sheltered the wounded monster for nearly a week. That was three days earlier, and the creature craved fresh flesh. It had been an easy thing to drop the small boulder on the deer's head and retrieve the battered carcass from the base of the precipice on which the monster had been recuperating, but skeletal remains of the four-point buck were all that remained. The time to hunt again had come. The creature rose. Its movements still showed signs of stiffness, but it healed much faster than other animals in the forest. The Crook County Sheriff's Office used lead-free pistol rounds and steel buckshot in its shotgun shells. There would be no blood poisoning or infection as a result of the encounter with Deputy Reed, and even in a slightly weakened condition the monster was more than a match for anything that breathed in the Black Hills.

Nonetheless, it wanted a quick and easy meal. Just at that moment, it noticed a bowhunter walking on a ridge about 400 yards to the west, silhouetted in the gathering dusk. The hunter became the hunted.

Stan Swenson took a deep breath and enjoyed the view around him. From the rim of the cliff overlooking the river he could see for miles. The top of Devil's Tower was silhouetted against an orange sky in the distant southwest. The fresh scent of a Black Hills evening filled his nostrils as a coyote howled at the sunset about a mile away. Stan lived for these moments. He'd left the hassles of big city life in Minneapolis seven years earlier and moved to a ranchette near Sundance with his wife and infant son. This was the kind of country where a man could raise a family without having to worry about crime, traffic, long commutes and overcrowded schools. He'd taken up bowhunting shortly after the move and it had become a passion. The flexibility of being a freelance software developer meant he could set his own hours, and this time of year he spent as many of those hours as he could wandering the hills in search of a trophy buck.

Stan started his descent to the valley below. About a half-mile downriver was a Forest Service road where his family was to meet him with the pickup. The day had been warm and Stan was careful to watch for rattlesnakes as he walked down the rocky game trail. It did not matter that he hadn't taken a deer. It was enough just to be outdoors, seeing the sights and smelling the...smells.

"What on God's green earth is THAT?" Stan grimaced as the pungent odor wafted up from the valley floor in the direction of the appointed rendezvous. The smell was unlike anything he had ever encountered in the Black Hills, and his instinctive response to it was also unexpected. Stan Swenson was afraid. He quickened his pace with about a quarter-mile to go to the truck. He saw the headlights moments later...one on top of the other instead of side by side. Then he heard the screams.

The creature had seen Stan on the opposite ridge and moved to intercept the hunter. In doing so, it had come upon a woman and child in a parked 2014 full-sized Ford F-250 extended-cab pickup. Not accustomed to taking food from one of the things some two-leggers used to move from place to place, the beast had taken a couple minutes to ponder the situation from the tree line adjacent to the driver's side before charging. In a fluid motion the monster reached under the running board and flipped the vehicle onto the passenger side with ease. Disappointment. The creature had anticipated turning over the truck and seeing its two occupants standing there, ripe for the picking. Instead it now stared curiously at the truck's undercarriage as the startled occupants, bruised and cut on a pile of glass that was the passenger window, screamed for help at the top of their lungs.

Stan Swenson drew his Diamond Archery compound bow until he felt his thumb knuckle gently touch the anchor point on his right cheek. The sun had set and it was getting darker by the second, but the glowing fiber-optic pins of his bow's sight still showed up nicely against the massive black shape 25 yards in front of him. He fought his thumping heart and surging adrenaline to hold the sight steady on the thing that was trashing his truck and threatening his family, then he touched off the release with his index finger and sent a carbon-shafted arrow tipped with a razor-sharp broadhead streaking through the gathering night at 300 feet-per-second. He yanked a second arrow from his quiver even as the first one hit home.

The penetrating power of a hunting arrow moving at high speed surpasses that of many firearm projectiles. On impact, hunting bullets start to expand and transfer the energy they carry into the target, resulting in shock and trauma to tissue surrounding the wound channel until the bullet's forward movement either stops or exits the target. Arrows, on the other hand, transfer relatively little shock and kinetic energy as they pass through an animal. Razor-like broadhead blades in the tips are intended to cleanly slice veins and arteries on their way through. Often times the cut is so fast and clean that an animal will not even realize it's been hit until it loses consciousness from blood loss. But things don't always go as the archer hopes.

It was most unfortunate for Stan Swenson that his arrow struck the back right shoulder blade of the beast. It may as well have hit the armor plating of a tank. The instant the broadhead struck the dense bone, the carbon arrow's energy had nowhere to go but back up the shaft, which shattered. Swenson was halfway through the draw of his second arrow when the creature swatted the weapon from the hunter's arms with its left forelimb and took hold of his throat with the right. A fast pivot and Swenson was airborne, flying toward the truck's windshield at a velocity that rivaled that of his arrow. Dead on impact, Stan didn't live to see the demise of his family now exposed through the open glass. The creature sat by the cab of the overturned truck and gorged itself on their dismembered bodies.

♦ ♦ ♦

Simon Standing Elk sat on a small bench at the end of a boat dock watching the sun dip below the mountain range across the lake before him. The crispness of a high-altitude autumn evening descended swiftly as the last golden rays disappeared behind the majestic peaks. For the last four days he had been at a remote Wyoming retreat in the company of the shaman and a handful of others. He had not spoken, since his hasty departure from the hospital, even as his father hugged him and said good-bye when they'd arrived at the retreat the following day. Since then, Simon had spent most of his time sitting by the lake deep in thought. Periodically, the shaman or one of the other Native Americans at the compound would place a small plate of food and some water next to Simon. He did not touch the food and drank only sparingly.

Simon glanced upward and noticed the first stars of the evening emerge from the gathering blanket of darkness. Soon the sky was full of glittering jewels. The beauty of the evening overtook the darkest corners of his soul. So many distant worlds. So vast a creation. So masterful a design. There was order. There was purpose. There had to be a plan. Then he heard, whether audibly or in his mind he did not know, the voice of his bear friend from the spirit realm, *"Since the beginning of all things, the invisible qualities of The Great Spirit, His power, and the nature of His being, have been clearly displayed in all created things. Those who see and doubt this are without excuse."*

Simon felt strangely warm. He noticed a beautiful handmade blanket someone draped over his shoulders. Traditional Native American markings and symbols covered the expanse of cloth. The shaman stood beside him, a tray of food and pot of steaming tea in hand. Simon looked up at the older man and their eyes met. For the first time Simon saw something different in the shaman, a depth and understanding that had eluded him until that moment. Not a word was spoken as the two men stared for several seconds, each into the other's soul. Then Simon tentatively reached out and took a sandwich from the tray. He ate. The shaman sat down on the bench next to him, never taking his gaze from the younger man's face. Simon reached for the second sandwich on the tray and alternated bites with sips of tea.

"I am ready now," said Simon as he dabbed at the corners of his mouth with a cloth napkin from the tray.

"I know," said the shaman. "We will begin in the morning."

"I must pray," said Simon Standing Elk.

"Indeed, you must," replied the old man as he rose from the bench. "Do not remain up too long in the night. You will need rest for tomorrow."

With that the shaman carried the tray and a plate of crumbs down the dock and up the stairs into the large log lodge. The old man set the tray down on the kitchen counter, walked through the main lounge area, and ascended a winding staircase to the floor above. He made his way to a room at the end of the hall, entered, and closed the door behind him. A weathered hand slipped into the ever-present leather pouch at his side and withdrew a plastic card, which was then swiped through a slot on the side of a small wooden desk next to a log-framed bed. On the desk sat a small lamp made of shed antler, a laptop computer, a telephone, a legal pad and a pen. No more, no less. Moments later the laptop screen came to life. The shaman sat down in front of it, opening an encrypted e-mail program. Creating a message, he began to slowly type with a single finger, one key at a time.

He will begin in the morning. The shaman clicked SEND.

Chapter Nine

"I am Dr. Jonathan Smythe," the man in the armchair began. "And the place you are now in is called Sanctum. It is the primary operation center, residence, research and training facility for The Watch. The two of you are here because you are members of a very select group. Only four people alive today have survived an encounter with a certain carnivorous species of anthropoid, and three of them are now seated in this room."

"Back the train up a bit, Doc," said Julie as she leaned forward to face the Brit. "I think you've seen one too many science-fiction movies on all those TVs over there." She cocked her head toward the huge screen and bank of monitors on the wall to her left. "I don't know anything about the anthro-whatever you're talking about but I do know the law, and you're in big trouble sir. While this mini-vacation has been interesting and even a bit relaxing, you're still holding us against our wills and have some serious charges to answer to. I'm talking two counts of forcible abduction involving transport across state lines, assault against a law enforcement officer, conspiracy to commit a felony, accessory to commission of crimes involving weapons, theft of law enforcement property, and enough other charges to put you and your friends in the Wyoming state prison for a couple of lifetimes. You and your cohorts, Dr. Smythe, are under arrest and any `watching´ will involve whatever you can see between the bars of a jail cell."

Dr. Smythe fought hard to keep a smile from his lips and did not entirely succeed. He noticed the resultant smirk seemed to irritate Julie and sought to calm her down a bit. "I understand why you would be upset..."

"I said you're under...." Julie began to stand up.

"Sit down Deputy Reed!" the man in the suit said firmly and with such authority that she immediately obeyed. "The Watch does not fall under the jurisdiction of any law enforcement or government agencies. As far as the rest of the world is concerned, at this moment the two of you are classified as missing persons last seen near the site of a forest fire that consumed nearly 200 acres. What happens to you from this point on will depend on decisions you make in the next few hours."

"Save it for the judge, Doc. No one is above the law!" Julie protested.

"There will be no arrests, no trials, no juries, Miss Reed," Smythe said evenly with just a hint of growing impatience in his voice. "You are given two choices. You can listen to what I have to say and offer you, or you can choose to wake up in the bed of your home in Wyoming with a hellacious hangover and absolutely no memory of what you've seen and heard or where you've been for the last several days. You will then fail a drug test administered by your employer and be forced to resign your career as a law enforcement officer without ever understanding why."

Julie was seething but remained silent. There was something about the way Smythe had said what he did that had her wondering if he could really pull it off. A total memory wipe? Could he, would he, even ruin her life?

"And I offer the same to you, Dr. Sanders," Smythe said turning to Jake, his tone more compassionate. "We can remove the dreadful memory of your wife's death and return you to your residence. We could remove her personal effects, photos, digital data and anything you possess that might remind you of Gail in order to minimize the trauma of her absence in your life, if you so wish. A cover story can be created about an accident that caused her death and left you with a brain injury resulting in trauma-induced amnesia to assuage her family's sense of loss and clear you of any suspicions. There will be no legal or professional consequences to you, just an outpouring of sympathy and a personal sense of emptiness that will eventually pass."

Jake thought for a moment. The offer did have some appeal if Smythe actually had that kind of influence, medical and technological expertise. A life without the painful memory of Gail's death, or...

"What is my other option?"

"Vengeance, Dr. Sanders. Vengeance and a new career that will introduce you to unsolved mysteries, untold challenges, a chance to study new species, and access to scientific advancements the likes of which the limits of human imagination are only now beginning to explore," Smythe responded with just enough excitement in his tone to hit key touchpoints in Jake's mind.

"What do I get if I pass on the hangover?" asked Julie.

"A cover story about how you bravely perished in the line of duty heroically attempting to rescue two campers from a raging forest fire. Along with a new career that will not only challenge your already impressive combat prowess, but expose you to foes far more formidable than any criminal you'd encounter as a deputy. All while protecting not only the citizens of your hometown and county, but those of the entire world."

Jake and Julie exchanged glances.

"We're listening," said Julie.

"I believe immersion education to be most effective," explained Smythe. "What I am about to share with you would seem so incredible, so unbelievable, that absence of any immediate supporting evidence would cause both of you to doubt anything else I tell you. Please accompany me."

Jake and Julie set their cups on the table as Smythe rose. Together they walked across what they perceived to be his large office and study. They paused behind him when he stopped before a section of the giant bookcase and spoke.

"Access. Dr. Jonathan Smythe."

A tile on the marble floor to the trio's right depressed and slid under the one next to it. In its place, a flat panel with the outline of a hand rose to waist height. Smythe placed his right hand on the outline and spoke what his guests thought to be a strange phrase.

"For what can be known of Him is evident in the things He has made."

"Confirmed," came a female voice from a speaker beneath the hand panel. "Voiceprint and handprint identity acknowledged. Facial recognition scan confirmed. Access is granted, doctor."

One of the bookcase sections swung slowly inward to the right. Dr. Smythe stepped forward with his guests in tow. Artificial lighting for the room they were entering activated as soon as they crossed the threshold of the large, newly created doorway.

It waited for them to the immediate left of the entryway, menacing glowing red eyes peering down over its large chest. Its massive presence was immediately felt by those entering the room. Jake looked up, gasped in terror and fell back against the bookcase door as he struggled to contain his bodily functions. Julie launched.

With lightning speed, the young woman pushed off with her left leg to leap up and to her right. Displaying almost superhuman strength, she used a bookcase shelf and her right leg to propel herself upward toward the beast's open jaws. With all the power she could muster, Julie kicked the monster's face. She felt her foot connect solidly, and was surprised by a snap and sharp backward movement of the beast's head. Spinning in midair, Julie righted herself and landed hard in a solid three-point stance between the creature and the two men with her. Before she could make her next move, the monstrous head landed on the floor between them. A puzzled expression on her face was met with the sound of a single pair of hands clapping slowly.

"Most impressive, Miss Reed," said Smythe as he continued to bring his hands together. He then stopped his praise and spoke in an admonishing tone. "But the taxidermy in this room is irreplaceable and I do ask that we look at, but do not touch, the exhibits."

Julie was livid. "What the HE..."

"Silence!" Smythe shouted to cut her off. "Profanity is forbidden at Sanctum!"

"Are you out of your friggin' mind, Smythe?" Julie retorted. "Where do you get off pulling a stunt like this? Look at that man over there." She pointed toward the bookcase as she continued to stare down Smythe. "He's likely going into shock! After all he's been through, no, after all WE'VE been through, how could you even think of bringing us in here you arrogant bast..."

"I shan't warn you again, Miss Reed," Smythe interrupted sternly. "Mind your tongue, your tone, and the hasty diagnosis you applied to the underestimated Dr. Sanders."

Julie, still seething, stole a glance toward the bookcase, but Jake wasn't there. Turning around she saw him, mouth agape, and several paces farther into the room they'd just entered. He was staring at the other taxidermy displays with complete incredulity. For the first time, she looked beyond the proximity of her always-in-place defensive perimeter and began to take in the contents of the enormous room. A shiver went down her spine.

"This...this can't be real," she unwillingly whispered.

"Oh, I assure you that it is, Miss Reed," Smythe said softly behind her, his confrontational and disciplinary tone replaced by one of near reverence. "Be assured, it most certainly is real."

Chapter Ten

Simon Standing Elk started down the stairs from the lodge on his way to the T-shaped dock where something inside him had changed the previous evening. Two Native American men were pushing away from the dock in a traditional birch-bark canoe outfitted with a pair of wicker seats. Two fishing rods, a landing net and a large tackle box between them betrayed their intentions. The shaman sat cross-legged on a thick woven blanket at the right cross of the T facing north, the first direct rays of the morning sun breaking over a mountain to the east gave the man's weathered face a bright orange glow. Simon started down the dock clutching a large mug of strong black coffee with both hands to ward off the chill of a beautiful autumn morning. The birch and aspen trees around the lake were at peak fall color, mirrored by the glass-like surface of the lake. The reflected image was only minimally rippled by the tiny wake of the departing canoe, its occupants skillfully dipping and stroking their paddles in silence while barely disturbing the water. Without turning to greet him, the shaman gestured to a second blanket opposite him and indicated that Simon should sit.

Doing so without spilling his coffee required concentration but Simon was soon facing the shaman. Once settled he took a sip from the mug, peering at the shaman over its edge. Steam from the hot liquid gave the older man a ghostly appearance that wavered as Simon drank. He couldn't help but notice half the shaman's face glowed in the sun, the other half was still cloaked in darkness that hid his full features. There was no reason Simon should have felt that odd, nor did he say anything because it occurred to him that, from the shaman's perspective, he also was half in the light and half in the waning darkness. As if reading his thoughts, the old man spoke.

"Light and darkness divide the universe as well, but not equally. Tell me, Simon Standing Elk, what are light and darkness?"

"Light is the absence of darkness. The reverse is also true. I suppose our eyes couldn't stand the intensity of too much light, nor our minds the depth of complete darkness without going mad," Simon answered. "So we spend our lives in the shadows made by the interaction, not that it's such a bad thing," he continued, allowing one hand to sweep toward the lake and view of the glorious mountain morning around them.

"Interesting," the shaman replied. Slowly, softly as if controlled by a dimmer-switch, the darker side of the shaman's face became lit evenly with the other. The man's long shadow cast from the dock onto the lake disappeared and Simon's eyes grew wide.

"How are you doing that?"

"What causes you to think I am doing anything?"

"The shadow on your face, on the dock and lake, it's gone! And yet I still see mine."

"How is that possible?" the shaman asked. "There is not a second sun rising in the west is there?"

Simon knew there wasn't but looked anyway. "No, yet you are being lit from some source of light. Where is it?"

"It takes time to teach and learn such things," came the reply. "But circumstances thrust upon us do not afford the time I normally take to teach them to those with eyes to see, ears to hear, and minds that are open. Events are in motion and you've shown promise of having a special gift that may allow you to grasp certain truths more quickly than other men. So I ask you again, where is the source of light that illuminates me?"

"I see no source. Nothing is shining on you but the sun in the east."

"Therefore?"

Simon felt foolish for what he was thinking. It wasn't possible. Or was it? He glanced beyond the shaman to the beauty of the trees on the shoreline. A fat trout leapt from the water, making a snack of a low-flying insect. The mournful cry of a loon echoed across the lake. The shaman's eyes were fixed on him, waiting for an answer.

"The light is…within you?" he speculated.

A faint smile appeared on the old man's face. A glint twinkled in his eyes.

"Do you…can you…control this light?" Simon asked.

"How can a person capture light, contain light or hope to control light?" came the reply.

"But if you are not controlling the light that illuminates you, how is it that I did not see it when I first sat down?"

"Exactly," the shaman observed.

46

"You're telling me I didn't see what was already there?"

The shaman allowed his smile to grow a bit broader. Not a full grin, no teeth showing, but a smile it was nonetheless. "Perception is important, is it not? And now I perceive the smell of pancakes and bacon."

The old man rose and Simon with him. The younger man reached out and touched the arm of his elder.

"This light you possess inside. Can I have it as well?"

"Where is your shadow?" the shaman asked.

Simon looked down and was startled. His own shadow had disappeared. But only for a moment or two. Then it slowly returned. Had he imagined it? Was it a trick of the mind or his eyes? "Wait. Sir, I just..."

But the shaman was already halfway down the dock heading back up to the lodge. Simon looked down again and, after making sure he saw things as they should be, followed his new mentor toward the source of the breakfast smells.

Chapter Eleven

Dr. Smythe reached down and gently took hold of Julie's arm, helping her to her feet. They were in a great hall the size of two gymnasiums. All along the walls and scattered around the interior were dioramas and displays featuring creatures one might encounter in the worst of nightmares or fantasy tales, as well as various artifacts and skeletal remains. Spaced here and there were benches where people could sit opposite LED panels mounted below the creatures.

Julie and Smythe started to walk toward where Jake was looking at what appeared to be a replica of a monster that had both canine and feline characteristics. Its front legs were longer than the hind legs and it had a broad chest bracketed by powerful shoulders, somewhat like a hyena but twice the size. The snout was flat, like a cat, with two big fangs protruding upward from a broad lower jaw. The tail was long and, like the hindquarters, striped. Its ears were small and round on the sides of the head instead of on top, and the eyes were abnormally large, round and dark as coal on the front of the face. Jake touched a button on the LED panel.

"The Beast of Gevaudan," a narrator began, his voice sounding very much like Dr. Smythe's. *"A large man-eating carnivore that terrorized the Margeride Mountain region in south-central France between 1764 and 1767 A.D. In addition to countless sheep and cattle, the beast is thought to have been responsible for at least 200 attacks on persons, fewer than 50 of whom survived. Of those that did, several suffered serious psychological trauma and at least five committed suicide. Those killed were eaten. Skilled at evasion, both cunning and tactical in its attacks, the beast demonstrated preference for the flesh of young women. Legend and lore describe it variously as a large wolf, a wolf-dog hybrid, a cross between an African predator and a wolf or bear, and some claimed it to be a werewolf. Attacks ceased after June 1767 when the creature was allegedly killed by local farmer and innkeeper Jean Chastel, who was also a skilled hunter and marksman. He used a German-made Jaeger Rifle in .54 caliber and a patched round ball projectile made of pure silver. Chastel also vanished shortly after the killings stopped. The specimen does not conform to known taxonomy classification and is therefore designated — species unknown."*

"C'mon, Doc," Julie turned to Smythe, her voice dripping with cynicism. "Werewolves, silver bullets, feasting on maidens? That's Hollywood B-movie horror stuff."

"Hold on," interjected Jake, "There are animals and people that experience allergic reactions to certain elements and metals. And predatory species can be drawn to women who are menstruating by the smell of blood. But even so Dr. Smythe, how did you know how to create this extremely realistic replica, let alone one of the creature that attacked us."

"Replicas?" asked Smythe.

"Dr. Smythe," Jake began, "You can't possibly expect us to believe this is taxidermy. It would be more than 200 years old, and the technology to create such realism that would last such a long time didn't exist in the 1700s. Even if it did, how can we know this is the beast the legends speak of?"

"Miss Reed, you're an experienced hunter and rancher who has been in close contact with animals on a number of occasions," Smythe noted. "Are you able to discern between real and faux fur?"

"Of course."

"Then I give permission to gently touch the beast and closely inspect its coat."

Julie stepped forward and carefully went up into the display. She ran a hand over the creature's right flank and drew it back with a start. "It's...it's real," she declared and then looked more closely at the fur. "The subtle color shading would be extremely difficult and time consuming to manufacture," she noted. "Smaller hairs underneath larger external ones, an undercoat that would have helped to protect the creature from cold and wet conditions. No seams visible. If it is dye of some kind, the whole animal skin must have been colored in various stages." She turned to Jake, "Um...if this is a fake, it's a really, really good one."

Jake looked at Smythe, who nodded approval. With almost reverential care, Jake stepped up to join Julie alongside the beast. He squatted and closely inspected both the front and back paws, noting the front claws appeared to be retractable, like a cat's, but the rear claws and feet were distinctly canine. "Miss Reed, please look at this."

Julie bent down beside Jake and the scientist pointed to dark brown splotches on the fur of the front right paw. "Looks like a blood stain," the deputy declared. "And you can call me Julie."

"Astute observations, both of you," said Smythe. "And while I'm certain you could spend hours, even days, examining all of the specimens in this collection, we must be moving on. There is much to do and little time in which to do it."

"Dr. Smythe," said Jake. "You're asking us to take in a lot here. May we please have at least a few minutes to look briefly at some of these other displays?"

"A brief tour, perhaps," replied Smythe. "AVADSA! Activate all LED panels with names and translations into English only."

"AVADSA?" queried Jake.

"Animatronic Voice-Activated Data and Security Assistant," replied Smythe. "She is our A.I. interface here at Sanctum. Not unlike those home digital assistants one can buy online. AVADSA, however, is considerably more robust, resourceful and versatile.

Panels next to each creature glowed and the trio began a slow stroll among the monsters. As they did so, Jake and Julie unconsciously found themselves walking closer together as if proximity meant mutual protection. The lineup was mind-blowing.

Camazotz – Mayan Death Bat collected in Belize, 1520 the display read in front of a man-sized animal with a human-like body, a vampire bat's head and giant bat wings.

La Lechuza – An anthropomorphic giant owl-like bird named by the Apache People. Collected in Arizona, 1855 the LED read.

Ahool – Resembled a prehistoric pterosaur and was mounted with wings spread out more than 12 feet wingtip to wingtip, *Collected in Indonesia, 1957.*

Jake and Julie looked up to see a snake more than 100 feet long and as big around as a small van hanging from the ceiling.

"Yacu Mama," declared Smythe. "The dreaded super-anaconda of the Amazon. She was collected from the river's western headwaters in 1984."

The three continued moving through the museum, passing more creatures with strange names from around the globe. Impundulu, Peluda, Ninki Nanka, Tatzelwurm and others. At times parts of the display hall

50

looked more like a section of Jurassic Park than a 21st century taxidermy collection. Jake and Julie occasionally glanced at one another when they came across something as hard to believe as the specimens themselves, such as collection dates going back to the 600s A.D. Smythe patiently kept his guests moving until they'd completed a quick circuit of the hall and returned to where the head of the beast Julie had kicked lay on the floor. Jake went to the LED near the creature.

Yakwawi – Shawnee, Mohican, Algonquian and Iroquoian: Known as the "stiff-legged man-eating bear." Collected in Vermont, 1610.

"Please come with me," Dr. Smythe prodded. "I'll explain as much as I can while I show you around."

The trio exited the display hall and the door system closed behind them when Dr. Smythe placed his hand on the scanning console near the entrance and commanded it to do so.

◆ ◆ ◆

It had killed four times since it feasted on the bowhunter and his family, and had discovered a pattern for success. The area was covered in dark trees that made resting in their shade during the day ideal for concealment of its black form. Hunting seemed best in the early morning and late evening along pathways where the two-legged animals with sweet blood and soft meat seemed to enjoy traveling in isolation. Sudden, violent ambush made pursuit unnecessary and it was pleased by how quickly and easily the creatures died. Their arrogance in moving about alone in its hunting ground was welcome but difficult to grasp. As was the way they sometimes moved.

The first of its recent kills had been a female who was strangely running from nothing down a forest trail. It thought she was naked with differently colored skin until it began to feed and realized the kill was covered in some kind of stretchy and tasteless secondary skin that seemed to have no purpose.

The second recent kill had been a male on a different trail. He came around a bend on a fast-moving device that held him atop two spinning discs and had slammed into its tree-like leg. That meal was also mostly covered in a second stretchy skin and the head was partially covered in a slippery shell. So it ripped the whole head off, tossed it off the path and fed on the torso,

51

organs and limbs. Once finished, the creature tossed the contraption with the discs up high into a tall pine tree.

Kills three and four had been veritable feasts. Those two-leggers were seated on the backs of large four-legged beasts that carried them around. The riders died easily, but the animals they rode were deceptively strong and fast. Killing them quickly had taken more effort. The flesh of the creatures ridden was different from other meat it had consumed since arriving and was not as agreeable, but it gave strength and sustenance needed to move on. And move the creature did.

It had traveled southeast through the wooded hills of Crook County, making its most recent kill near the intersection of Orr Road and Government Valley Road northeast of the town of Sundance. It traveled at night, taking care to avoid larger roads where it sometimes watched from the shadows as metal shapes carrying the prey creatures raced rapidly by. It remembered the sharp pain of being struck by one of them and desired not to repeat the experience. When it came to Interstate 90, the monster almost turned back north but then saw a way beneath the big path on which the metal boxes passed more frequently than on others it had seen so far. Dropping to move on four legs, it loped under the big path onto a smaller one – Moskee Road – which it paralleled for a time before heading east into more of the wooded hills where hiding was easy. Instinct drove it toward higher elevations.

Chapter Twelve

Simon Standing Elk and the shaman walked along a hiking trail in the woods behind the lodge. Energized by a hearty breakfast, the two men were silent until the view and sounds of the lodge had vanished behind them.

"Shaman," began Simon, "Forgive me, but I don't recall your name."

"That is because none was given."

"How do you want me to address you then?" Simon asked.

"Summarize our relationship thus far, from the time we met at the hospital to our conversation on the dock this morning. What do you think I should be called?" the shaman asked.

Simon thought in silence for a while before answering, "Wicasa."

"Mmmm," the shaman responded with a slow nod. "You think me a sage, do you?"

"As you will not tell me your name, I chose one that seems to cover our relationship to this point and where I think it may be going," stated Simon. "Do you object?"

"Let it be so for now. I will answer to Wicasa," the old man replied. "Time is against us. Ultimately the name may fit you better than I, Simon. There is strong medicine inside of you. You have seen the spirit realm but also experienced the bridge. As uncomfortable as the remembrance may be, we must speak of the creature that terrified you and changed the color of your hair."

"It was a powerful vision, Wicasa," began Simon. "I was in the sweat lodge speaking with my spirit guide, an old bear, when he left me alone in the forest. He spoke of old things passing away and new things to come, but was very sad. After the bear left I was thinking on his words when I felt a darkness overshadow me in the vision. Then I turned and looked up into the face of Yakwawi."

"Did Yakwawi speak to you?"

"No."

"Then how do you know it was Yakwawi?"

"I…I guess I don't know," said Simon as he stopped on the trail. "In fact, I have never heard of Yakwawi and don't even know what it is!"

"It is the name given a monstrous forest beast by this land's indigenous people of the Northeast. The Shawnee, Mohican and Iroquois spoke of them in legends. Fierce, bloodthirsty and stronger than 30 warriors, Yakwawi was very hard to kill. Describe it to me," Wicasa requested.

"The beast I saw was massive," Simon began. "Perhaps twice the height of a man, with a broad and thick torso. Long forearms, bulging with muscles, ended in hand-like paws with four fingers, two thumbs and short but thick claws that looked very sharp on each of them. The head was shaped like a football with a snout shorter than a wolf's but not as flat as a human. Big fangs jutted both upward and downward from its jaws."

"Tell me of the legs and the fur," Wicasa prodded.

"The legs were thick as trees with no visible knees or joints, like columns holding up a living building, yet they still bent. It was covered in short, coarse black fur. So black that light seemed to disappear into it. Almost like a black living cutout against the green forest plants behind it," continued Simon. "It reeked of death and filth. And the eyes … red as fresh blood but glowing with the intensity of a full moon," the man shuddered. "I hope I never see such a sight again. Even if it was only in a dream."

"What makes you certain it was a dream?" asked the shaman. "After all, when was the last time you smelled something in a dream?"

Simon mentally acknowledged that the older man had made a good point but he could not accept the existence of such a monster as reality.

"With respect, Wicasa, such monsters are the things of legend and myth. All cultures have stories about mystical creatures and monsters, do they not? The Greeks, Babylonians, Egyptians, Mayans, Aztecs, Chinese and many more? The legends of our own people speak of strange creatures that live in the woods, such as Bigfoot. These are but scary campfire stories and bogeyman tales for frightening children."

The shaman stopped in his tracks and fixed a stern gaze at Simon, his dark eyes blazing with admonition. "Be very careful, Simon Standing Elk. Do not so readily dismiss the stories of old, and do not disrespect Chiye-tanka while in a forest."

"Who?"

"Chiye-tanka, the Big Elder Brother whom you dismissively call Bigfoot. You and he may share a similar gift," the old man replied.

"Whoa, wait a minute," Simon objected. "You actually believe in Bigfoot? You sincerely think there is credence in the monster stories handed down by our ancestors? If such things existed then, or do even now, how is it that there is no evidence? Where are the bones, the bodies and the proof? Scientists have combed the forests, mountains and seas for generations in search of mythological beasts and none have yet to be found. If you want me to take you seriously, Wicasa, please explain."

The older of the two men gestured to a fallen log just to the right of the path they were walking along. Once seated, the shaman closed his eyes and took a deep breath. The scents of the forest seemed to nourish him and, just for a moment, Simon thought he saw the older man's weathered face lighten a few shades. Then the shaman spoke.

"I knew your father when you were a boy. He and I spent a great deal of time hunting and fishing together. When you were old enough, we took you along. Do you remember?"

"Yes," Simon replied, "I have many good memories of that time."

"The land where we hunted deer and pronghorns was home to other creatures as well. There were many coyotes, foxes and even some mountain lions in the area."

"I remember sitting by the campfire and hearing the coyotes call to one another," said Simon.

"Did we ever find coyote that died a natural death on any of our hunts?"

"No shaman."

"Did we ever see the bones of a mountain lion?"

"No."

"And, Simon Standing Elk, I encourage you to ask anyone who hunts or hikes through the wilderness how many times they have come upon the carcass or bones of a bear, moose, fox or wolf that was not killed by humans. You will find it rare that anyone has. Yet we know these animals exist."

"But that's because we see them often in the wild," said Simon. "We see deer and elk grazing in the meadows, bears turning over logs looking for grubs, and the howl of the wolf is common at night in areas where they live.

Plus, we have other evidence in the form of tracks, scat, fur, antlers, bones and photographs."

"You are right, my friend," the old man responded, "But people take hundreds of photographs every year of animals they cannot identify. We rightly are saddened when we hear of species threatened with extinction, but do you know how many new species are discovered annually?"

"I don't," replied Simon. "Perhaps one- or two-dozen? After all, it's getting harder and harder for any creature to avoid detection with such things as drones, thermal imaging and destruction of habitat."

"No. Many more than two-dozen. Far more than people are lead to believe," instructed the shaman. "Thousands of creatures are identified as new species each year. As many as ten or twenty thousand every circle of the sun."

"That's impossible," said Simon.

"Only for those who limit the scope of their search," the old man continued. "Many of the new species documented are insects or new kinds of sea creatures, but larger animals never before seen, or even thought to have been extinct, turn up as well. Wild giant ape-men reportedly lived in some African hills but were dismissed as myth until they were more correctly identified as mountain gorillas as recently as the early 1900s. The legendary Kraken sea monster is now assumed to be a giant squid, but a live one wasn't filmed in its natural environment until 2004. A pilot crash-landed in the Pacific early in the 20th century and, upon being rescued, spoke of fearsome dragons on nearby islands. We now know them as giant monitor lizards called Komodo dragons. All who first encountered these animals were thought to have been crazy or exaggerating. Now we realize they were speaking truth about what they saw, even if some were unable to use the right words to describe the creatures accurately."

"So you believe stories of Bigfoot, Yakwawi and other legends of our ancestors may have been about real animals they encountered?" asked Simon.

"You insist on using the past tense, my young friend. Never forget it is very difficult to disprove the existence of something that wishes to remain hidden," the shaman replied. "This is especially true if the creature in question can cross unseen barriers, barriers that exist all around us but are never considered by most."

"What on earth are you talking about?" asked Simon.

"Who said I was speaking of things on earth?" the older man answered.

"With all due respect, I cannot accept that mythological creatures are from outer space," Simon exclaimed with exasperation.

"Extraterrestrial doesn't necessarily mean from outer space, Simon," the shaman said calmly. "Just not of this earth, at least not initially."

Simon Standing Elk would hear no more. He rose quickly, "You're asking me to accept too much, shaman."

He left the older man and started walking quickly back down the path in the direction they'd come from. Undiscovered species he could, in theory, understand and recognize as a plausible reality. Perhaps even in the numbers the shaman claimed. But otherworldly monsters arriving on earth from who knows where? That was too much.

Simon quickened his pace, wondering what was happening to him. Visions of a horrible monster that could be linked to a creature other native tribes may have known of in the past? Days recovering from shock, and then a room at a lodge in some hidden valley of mountain beauty in the company of a strange man he thought he knew? Then seeing that man glow, even thinking for a moment he himself was glowing? And now a weird walk in the woods talking about space invaders past and present. He decided he'd reached the limits of what his mind could take in or accept.

Simon Standing Elk rounded the last bend in the trail expecting to see the backyard of the lodge. He stopped, frozen in his tracks with his mouth hanging open. Between him and the lodge the shaman he thought he'd left behind him stood erect in the path ahead holding his walking staff. Next to the shaman an eight-foot tall apelike animal stood upright on two legs.

"We are not finished," the shaman said before turning to the Chiye-tanka and nodding. The large creature with no visible neck turned its upper torso toward the shaman and made a barely perceptible nod of acknowledgement. Then it turned and fixed its gaze on Simon, a gaze that contained an odd mix of friendship and warning at the same time. The man and beast stood looking into one another's eyes for a few moments. The Chiye-tanka turned and strode off the path, vanishing silently into the forest.

Simon couldn't believe what he'd seen. The animal was there and then it wasn't. Had it actually dematerialized or was it an illusion created by the way it moved into and became one with the forest? Simon realized during the whole encounter he had not felt even a twinge of fear, only awe. He dropped to his knees on the path, mouth still agape.

"Now," the shaman broke the silence. "Please close your mouth and listen or I'll ask Chiye-tanka to pay you another visit. Time is short and we must verify what I suspect. That you are among the gifted ones."

Chapter Thirteen

Jake was the first to break the silence as the trio crossed the office area. "You've given us a great deal to absorb in a short period of time, Dr. Smythe."

"Indeed. But I'm afraid we're on an accelerated timeline. As you've both doubtlessly surmised, we have what may be a Yakwawi on the loose in the Black Hills. It's the first UKS we've had to deal with in that area in many years. Since you both know the region from recent work there, The Watch hopes you can help us destroy it."

They'd been walking toward the main entrance to the office but Smythe's comments caused Jake to halt.

"Why must it be destroyed, Doctor? Think of the scientific knowledge that could be acquired from close examination of a living specimen. If a creature of that size and power has somehow managed to elude being seen or killed, it must possess some amazing biological characteristics. And its presence means there could be more. I mean it can't be the only one in North America. It had to come from somewhere."

"That thing did come from somewhere," Smythe responded a bit too sharply. "And need I remind you of what it did to your wife? What's more, perhaps you'd benefit from knowing at least nine deaths have been attributed to the creature so far and more will follow the longer we delay."

Smythe's response hit Jake like a slap in the face. Julie saw it and intervened. "What's UKS?"

"Unknown species, Miss Reed," replied Smythe correcting his tone. "And I apologize for being abrupt. It's been years since The Watch has taken in any new recruits and I sometimes forget how overwhelming this can be for them. Especially when it is necessary to cram what is typically months of training and preparation into days. Let's sit down and order lunch to be brought in. That way I can run through answers to some of the many questions you doubtlessly have as we eat. Is that acceptable?"

Jake and Julie agreed. A side door to the office opened as they seated themselves opposite one another on the couches. Smythe sat down at the end of the table. A short, stocky Asian man dressed in a chef's outfit walked in and inquired what those around the table would like to eat.

"Do you have a menu like the ones in our rooms?" asked Jake.

"That won't be necessary," replied the chef with a hint of an Indian accent. "I can prepare anything you'd like."

Jake decided to keep it simple and asked for a ham and cheese sandwich with a side of fresh peas in the pod and a cola in hopes of finishing quickly in order to get back to the discussion.

Julie ordered a salad containing lettuce, sliced chicken strips, green peppers, tomatoes, egg slices, red onions, croutons and Italian dressing, and iced green tea with ginseng.

Smythe opted for a dozen oysters on the half-shell accompanied by a small bottle of hot sauce and hot black tea. With orders taken, the chef disappeared through the same door he'd entered.

"I'll give you the high-level and abridged version," began Smythe. "That will doubtlessly raise as many questions as it answers, but will also serve as a contextual framework regarding what's going on."

Jake leaned in attentively. Julie swung her right leg over her left and put an arm out along the back of the couch as Smythe began a tale both of them found fascinating and hard to believe.

"You've deduced the creatures in our little museum are, in fact, taxidermy. It's likely you have also concluded several of our specimens are very old. Each of you has had experiences since you arrived here at Sanctum that have likely led you to correctly surmise that The Watch possesses technology far more advanced than anything you've encountered elsewhere. It does, and has always been decades ahead of the rest of the planet in both technology and the unique capabilities of its personnel. The Watch has representation in, and or influence upon, every government in the world, and is itself in possession of more wealth than any nation. This allows us to operate globally, across all borders and sectarian or political divisions not only with impunity, but also with the gratitude of the global community at the highest levels. We answer to no human authority but have proved our benevolence to those in positions of power for generations. We do not interfere in the affairs of governments at any level beyond what is necessary to accomplish our mission, nor do they interfere with ours."

The chef returned with the requested food and drink orders but neither Jake nor Julie reached for anything on the table as Smythe continued once the chef had gone.

"Immediately you'll wonder how it's even possible for a secret order to be the richest entity on Earth. The answer is quite understandable. The onset of a so-called global economy during the last century resulted in the vast majority of the world's countries abandoning the gold standard and the issuance of fiat currencies, the values of which are not tied to any commodity. Throughout its long history, The Watch has been in a position to accumulate huge stores of gold, silver, diamonds and a host of other precious metals and gems. These are stored in various secret locations, unknown even to the countries in which they are located, and drawn upon to fund our operations. At current commodity exchange rates, The Watch possesses the equivalent of several trillion American dollars in solid tangible assets and we'll leave it at that."

Jake finally reached for his sandwich after Julie picked up her salad and began to pick at it while listening. Neither spoke, though the quick glance between them communicated the same message silently – *Are you buying this story?* Smythe went on.

"The Watch has existed for nearly two millennia. That's all you need to know for now, suffice it to say that its membership has observed and recorded first-hand accounts of some of the most momentous events in world history. Its objective is to defend humanity from extraordinary threats to life and property that occasionally appear in our plane of existence. I won't delve into space-time science or the metaphysics surrounding the intersection of planes of existence other than to point out that those who have proposed there are dimensions other than our own are correct. The reality is, we live in a multiverse. Scientific analysis in support of this conclusion has been underway for some time, most notably at Durham University in northern England and other prestigious academic settings using a simulation called EAGLE, the Evolution and Assembly of GaLaxies and their Environments. Findings have been published in various journals, including those of the Royal Astronomical Society, but few of the world's major news outlets cover such things. With the attention span of most people today measured at fewer than 7 seconds, stories that demand even rudimentary knowledge of mathematics, science and physics don't drive enough ratings, clicks or social-media shares to produce revenue, so they are avoided in favor of more salacious tabloid-like content."

"As a scientist, I know that all too well," interjected Jake. "It's been more than a year since I was interviewed about predator behavior by any reputable news outlet."

"Indeed," Smythe continued. "These alternate dimensions or existential planes intersect our own and, occasionally, what can loosely be described as portals, doors or windows open between such planes and our own at various places in the universe. During the time such portals are open, crossovers can occur in which objects, creatures or entities from our existence are swept into alternate realities and vice versa. Most of the time, living things do not survive the transition from one plane to another as the portals open in space. But others do open on or near Earth. Now two-thirds of our planet is covered by water, so any interdimensional land-dwellers unfortunate enough to pass through an opening over or in one of our oceans usually quickly die. Even sea creatures that make it through are likely to encounter challenges adapting to the temperatures or salinity of our waters. But there are times when a living thing passes between planes of existence only to find life-supporting conditions on our side to be favorable, if not more so, than where it came from. Unless dealt with swiftly, there is a remote possibility that such living organisms originating elsewhere could establish a toehold in our reality and multiply. The purpose of The Watch is to be on the lookout for these crossover entities, ascertain the threat level they pose, and then take appropriate action."

Smythe paused to take a sip of tea, put a drop of hot sauce on an oyster and slide it into his mouth. He then dabbed the corner of his mouth with a napkin.

"I want to be sure I've got this right," Julie remarked. "You're telling us that there are parallel universes, dimensions, planes, or whatever, and stuff is jumping around between them? C'mon, Dr. Smythe. I'm still trying to wrap my head around the fact that I went head to head against some inhuman monster, one of which you've got stuffed in a big closet. I actually don't give a fu-f-fudge where the thing came from. I just know it killed this guy's wife in front of both of us and now, if what you say is true, it's killed even more people. With that shi-er-crap going down in my jurisdiction, I need to get back there and take that thing out."

"Thank you for your linguistic restraint, Miss Reed. You shop at Walmart in Spearfish occasionally, don't you?" Smythe responded with a question that really wasn't one.

"How did you? Oh never mind. I guess your Illuminati and Bilderberg friends know everything, so yeah. But what's that got to…"

"And don't you stop each time to look at the wall near the exit where posters of missing persons are on display?" interrupted Smythe.

"Of course. In case I … wait … are you telling me?" Julie's expression suddenly looked far less cynical and much more concerned.

"Few are aware that nearly a million people go missing in the United States alone each year," remarked Dr. Smythe solemnly. "It's true that about half are runaways, another quarter are abductions related to family custody disputes and most of those are eventually found. But that still leaves tens of thousands of Americans that disappear without a trace annually, never to be seen or heard from again. Globally the number is more than eight million – a year. True, only a comparatively small number of unexplained disappearances are related to existential plane crossover but unfortunately we cannot control when or where that happens. Likewise we have uninvited arrivals in our world regularly."

"Dr. Smythe," it was Jake's turn. "If I assume what you say is correct, there could be considerable size variances in these cross-universe openings, right?"

"An astute observation, Dr. Sanders."

"So whatever is exchanged between these so-called planes of reality would be dependent on how big the opening is, correct?"

"Again you are spot on doctor," came the reply. "And it should be noted that the size of the opening could be very small but still pose an existential threat to humanity. A single virus or antibiotic-resistant bacteria could pass through a tiny portal but still have the potential to wipe out millions of us. This has, in fact, happened but I won't elaborate now. We've also experienced openings big enough to allow large animals to come through. Some of them very large indeed."

"What's the biggest door to open so far?" asked Julie, now fully engaged.

"Perhaps you've heard enough unbelievable stories for one day," suggested Smythe.

"Humor her," said Jake with genuine curiosity.

"There is a reason, my newfound friends, why almost every culture on earth has stories about dragons," Smythe commented as he reached for another oyster. Jake and Julie again exchanged glances of incredulity as Smythe continued. "But as to the largest openings that we know of, well, do you know what happened to the Anasazi?"

"You mean the Pueblo Indians who lived in remarkable dwellings built into the faces of steep cliffs in what's now southwest Colorado?" asked Julie before taking a sip of her green tea. "My understanding is something catastrophic went down and they migrated south."

"Compliments, Miss Reed," said Smythe. "That is the story anthropologists are sticking to at the moment. Reality suggests an entire civilization spent most of its existence living in fear, a fear that drove them to live in a way that meant even acquisition of necessities such as food and water exposed them to the danger of plunging to certain doom. Then, after generations of living in fear, a people is abruptly gone, leaving only ruins and a few artifacts behind."

"Dr. Smythe," Jake responded, "You can't expect us to accept a rift between planes of existence swallowed up everyone in an entire region of the country. What happened to the Anasazi was unique and likely explainable by natural circumstances such as drought."

Smythe finished the last of his shellfish, leaned toward Jake and spoke, "Unique, you say, Dr. Sanders? The Olmec of Mexico, Ethiopia's Aksumites, Peru's Moche, the Mycenaean civilization in Greece and the Cahokia of Illinois. I could go on, but there are many instances of large people groups mysteriously disappearing from various places across the globe throughout history. The Watch believes they will not be the last."

"Haven't archeologists found clues that indicate what happened to them?" asked Julie. "Climate change, foreign invaders, plagues and such?"

"Those are some of the narratives accepted and we're content to let them be so," Smythe replied. "It quells the need to dig deeper and discover more disturbing and ominous explanations. But let's return to the matter at hand. Dimensional crossover inevitably occurs and occasionally deposits unfortunate challenges in our world. For now, our focus must return to the one at hand – Yakwawi and how to stop it. It's time to head to the operations and technology wing."

Dr. Jonathan Smythe rose and indicated for the others to follow him. They did so, heading out the big oak doors and down the corridor.

Chapter Fourteen

Simon Standing Elk was seated across from the shaman at a small round table on the patio behind the mountain lodge, a pitcher of lemonade to one side as the men conversed over two tall glasses. Simon was so shaken by his encounter with The Elder Brother that he'd momentarily desired a stronger form of drink.

"Is Bigfoot friendly" he asked the older man.

"Friendly is a human term not always applicable to creatures that are not human," the shaman replied. "And let us call him Chiye-tanka, the name our people give to his kind. As to his disposition, he and his kind are vigilant, strong, quick and mostly silent with a desire to be left alone. They are the watchers and guardians of our wilderness and wild places. Respect the wilderness and you'll likely never encounter Chiye-tanka but if you do, the encounter will be peaceful. Disrespect the wilderness and his kind will frighten or harass you. Pursue or show aggression to Chiye-tanka and you will know wrath. In such respects, Chiye-tanka differs little from other large wilderness dwellers but there is one distinction. Chiye-tanka is gifted."

"Please explain. What is the gift of which you speak?"

"There are deep secrets The Great Spirit has hidden from all but a few," the shaman began. "What I tell you now I would rather have revealed over a period of many weeks but circumstances do not afford us that luxury. You are already overwhelmed, Simon Standing Elk, and if I continue to reveal The Knowledge, there will be no going back."

"I don't understand," confessed Simon staring at condensed droplets of water running down the glass containing his cold drink.

"If I continue, you will become a part of something much larger than you, than me, than our people, or anything else. To hear of The Knowledge is to cross a line of no return. To hear me is total commitment to the protection of all humans and nature alike. Refuse to hear me and you'll awaken tomorrow in your hospital room at Rapid City with no memory of recent events. Friends will tell you there was an accident in the sweat lodge and you passed out. You'll feel unwell for a few days but then resume life as it was before the Bear Butte incident. But there may be a lingering problem."

"What kind of problem, Wicasa?" asked Simon.

The shaman sighed. "If you are, in fact, among the gifted, there is a possibility Yakwawi will sense your presence if you venture too close to its self-declared territory. Should that occur, it will come for you."

Simon Standing Elk knew he was at a crossroads. One path would lead back to the life he'd known before his terrifying vision. A chance to be free of that haunting image in his mind. But he loved the Black Hills passionately. The Paha Sapa, as his people knew them, were sacred lands and the thought of always having to be alert for the presence of a demon creature stalking him whenever he went near the tree-covered mountains was a future he couldn't tolerate.

Besides, his sense of wonder and curiosity over what he'd seen the last few days made the choice easier than he thought it would be.

"Teach me," he said looking up into the eyes of the shaman. "Teach me this Knowledge of which you speak."

"Very well," the older man began. "But understand that the path you've chosen will require great courage. You will see wonders unseen by most of humanity. You will encounter that of which myth and legend are made. But in the end, if you persevere and survive, you will become legend yourself and our people will tell your story in songs for generations to come."

The shaman began by revealing his real identity as a covert agent of The Watch and went on to explain the intersection of existential planes in the multiverse. Simon listened intently. Nothing surprised him much at that point, including the sounding of the dinner chime after what only seemed like an hour instead of five. When he asked the shaman to tell him more about the role of the gifted, the old man rose and told him they would speak again in the morning.

After the evening meal, the shaman retired to his spartan quarters. As before, he swiped a card to activate the encrypted laptop on his desk and he slowly typed a new message.

A watchman is born. Gifting probable.

He slid the cursor over the SEND button and tapped his finger.

♦ ♦ ♦

Hunting had been good along the new path it found. The creature had no way of knowing it was called Sand Creek Road by the locals, but it did understand that the number of two-legged creatures with soft, tasty flesh traveling along the path had increased once it turned to follow it north. On cloudy nights it could see the sky to the northeast reflecting a large concentration of lights below and had come to associate such light with the presence of its favorite prey.

The time of year also benefited the creature as bowhunters pursued deer and elk, while those preparing for upcoming firearm seasons were out scouting for signs of big game. An increase in people walking the deep woods kept wild game moving around. The beast knew the two-leggers carrying the objects that hurled the stinging sticks could be dangerous, so it seldom stalked them.

Instead it waited for them to move along game trails around dawn and dusk as they walked through the forest to find places to hide and ambush prey. It let them, knowing that their success meant more meat for itself. Three times in recent days it had caught hunters as they carried parts of their prey back toward the direction of the lights. When doing so, they could not react quickly with the stick-shooting weapons and were vulnerable. Using the disguise of darkness along the trails, there had been no pursuit involved in its killings. A single crushing blow to the heads of the two-leggers either killed them outright or stunned them enough for the creature to break necks and spines. It discovered the blood flowed more freely immediately after the killing blow and now preferred to drink them dry before feasting on the flesh. Then it would dismember its prey and hurl bones as high and far as it could so as not to leave much behind at the kill site that could alert other animals and two-leggers to its presence. Once disposal of the remains was accomplished, the creature would take what the hunter had killed and use its scent to find out if there were any leftovers in the direction from whence the two-legger had come. It had been rewarded for following this tactic. Blood-filled organs had been found near the remains of the four-legged prey in piles that also contained digestive organs. It had been able to eat its fill of meat and blood organs regularly, but had also learned it was not the only predator in the forest.

Twice it had encountered skulking, tan-colored, four-legged creatures that moved with great stealth and silence. Both times these beings had been found lurking around carcasses of the four-legged beasts that had spikey sharp bones sticking out of their heads. Those were the kind of creatures the two-leggers were trying to kill, the kind that had sustained it until it discovered a preference for the flesh and blood of two-leggers. The tan predators had objected to the monster's attempts to take their kill and attacked it. Though they had very sharp claws and teeth, and were able to move with great speed and agility, killing them had been nearly as easy as killing two-leggers. Once the great beast got hold of one of the predators, it simply ripped them apart. The flavor of their flesh was not as pleasing to the creature as that of other animals it had sampled, so it just tossed their remains high into a tree.

Then there were the pack hunters. It had only encountered them once but found them more formidable than the sleek tan predators because they coordinated their attacks from different directions simultaneously. When the beast was able to get a partial hold on one, two others would leap up and bite its paw-like hand while others harried the backs of its ankles. It had killed one and chased the others off. While the flesh and blood of the gray pack hunter was better than that of the tan one, there were more preferable menu options.

Smell had drawn it to the edge of the denser forest where a group of four-legged animals nearly the size of those it had killed carrying riders several days earlier was gathered around a muddy depression in meadow grass. One of them was rolling around in the mud as others grazed nearby. It had learned from experience that success depended on approaching prey with its face into the wind so it moved toward the animals, stalking them from downwind with surprising stealth for a creature of its mass. Dropping to all fours and eventually a crawl, the beast edged closer to the group.

Predators understand the need for patience and choosing the precise moment to strike. A full hour passed as the creature watched the other animals graze and wallow in the mud just 10 yards away. It was as still as a big black boulder, hind legs tucked underneath like large, spring-loaded logs.

Something in the trees beyond caused the animals to all look in a direction opposite the beast. The nearest of them was smaller than the others and close. Close enough for the monster to catapult forward, front limbs outstretched, and catch the young elk. It grasped the animal's hind legs and held onto them, swinging the elk violently into the trunk of a nearby ponderosa pine. The beast rose to full height, hanging onto its stunned prey. It crashed the elk's head into the ground as it squirmed to escape, but the ground was soft near the mud. Without warning, the beast felt a sharp stab in its lower torso and wheeled around, still holding one of the young elk' s hind legs the grasp of a forelimb. The herd's dominant bull lunged forward toward the hulking black menace again, pushing a pair of massive antlers forward toward the threat with all the power it could muster. But the monster's reach was longer than that of the antlers and its free arm swatted the side of the charging bull's head with enough force to send it staggering sideways and backwards into the mud. The bull shook off the blow and recovered to set up another charge. This time the monster swung the smaller elk over its own head and brought it crashing down onto the antlers of the charging bull like a heavy living club. The impact snapped the neck of the bull and impaled the younger elk on its antlers clean through, killing both animals.

It sought to relieve the discomfort caused by the bull elk's initial charge into its back, so the beast dragged the younger elk's carcass to the edge of the wallow and dropped it before rolling in the mud itself. The moist dirt created a sensation the monster felt pleasing. It eased the sting of the antler stab wounds, which had not penetrated far into the beast's dense muscle. It slid to the edge of the wallow and began to feed. In time, the monster rose to leave, but not before ripping the heart and liver from the big bull elk to take along as a snack. The creature became one with the forest once again, oblivious that its savage attack on the elk had not gone unnoticed.

In the trees beyond the wallow, an elk hunter sat trembling in soiled camouflage pants reviewing video he'd taken of the entire fight and subsequent events on a smartphone.

Chapter Fifteen

Dr. Smythe led Jake and Julie to an elevator at the end of a hallway. Its outer doors were handsomely polished hardwood but the entire interior was bright, burnished metal that somehow didn't hold reflections of the occupants. Smythe pressed his right thumb against a small reader where elevator floor buttons would typically have been.

"AVADSA," he spoke to no one in particular, "Operations and technology please."

"Yes, Dr. Smythe," came the reply from an overhead speaker.

There was no sensation of movement up, down or otherwise and just as Jake was going to ask if there had been a malfunction, the elevator doors slid open to reveal a catwalk separating two large sunken, open work areas. Below them on the right was what appeared to be an incredible tactical operations center. Julie let out a whistle at the site of high-definition flat-screen monitors lining the walls and two rows of workstations arranged in concentric semicircles at which sat a dozen workers wearing microphone-equipped headsets. Seated behind and above them on an elevated platform in a chair that looked like what one might expect to see on the bridge of a futuristic starship was a man with a mane of flowing white hair and a beard to match. He swiveled toward the new arrivals and looked up at them to reveal a deeply tanned face.

"Jonathan," the man began with a smile, "To what do we owe the honor of your presence today? We've had no activity out of the ordinary and all five operations currently underway are condition green."

"Hello Moses," Smythe smiled in return. Jake and Julie immediately noticed a resemblance between the depictions of the Old Testament prophet in artwork and the man below them. "Allow me to present Dr. Jake Sanders and Deputy Julie Reed." He turned to this two guests and gestured toward the man below. "Dr. Sanders, Miss Reed, I present Moses Davison…The Watch Operations Center Commander on Duty, a position we affectionately call COD."

"Ah," said Moses standing with a smile. "The preeminent scientist and the renowned smiter of backside. A pleasure to finally meet you two. Welcome to The Watch."

"I don't know about the preeminent part," replied Jake. "But thank you Commander."

"Call me Moses," the man said. "And commander's a job description, not a title or rank."

"What's this smiter of backside stuff?" asked Julie.

"We keep the language clean around here, young lady," Moses responded. "It was a polite way of saying I'd bet against anyone stupid enough to try to take you in a fight."

"Gotcha," acknowledged Julie with a smile. "Nice to finally get some respect."

"Did he say something about five operations going on?" asked Jake.

"Indeed," responded Smythe. "Intersection of existential planes is nearly constant, though such intersection doesn't always result in openings and or crossovers. Right now, watchmen and women around the globe are on the alert for signs of anything that might warrant our close attention. Most alerts turn out to be false alarms but when we do get a hit on solid lead, teams are dispatched to investigate. Moses just told us we have five teams in the field conducting investigations at the moment and everything is proceeding as planned."

Jake shifted his attention from the operations center to the technology side of the room on the other side of the walkway. It looked like a sophisticated science laboratory and was sectioned off from the rest of the entire area by a thick, but unbelievably clear transparent barrier.

"I assume this is to seal off the area in the event of a mishap?" he asked turning to Smythe.

"Yes. It's impenetrable and airtight. You'll note the large ventilation panels on two of the walls, and those lockers in each corner contain hazmat suits. Beyond that door there," Smythe said pointing, "Is a decontamination center capable of neutralizing any contaminant or biohazard."

"Any hazard?" questioned Julie. "Pretty confident about that aren't we? After all some stuff from another dimension might not be killed that easily. Aren't there microorganisms that can live in the most hostile environments like volcanoes on the ocean floor? What if something is so resistant to heat, cold and known substances that your decon system can't handle it?"

"Rest easy about that, Miss Reed," replied Smythe. "We've yet to encounter anything able to withstand disintegration at the sub-molecular level."

"Wait," interjected Jake. "You've got some kind of a science-fiction disruptor beam here?"

"Who do you think gave Hollywood writers the idea for one?" answered Smythe with a glint in his eye. "Oh, it's not portable. Not yet in a practical manner anyway. But when particularly difficult bacteria, viral or fungal agents are discovered, our system has been most effective in eradicating them."

"And what of the hosts carrying those bugs?" asked Jake.

"Unfortunate sacrifices must sometimes be made to protect humanity," Smythe replied somberly. "That only happens when the contaminant is deemed lethal and the host irreversibly terminal. Fortunately, such instances are quite rare and we make every effort to minimize any discomfort on the part of the host when it happens. Please understand that gives us no joy, but there have been a few instances, and I emphasize few, where infectious foreign agents entered our world that, had they been allowed to spread, would have made such things as Ebola and Marburg look like a case of the sniffles. But today we are dealing with potential threats one doesn't need a microscope to see. Speaking of sight, do you both see that black basketball on the right end of the center table?"

Jake and Julie directed their eyes to a black sphere where Smythe was pointing.

"Miss Matthews," Smythe called down to one of the six workers in lab coats on the floor below. The airtight barrier apparently did not impede the transmission of sound. "Please be kind enough to show our guests the ultra-black project."

The thirty-something redhead with short hair and safety glasses walked to the black ball and picked it up. Then she turned it to reveal it wasn't a sphere at all, just a perfectly round piece of cardboard with one side covered in paint so black that it gave the illusion of being a sphere. What's more, it looked like a bottomless hole in the table when she laid it flat.

"Everything we see is seen because some amount of ambient light reflects off it and registers with our eyes and brains," Smythe explained. Some scientists have perfected paints that absorb up to 99.65 percent of light, with some help from a few of our covert science agents. Our version absorbs 99.99 percent of light shown on it from any angle. Miss Reed, can you think of any application for such technology?"

"It'd make a heck of a hard-to-see ninja suit for tactical night ops," she replied. "Any operative wearing it would still be vulnerable to detection from thermal scanners and motion-sensing optics though."

"And what if I told you we'd just perfected suits of that color on the outside interwoven with a special thermal-dispersing material regulated to match the temperature of the environment externally while optimizing the comfort of the wearer?"

"That'd be a tremendous advantage to anyone conducting night operations," Julie acknowledged.

"Did you notice anything about the color of the beast that attacked you?" queried Smythe.

"Come to think of it, that monster was blacker than any animal I've ever seen," answered Jake. "Maybe not as black as that stuff down there but it would be very hard, even impossible to see it at night in a forest. Even if you did, you might not know what you were looking at until it was too late. The thing could bunch up against a rocky hillside and look like the opening of a cave. Anyone who got curious and ventured too close would likely be killed."

"Using that knowledge, Dr. Sanders, tell me how you think Yakwawi hunts?"

"If it's strictly carnivorous, it's an ambush predator. Patient, cunning, tactical and quick when it has to be. But its downfall is the overpowering stench it gives off. To succeed, it would have to understand that and position itself downwind of prey."

"Astute, as always doctor," Smythe commented. "But what if the odor you speak of was the ambient smell in the land of its origin?"

"Property values would suck," quipped Julie before she could catch her sarcastic wit, earning her a stern glance from Smythe. "Sorry. Continue."

"It would have to learn that and adapt in order to overcome the liability," answered Jake.

"How?" asked Smythe. "What would a being of significant animal intelligence do to change the way it smelled or the way its smell carried?"

"I suppose it depends on the level of intelligence we're talking about here," surmised Jake thoughtfully staring off to one side but not looking at anything in particular. "Scent suppression can be achieved by masking or taking on the scent of something else, but also by paying attention to atmospheric conditions. Many odors don't transmit as well in thinner air found at higher altitudes."

"AVADSA," Smythe commanded, "Proximity hologram. Topographic map. Crook County in Wyoming and adjacent counties please."

Between Smythe and his guests appeared the map he'd requested. He stepped through the hologram to view it from the same perspective as the others and the map adjusted accordingly with his hands to show them all the same view.

"AVADSA, plot suspected kill sites of entity designated Yakwawi since known arrival."

Red dots appeared on the map with a key indicating human fatalities at red locations. Yellow triangles appeared where animal kills were suspected. Numerals indicated the order in which the sites had been found. Smythe used his fingers to manipulate the map, zooming in tighter on the area between the towns of Sundance in Wyoming and Spearfish in South Dakota. Though not a straight line, there was a general eastward track between the two towns.

"AVADSA," said Jake as Smythe turned to him with a raised eyebrow, "Show elevations of highest hills in or near the displayed area."

"Dr. Smythe, shall I grant Dr. Sanders access to my interface?" the computer asked.

"Clearance level five for now, AVADSA," came the reply. "And the same for Miss Reed."

The computer responded by plotting elevations on the map. Jake studied it closely for a few moments before drawing his initial conclusions.

"The highest elevations in the apparent path of the beast are all in Lawrence County, South Dakota," Jake noted. "Crow Peak southwest of Spearfish is the shortest of the tall ones at close to 5,800 feet and it is near abundant human-associated food sources. But there are two hills near Tinton on the state line with Wyoming closer to 6,000 feet. There's also some pretty rough terrain in that area for seclusion but if it wants to eat people, hunting might not be as good there. But look at Terry Peak near Lead and Deadwood. It's more than 1,000 feet higher than the others with a lot of prey in a concentrated area. If I'm not mistaken, it's one of the highest elevations in the Black Hills formation. But it's also the greatest distance from the last mapped kill."

"Hey guys," Julie interjected. "The fall colors will be peaking in Spearfish Canyon about now I should think. That's a huge tourist draw this time of year and it is right between the last known kill and Terry Peak."

Almost on cue, a red strobe light activated on the ops center side of the catwalk and attention turned from the map to what was happening.

"Report please," Smythe called down to Moses.

"We have a situation near Spearfish, South Dakota, Jonathan," the commander replied.

"Initiate containment per standard operating procedures," ordered Smythe.

Chapter Sixteen

50 minutes earlier

Chad Barrick had been hunting in the Black Hills since he was a boy. He'd seen coyotes, mountain lions, bobcats, even two black bears and a wolf, which weren't formally acknowledged to exist in the area. At five-foot eleven and 180 pounds, the 29-year-old construction worker was fit and a formidable archer. Rarely did his deer or elk tags go unfilled during bowhunting seasons. In spite of more than a decade of experience stalking game through the forest and having his share of close calls with everything from rattlesnakes to rockslides, nothing could have prepared him for what he'd seen. As soon he was certain the monster was gone, Barrick ran through the woods as fast as his legs could propel him until he reached his pickup, a red 2007 Chevy Silverado 1500.

Once at the truck, he stripped off his filthy camouflage and underwear. Barrick grabbed one of the rags he kept in the large tool chest across the back of his pickup bed and a jug of orange-scented hand cleaner. After doing his best to clean himself up, Barrick reached behind the driver's seat for a pair of Wranglers and a clean T-shirt he'd stowed there for times his friends or family wanted to go out after work. In clean clothes and reasonably presentable, Barrick pointed his truck down the Forest Service road and raced toward Interstate 90.

♦ ♦ ♦

Ranger Lisa Sutherland was nearing the end of her day shift at the U.S. Forest Service Northern Hills Ranger District Office. She wore her dark hair in a ponytail under her standard-issue ranger hat. Combined with a uniform that fit her very well, the look took about a decade off her 44 years. As Lisa was closing the blinds on the front window of the office, a Chevy pickup roared up to the main door and screeched to a halt. A man wearing a T-shirt and jeans tumbled out of the driver's seat looking quite distressed.

Anticipating the report of a fire or some other emergency, Sutherland just managed to get behind the main desk as Chad Barrick barged in out of breath. Not knowing what to expect, Sutherland's right hand reached for a can of bear spray she kept under the counter whenever she was alone in the office.

"Please," gasped Barrick. "I need to show you something you'll never believe."

Not really knowing how to take the desperate-looking man's remarks, Sutherland flipped the safety on the bear spray off before responding.

"Good afternoon, sir. Are you alright? Please calm down and tell me how I can help you."

Barrick, suddenly realizing how things might look, took a moment to slow his breathing and stepped back while raising his arms halfway to show he had no nefarious intentions.

"Please ma'am, I have to report something I saw in the hills near the Wyoming border. Something you're not going to believe because I'm not sure I do. I was bowhunting east of Sand Creek and got something on video I have to show you. People need to know it's not safe."

Sutherland could see now that what she'd initially thought could be aggression on the visitor's part was not. It was fear. Something had scared this hunter and he apparently had video of whatever it was.

"Okay, let's just take it easy and tell me what you saw."

"It was the biggest predator I ever saw, ma'am," Barrick began. "I was watching a small elk herd at a wallow when all of a sudden it was just there. It grabbed a calf and when the dominant bull charged the thing, it clubbed it to death with the calf."

Sutherland appraised the man carefully. His eyes were not dilated. He did not smell of alcohol but, oddly, did smell like oranges.

"I am Ranger Sutherland, but call me Lisa," she began. "I want to understand what you're telling me. You were hunting east of Sand Creek. You saw a herd of elk attacked by a predator. A predator that killed an elk with a club?"

"Ma'am, I know how this must sound. You must think I'm nuts. You're thinking I come barging in here with some wild story about elk getting killed and probably think I'm high or drunk. We'll I am as sober as you are, Lisa.

Call me Chad, by the way, Chad Barrick. Yeah, I smell like an orange but that's because I was so scared I crapped myself and had to clean up with some stuff I keep in the truck before coming in here. I've got a pile of smelly camo in a plastic bag in the pickup bed if you don't believe me. But I've got proof right here," he pulled his phone from his back pocket. "And believe you me, when this gets on the news there's gonna be a full-on search and destroy mission for whatever that thing is!"

Lisa was beginning to believe the man saw something that had shaken him badly. She pulled a U.S. Forest Service map of the Black Hills from a display on the counter, opened it up and folded it so the area around the northern Black Hills was on top. Taking a pen from her shirt pocket, she handed it to Chad.

"Are you able to show me the area where you saw this happen?"

"I can show you exactly where it happened," and Chad put an X on the map precisely where the wallow had been. Then he wrote GPS coordinates next to the X. "There. That's where I was. Now let me show you the video."

Lisa suggested they sit down and gestured to a small table with three chairs in the entryway lobby area. The blinds were still open on the window next to the table so people outside could see in, adding a measure of safety in case she'd misjudged the man's intent. Once seated, Chad opened his phone's video app and hit play. The ranger fought to keep herself composed as she watched the scene at the elk wallow unfold on the screen. Chad's hand began to shake so badly that Lisa had to take the phone from him in order to see the end of the clip clearly. Then she rewound and played it through two more times.

"See…see…I ain't crazy, ma'am! If you know what that thing is, I want you to tell me right now. And don't go telling me it's a big bear or even a freakin' Sasquatch because I've spent a lot of time in those woods and know what is and isn't up there. At least I thought I did."

"You're right," Lisa replied, keeping her voice calm and steady in spite of dread welling up inside her. "We need to get some help on this right away. Please stay here because I'm certain we have people who will want to hear your story and see your video. Have a drink from the water cooler behind you. I need to make a phone call."

U.S. Forest Service Ranger Lisa Sutherland knew what she had to do and didn't like it. She'd been a ranger for nearly 20 years and enjoyed her work. But she also had a higher oath to uphold, a promise made to a man who had saved her life many years ago. Once behind the front counter, she reached into her purse beneath it, skillfully picking up the telephone receiver at the same time with her other hand and pretending to dial a number. She felt for a small square metal container inside the purse, which she flipped open to expose a small button. She pressed it as she spoke to no one on the telephone.

"This is ranger Lisa Sutherland at the Northern Hills Office in Spearfish requesting immediate assistance. There's been a major animal attack by a large predator and we're going to need to get some people on it ASAP. And we'll need a Game, Fish and Parks conservation officer in the area to look at a video and take a statement. Yes. I understand. We'll be waiting. Thank you."

She returned to Chad and sat down at the table with him. He'd looked at the video again and there were what appeared to be tears in his eyes.

"Help should be here shortly," she said in a reassuring tone with some tears of her own beginning to form. "I am so sorry for what you've been through, Chad. And I'm sorry I was skeptical of your story at first. It's just... well...so unbelievable."

"Ma'am, I wish this had never happened," Chad said lifting his eyes to meet hers. "I got a hot wife and the cutest little girl waitin' on me at home, expecting maybe tonight would be the night I'd bring home the bull elk I've been watching up there since July. Lord knows we could use the meat because the construction biz hasn't been what it used to be with the economy and all. I'm just afraid of what would happen if someone else...a hiker, another hunter or anybody else came across whatever that thing is. Ranger Lisa, please tell me this isn't the first time someone saw this. Please tell me what that creature is."

"I wish I could, Chad, but I honestly don't know. It's unlike anything I've ever even imagined in my worst nightmares and I gotta tell you it's going to be a while before I venture up into that part of the forest. At least until I hear that thing's gone for sure."

"But what was it?" Chad persisted. "I told ya what it isn't. It's like something from a bad horror movie, an experiment someone messed up and got loose or something. Where does something like that come from?"

The front door opened at that moment and two men built like inverted pyramids entered wearing official U.S. Forest Service ranger uniforms. Their shirts struggled to contain their muscular chests and arms. Full duty belts were wrapped around their slender waists, each of which held a holstered 10 mm Glock semiautomatic pistol. The men turned toward the two at the table who rose to meet them.

"I'm Ranger Rick and this is Ranger Smith," said the closest one extending a meaty hand.

"Seriously guys," Lisa thought noticing that Chad's eyebrows raised as if he wasn't buying the men were rangers. They weren't, but Lisa quickly grasped the extended hand and shook it eagerly before extending hers to the second new arrival. Her actions seemed to relax Chad a bit as he'd tensed at the sight of two men who looked more like professional bodybuilders than forest rangers.

"Ranger Steve Rick, Ranger Tim Smith, it's great to see you again," Lisa said making up fictitious first names for the pair. "Mr. Barrick here has something to show you."

The two men stood either side of Chad, each a full head taller than the hunter, and looked over his shoulders as he played the video.

"Mr. Barrick, you've got something mighty strange there," the man designated as Steve said after the clip had played. "I'm going to ask you to help us by doing something that may be hard for you. Will you accompany us back up to the place where this happened?"

Chad had hoped to file a report, give them a copy of the video and go home to his wife and daughter.

"Sir, is that really necessary? I mean it will be dark soon and believe me, that thing is something you don't want to tangle with in broad daylight, let alone in the dark. Besides, if we do see it what will you do? You two look like you can handle yourselves but that thing took down a six-by-six bull elk without a weapon and those pistols of yours won't be much use against something that big and powerful."

"I assure you that it will be fine," it was Tim's turn to talk. "We have two trackers with dogs lined up, along with four more rangers armed with rifles and two conservation officers who will either have shotguns or rifles in addition to side arms. The team is assembling and waiting for us just off I-90 near the border and everyone will be there soon. You'll be well protected."

"Wow. That was fast. Okay, I guess. That sounds like a lot of firepower. But how did you know you'd need that much and where to go?"

"I can't comment about an ongoing investigation, sir," Tim began to cover their story. "But between us, I'll tell you this is not the first sighting of that beast this afternoon. We had another hunter on the Wyoming side turn in some digital pictures this morning and started assembling a response team a couple of hours ago."

Chad bought the story but had one more question. "Can I call my wife and tell her I'll be late?"

"Let's do that on the way if you don't mind," replied Steve. "Before you do though, may I please have your phone to transmit the video to the team? We have high-speed mobile Wi-Fi in our truck just for such things."

The three men walked out the front door of the ranger station to a Forest Service pickup. The two in uniform got into the front seats, motioning for Chad to get in the rear cab. In minutes they were on I-90 heading west toward the Wyoming border.

Lisa Sutherland unzipped a compartment in her purse and withdrew an envelope she never thought she'd use. Inside was a letter requesting an immediate leave of absence of undetermined length from the U.S. Forest Service, citing a family health emergency as the reason. In two weeks she'd submit her formal resignation. She regretted leaving a job and town she'd grown to love, but as a covert operative of The Watch, she knew what must be done.

Steve, Tim and Chad were racing down I-90. As Tim drove, Steve took an exact duplicate of Chad's phone from a pocket on the truck's center console, discretely copied everything from the original to the duplicate, and replaced the video of the attack with a different one on the cloned phone. Chad had drifted off into a dreamless sleep, unaware of the colorless and odorless gas seeping into the rear cab through the air vent. Nor could he see the invisible airtight barrier that separated the men in the front of the truck from the back seats. Seeing their passenger unconscious, the two fake rangers slowed and waited for a driver in Chad's truck to catch up.

Both vehicles exited the interstate and made their way to a second turnoff heading up into the forest where The Watch had a special sanitizing crew waiting.

◆ ◆ ◆

It was dark when Chad Barrick woke with a start in the driver's seat of his truck, which was parked precisely where he'd left it at the beginning of the day's hunt. He was wearing the same camo garments he'd put on earlier in the day but they were clean, exactly as they'd been when he left home. Pulling his phone from his pocket, he found a video of the elk herd he'd been watching at the wallow. Then he whispered to himself in the clip that it was time to set up a shot on the big bull and the video went dark.

Chad exited the truck and looked behind the seat. His extra clothes were as he'd placed them days ago, his bow and arrows where he normally transported them. Moving to check the bed of his pickup, Chad let out a gasp at the site of the big bull elk's partially caped head and shoulders. Also in the truck bed were four quarters of the elk with the appropriate tag filled out and signed by him as he'd have done after a successful harvest. He then noticed one of his arrows next to the bull, bloodied tip to vanes as if it had passed right through an animal.

Head spinning with confusion, the hunter had no evidence to support the fearful encounter that was becoming an increasingly fuzzy recollection in his mind. There were no memories of drawing on the elk or loosing an arrow, let alone packing out the elk to his truck. But how could he explain the evidence in front of his eyes? Even his orange-scented cleaner and rags were where they should be with no trace of having been disturbed. The bewildered hunter climbed into his truck and started for home, oblivious to two pairs of eyes watching over his safe departure.

One belonged to a powerfully built man in a ranger uniform. The other set of eyes was an almost luminescent shade of sapphire blue and disappeared with a moonlit flash of gold and white into the gathering forest mists of night as soon as the truck was out of sight.

It was 11:00 when Chad pulled into his driveway and saw a county sheriff's SUV parked in front of his home. A deputy was talking with his wife in the front yard. At the sight of his truck, the woman called into the house and ran toward him. A young girl, his daughter, bolted out the front door and followed close behind.

"Chad!" the woman exclaimed. "Oh baby, I'm so glad you're home. Are you alright? We were worried sick when it got so late. I called the sheriff and we were about to come looking for you. Why didn't you call?"

"I...I...ah...I got a nice elk"

"What!? And you didn't think to call?" the woman's tone switched from relief to anger.

"I must have gotten dehydrated or something packing it out, sweetie. Honest, I passed out or something and woke up in the truck a half-hour ago. For a while I even forgot where I was," Chad speculated. "And I had this horrible nightmare. I'm really sorry."

"Mommy, mommy, look at the big elk daddy shot!" his daughter squealed with excitement after jumping up on the rear bumper and looking inside the pickup bed.

"We'll talk more about this later," the woman told her husband as the deputy approached.

"Are you alright, Mr. Barrick?" the lawman asked. "Your family was getting worried."

Chad eyed the large, muscular law enforcement officer. He felt he should know the guy but couldn't place where he'd seen him before.

"Yeah," replied Chad. "Guess I just overdid it trying to get the elk packed out and all. But I think I'm okay now. Sorry for causing all the worry and trouble."

"No problem, sir. That's what we're here for. Just glad everything is okay. Nice bull, by the way," remarked the deputy peering into the truck bed. "Your family will be eating well for quite a while. If there's nothing else, I'll be on my way."

"No, and thank you so much for coming so quickly," Chad's wife replied wiping tears from under her eyes.

With that the lawman entered his SUV and pulled out his phone. Opening a highly encrypted text messaging app, he typed in all caps CONTAINED AND SANITIZED before driving off.

Chad hugged his wife and girl. Then the three of them headed into the house. It was cool enough to let the rest of the work on the elk meat wait until morning.

Chapter Seventeen

He had risen before dawn, unable to sleep soundly following the previous day's strange events and conversations. Simon Standing Elk sat on a blanket with another wrapped around him, staring across the lake from the end of the dock's right "T". The reflection of the stars on the calm water's surface was fading slowly as the eastern sky began to lighten and push night slowly westward. The sounds of morning birds increased and the distinct laugh of a loon echoed across the still water. Far in the distance, a wolf howled and was answered by another somewhere in the forest on the mountain behind the lodge.

"Great Spirit," Simon bowed his head and softly prayed with an earnest heart, his voice barely a whisper. "I do not understand all that the shaman has told me. It is said you give wisdom generously to those who seek it from you. That is what I now seek. If there is a greater purpose to my existence, a special plan for which you created me, please open my heart and mind to receive it. Please remove the fog of doubt and give me strength, Great One. I surrender all that I am into your care and purpose. Please give me eyes to see, ears to hear, and wisdom to not be deceived."

When he raised his head, a column of gray lake mist stood on the water before him. Glancing right and left, Simon noticed no other mist than what was right in front of him. Believing it not to be a coincidence, the Lakota man stared intently into the mist. Shapes began to move inside the small rectangular cloud as if he was peering through a fogged glass door. At first they lacked definition but the more intently he looked and concentrated, the greater the clarity of his vision. A familiar forest path. His bear friend walking away. A flash of light followed by a series of rapid images that appeared to be from a complex on a tropical island. A white man he did not know and a woman that looked familiar. Deep blackness for a moment. Then rapid fire images of more than a half-dozen people with looks of abject terror on their faces. Bloody remains of two elk. A monstrous dark form moving slowly through a pine forest. Its head snapped around to glare through the mist at Simon with glowing red eyes. Yakwawi! It saw him. It knew him. The flash of a flaming sword through the mist and then nothing but the placid scene of a mountain lake at dawn.

"Tell me all you saw." The shaman had silently walked out on the dock to stand behind Simon.

The younger man began to recount his vision to his mentor.

Unseen to both men, high on the mountain rising from the shore opposite the lodge's dock, stood a solitary figure clad in a knee-length tunic whiter than the whitest snow. Polished gold vambraces covered his forearms. Matching greaves were on his shins above sturdy sandals laced to the ankles. Around his slender waist was a broad belt of polished dark-brown leather with a round gold buckle in the shape of a roaring lion's head, the mouth of which contained a symbol that resembled the anchor of a large ship. Between his broad shoulders was a large sword slung at an angle across his back. Piercing sapphire-blue eyes contrasted the bronzed skin of his face. Flowing blonde hair stirred gently in the early morning breeze. His gaze shifted from the dock to the mountain behind the lodge, eagle-like eyesight scanning the tree line before locking on another figure in the distance.

The entity would have been missed were it not for the keen eyes of the sentinel across the lake. It looked like a human-wolf hybrid wedged between two giant boulders, staring intently at the men on the dock below. Sensing it had been spotted, the being lifted its gaze to the edge of the snowfield on the mountain opposite the lodge. Just then the rising sun's rays glinted off gold in the distance. It bared sharp fangs when eyes black as coal zoomed in to be met by the stern stare shot at it from a pair of bright blue eyes more than five miles away.

A rectangular white cloud of mist formed behind the sentinel, engulfed him, and dissipated immediately. The dark creature took its cue to depart and a black hole in the fabric of space formed around it just in time. It disappeared into the void just as a column of white mist formed feet away and the sentinel emerged. He took a quick scan of the area, looked down at the dock below, stepped back into the mist and also vanished.

Simon Standing Elk finished describing his vision to the shaman who seemed increasingly distracted, occasionally glancing up at the mountain in front of him and also over his shoulder to the one behind the lodge.

"What does it mean, Wicasa?"

"It means three things, my friend. First, you are gifted. Some may say cursed. It's a matter of perspective that you will decide. Yesterday we spoke of planes of existence and it seems you have the gift to be able to see at least partially across this plane into events of the recent past. Perhaps the future as well," the older man explained. "Second, we must conclude that Yakwawi also has such a gift and is able to see or sense you as I warned. And third, other parties appear to be taking an interest in us. There is new danger now and we must leave this place at once."

◆ ◆ ◆

Despite being comfortable since she'd first awakened at the Sanctum, Julie hadn't slept well. She'd had a late dinner with Dr. Sora Wu after watching events of the previous evening unfold in the operations center. In the conversation she'd confided she wasn't a silk pajamas kind of gal, much preferring panties and a large loose cotton T-shirt. The good doctor had acted quickly and an assortment of tees crafted of the softest cotton she'd ever worn was hanging in the closet of her room when she retired after the meal. Not doubting Dr. Wu's kind intentions, the relatively insignificant presence of the shirts was just the latest on a list of things that bothered her about The Watch and Sanctum.

Julie was a private person. The thought of people coming and going in and out of her room when she wasn't there disturbed her. Watching the incredible operation unfold around Spearfish the previous evening, and seeing how quickly The Watch's assets could be brought into play in a small Black Hills town she doubted most Americans had ever heard of, was also disquieting.

"How many operatives were there? Where were they stationed? Given how hard it was to keep anything secret in the age of the internet and social media, how had The Watch managed to operate so effectively without being discovered and exposed?" Julie asked herself. She'd gotten very quiet when she saw how The Watch turned a terrified man with video evidence of a horrific monster into a successful elk hunter with no memory of the creature or the hunt. And then they'd intercepted the missing person call from the man's wife, perfectly

impersonated a law enforcement officer, and managed to create a happily-ever-after ending to the man's day with no one being the wiser.

Lying in bed, staring at the ceiling in her room, Julie wondered how many cameras and microphones were monitoring her that very moment. *"Had they watched her in the shower, in the bathroom or testing the apparently impenetrable screen door leading out to the beach?"* Every article of clothing and footwear in the room fit as though it was made for her. Three days earlier, a supply of feminine hygiene products had appeared in a box on the shelf of her bathroom just in time for her monthly cycle. *"How did The Watch know so much about her? Did they have as much information about everyone on the planet?"* The way they'd manipulated all the little details involving the Barrick family the previous evening had her wondering. If knowledge was power, The Watch could very well be the most powerful group of people in the world. Julie inherently questioned the ethics of consolidating such power in the hands of one organization, or even a few. From what she'd seen so far, that power had been used to the benefit of the greater good. What made her uncomfortable was the potential for the abuse of such power.

Turning onto her side to stare out the screen door, Julie considered the creatures in the museum as she listened to the call of seagulls and the gentle swish of ocean surf against the beach. The sounds of nature quieted her mind to a point where she was just about to fall asleep. Then the phone on her nightstand rang and she reached for the wireless handset.

"Good morning, Miss Reed." It was the voice of Jeff, the stocky Australian.

"Um, hi. What's up?"

"Breakfast pre-operation briefing in thirty minutes. In meeting room three off the main dining area. Is that enough time for you to shower and get ready?"

"Yeah. But this is one of those mornings a tea drinker like me might go for a butter-rum latte to jump-start my motivation," Julie said in a mildly sarcastic tone.

"Crack open your door a smidge sheila," Jeff responded, using the Australian slang term for a young woman.

Curiosity got the better of her. Julie told him to hang on and tossed the covers aside. She pulled down on the T-shirt for maximum modesty and stood behind the door while she opened it enough to see what was going on. Jeff was in the hall and handed her what appeared to be a Styrofoam latte cup through the narrow opening, grinning as Julie's eyes about popped out of her head. She took the cup, staring at it in disbelief.

"Ain't butter rum. Sorry to disappoint," said Jeff cheerfully. "Had you pegged for more of a hazelnut mocha gal. Hope you like it. See you in thirty."

Julie slowly shut the door and stared at the latte for several seconds before tasting it. She didn't know whether to smile or be even more concerned. It did taste better than the occasional butter-rum latte she usually ordered back home. After a few more sips, she entered the bathroom, set the latte on the vanity and turned the shower on hot without activating the ceiling ventilation fan. Only after a fog had formed did she disrobe and step into the shower thinking any visual or thermal cameras would have trouble finding her in the steam.

Chapter Eighteen

The large table in the center of the conference room was U-shaped so that everyone could see and interact with the other participants. Jake was the last to arrive but the meeting hadn't started yet. Invitees were still helping themselves to breakfast items on side tables where an assortment of fruits, pastries, coffees, teas and juices offered an ample selection. Dr. Smythe was already seated in the center chair going over something on a tablet and jotting down notes on a legal pad. Also in attendance, Jake noted, were Scott, Ibutho, Dr. Wu, Julie, Moses and three people in unique 3-D camouflage uniforms he had not yet met. The camo-clad trio, two men and a woman, had the distinctive physiques and bearings of professional soldiers. Soon everyone was seated and Smythe began the meeting.

"Good morning. We start with introductions as Miss Reed and Dr. Sanders do not yet know everyone here." Smythe gestured toward the three in uniform.

"Allow me to introduce Cora Sanchez, Domingo "Dom" West, and Anatoly "Tol" Petreykin, all members of The Watch Tactical Division. Cora will be our security team leader on this operation, Dom is our logistics support officer, and Tol is a marksman and weapons specialist. The floor is yours, Cora."

Cora Sanchez was a muscular middle-aged woman of average height with black hair, light brown skin and deep brown eyes. The wall nearest the open end of the conference table lit up with a map of the northern Black Hills and the room's lights dimmed slightly when she began to speak with what Julie pegged as a South American accent.

"I begin by welcoming Dr. Sanders and Miss Reed to our briefing. She smiled and nodded at the duo, then turned to the projection. What we're looking at is an updated map of the area where what we suspect is a Yakwawi has been recently active. The conclusion about what kind of target we're dealing with was arrived at by comparing hair and blood samples and plaster casts of footprints from the site where Miss Reed engaged the creature just more than a week ago, and comparing them to similar samples collected at a location you're about to see. DNA samples from our database were compared with those collected and the casts compared with our museum specimen to make an initial ID. We'll now look at video shot by a hunter near the Wyoming border with South Dakota yesterday. The man was not seen by the animals and has no recollection of the encounter, thanks to superb work by the containment team we'd pre-positioned in the area following the attack on Dr. Sanders and his wife."

The room got darker and the video began with the peaceful scene of a small group of elk grazing around a wallow surrounded by ponderosa pine trees. A stifled gasp was heard from the hunter when the massive predator seemed to suddenly rise up out of the ground to grab an elk calf. Jake and Julie were initially startled by the appearance of the creature on the screen, and there were several audible reactions from those around the table when the monster used the calf to club the bull elk to death. The only audio apart from the sounds of the combat between large animals was the heavy breathing of the hunter punctuated by both profanity and urgently whispered prayers to Jesus for protection and deliverance. Oddly, no one looked away when the beast made a gory mess by ripping into the animals it had just killed.

Smythe glanced at Jake to see his reaction and noted the scientist staring attentively at the screen, his face set like flint with no indication of emotion. Jake's eyes revealed intense concentration. It was evident the man was making mental notes concerning the predator's behavior. Smythe, who had already seen the video several times, noted Julie was also studying the beast's movements but not as a scientist. Hers were the eyes of a rival predator sizing up its prey. Smythe surmised she was studying every movement the monster made in search of any potential vulnerabilities or possible angles of attack. The video was played three more times before the lights came back up and Cora resumed her presentation.

"Our map now displays the locations of human and animal fatalities we attribute to the Yakwawi in order of occurrence. It reveals a general eastward track toward more rugged terrain that is also higher in elevation and more heavily forested than the area in which the creature was first encountered. We'll now open the floor for discussion and begin planning our tactical response."

"It is large and powerful," noted Ibutho. "A young elk weighs maybe 250 to 300 pounds this time of year. Yakwawi swung it around as easily as I would swing a hammer. It is also quick. With that speed and power we must not get within its reach or it will tear us apart."

"We could engage with high-powered, armor-piercing ammunition outside its range of reach," suggested Tol in a thick Russian accent. "A .338 Lapua at 100 yards should do the trick."

"How was the one on display killed?" asked Julie to no one in particular. She couldn't help but notice how everyone at the table turned to look at Dr. Smythe for an answer.

"Before I answer that question," Smythe replied, "I think it important to understand what we know of Yakwawi anatomy. AVADSA, display three-dimensional hologram of a Yakwawi male and prepare for both layered and cross-sectional analysis."

A semi-opaque scale model of the monster appeared inside the "U" of the table. It began to slowly rotate in order to afford everyone the chance to view it from a number of angles. Smythe rose and began to speak.

"Yakwawiak, the plural for Yakwawi, were known to a number of pre-Columbian Native American tribes by various names. Among those familiar with the beast were the Amangachtiat, Yagesho, Tagesho and others. Tribal lore concerning these creatures is most prevalent among the stories passed down to us from the Shawnee, Lenape and Mohican people. The closest English translation can come to these names is giant stiff-legged bear, big-rumped bear and naked bear. The latter we ascertain due to its extremely short and densely packed black fur."

"Wait," said Julie. "You're telling us that hundreds of years ago there were tribes of people coexisting with this thing and they called it a big-ass nude bear?"

Jeff snorted and Jake would have sworn he saw some orange juice shoot out of the Aussie's nose into a hastily grabbed napkin. Ibutho began a deep, booming laugh and even Cora slapped her hand over her mouth to hide her spontaneous amusement. Smythe shot Julie a scathing look until he noticed that even Moses was grinning ear to ear, his head wagging. Realizing that a moment of likely needed levity had been interjected into the meeting, Smythe softened his look a bit. "Well played, Miss Reed, but we all know what this beast is capable of. I ask that we proceed without further interjections of sophomoric humor. May I continue?"

"Please do doctor," Julie replied with a sly smile. "But as one who has been up close and personal with this monster, I'll verify what the legends tell us. It's more than four feet in diameter all the way from its armpits to its, ah, derriere, and broader across the shoulders. We'll need serious penetrating power to take it out. My .45-caliber service weapon barely seemed to sting it. Also, I don't know where its vitals are but I do know something vital. It is a male and likely a bit tender in its boy parts where I blasted it with buckshot so the doc and I could get away."

"Thank you, Miss Reed," said Smythe with a hint of admonition in his voice before moving on. "Some of you are aware The Watch has had a presence in North America for more than one thousand years and had operatives in contact with the Abenaki, Penobscot and Mohican people among others. It was from the Mohicans that The Watch first learned of Yakwawiak and the danger the creatures posed. The scope of the stories involving these beasts covered too large an area and timeframe for there to have been only one, and we eventually discovered a small breeding population in what is now the northeastern U.S.

Smythe enlarged the projection of the beast and continued, "Adult Yakwawiak were notoriously difficult to kill, so tribes in the areas they inhabited would ambush their young with arrows or spears and then flee. The Yakwawiak reproduction cycle was even slower than that of the North American grizzly bear. Sexual maturity was reached at about six years of age and females were only fertile until about 20 years of age. Lone offspring remained with the female for up to five years. Gestation was roughly a year, so female Yakwawiak could conceivably have only two to three offspring during their lifetimes. Eventually, slaying of the young diminished the population and pressured the Yakwawiak south and west into an area south of the Ohio River that is now known as Kentucky."

As the hologram rotated within the "U" of the conference table, a map of the area Smythe had been referring to appeared on the wall behind him. The man continued.

"The state's Department of Tourism says Kentucky's name is a derivative of the Iroquois Indian word ken-tah-ten, which means `Land of Tomorrow´.

The Watch is content with that conclusion as it serves our purposes. Kentucky is actually a much older word given to the area by an advanced civilization that once inhabited the region. The ancients are known from sophisticated artifacts and their construction of elaborate buildings that time and erosion have turned into interesting mounds for archaeologists to fuss over. Those people possessed weaponry more advanced than other Native American tribes in the mid-Holocene epoch. Among these advances were edged weapons and arrowheads made of obsidian. When carefully crafted by a skilled workman, the cutting edge of an obsidian blade is more than 100 times sharper than surgical steel. So sharp, in fact, that it cuts animal and human tissue between individual cells. The Watch has overseen modern surgical procedures conducted with enhanced obsidian instruments and noted that the cuts are so fine that no visible scars are present on the patient following recovery. Now imagine the effect of such cutting capability delivered by force."

"Like an arrow, spear or knife," surmised Ibutho. "The cut would go very deep, even into Yakwawi."

"Indeed, my warrior friend," said Smythe. "So when the ancients encountered the Yakwawiak entering their domain, a major effort was launched to eradicate them. The battle was far from easy, even with powerful bows launching obsidian-fitted arrows, long obsidian-tipped spears, battle hatchets similar to those we now call tomahawks, and obsidian-bladed knives such as this."

Smythe paused to open a wooden box on the table near his chair. He removed a beautiful Native American knife with an antler handle and polished black obsidian blade. He handed it first to Cora, indicating she should pass it around the group, before continuing.

"The Yakwawiak possessed extreme intelligence for carnivorous brutes and, while they had typically wandered and hunted in individual family groups, they eventually formed into clans for mutual survival. Clashes between the humans and the beasts were horrific in their carnage and butchery. Some say between ten and twenty warriors were slain for every Yakwawi killed. Ground where the battles took place became soaked in blood and gore. Some Native American tribes allied with the ancients. Others stood on the sidelines to see who would win. In any case, though the

95

ancients eventually prevailed against the Yakwawiak, victory came at a terrible price. Casualties were catastrophic and the decimated survivors of the conflict were unable to restore their civilization to its former glory. Some were killed by other Native American tribes. Others were integrated into them. Still more disappeared in a migration southwest. A few became members of The Watch. The collapse of the ancient's control over the region led to war between other native tribes in the area over the spoils. Bloodshed so characterized the region that it became known in native tongues as a place of `dark and bloody ground´ – the true meaning of the word Kentucky. That is why, at the signing of the Treaty of Sycamore Shoals in 1775 between the Transylvania Land Company and Chief Dragging Canoe of the Cherokee, the chief said…"

Smythe paused and an audio recording played over the room's speaker system. It was a male voice speaking a language no one in the room understood as a picture of a Native American warrior was projected on the wall where the map had been moments before. Above his head the title read, *"Chief Dragging Canoe of the Cherokee, 1775"* and below subtitles in English tracked the man's speech as he congratulated representatives on securing "a dark and bloody ground."

Little surprised Jake and Julie anymore, let alone an apparent photograph and audio recording of a Native American chief roughly a century before such technologies were known to have been invented.

"So let me get this straight," stated Julie. "An obscure ancient civilization I'd never heard of went to war with an ancient species I'd never heard of and the end result was Kentucky? Sounds like a great science-fiction movie, doctor, but you still haven't answered my question. How exactly is a Yakwawi killed? Will Tol's .338 with AP ammo get the job done?"

Smythe extended an arm toward Dr. Sora Wu, "It may not. I'll let Dr. Wu take it from here."

Chapter Nineteen

Simon Standing Elk and the shaman moved quickly through the lobby of the lodge into a small room behind the kitchen. The older man twisted a can of soup on the pantry shelf. Part of the floor recessed slightly before sliding to one side to reveal a staircase leading down. The men descended.

A large dock, actually more of a pier, was situated alongside a subterranean canal at the bottom of the stairs. Two unique watercraft resembling stingrays were moored nearby. As if on cue, a hatch atop one of the craft opened and a very fit, jumpsuit-clad woman climbed out.

"We can depart as soon as you're ready," she said addressing the shaman.

"We go now," the shaman responded, extending an arm toward the craft and looking at Simon to indicate he should go first.

The woman descended into the hatch and called up that the men should watch their steps as they followed her down a ladder. At the bottom twelve seats in two groups of six arranged in pairs were separated by a center aisle. The front two seats in each section faced the rear of the craft. The other eight faced forward toward what Simon perceived to be the cockpit of the watercraft.

Though there were places for both a pilot and copilot, the woman sat alone in the left seat of the cockpit and donned a helmet that looked like something a fighter pilot would wear.

"Where to, gentlemen?" she asked turning over her right shoulder.

"Please arrange a rendezvous with the nearest Albatross able to take us to Sanctum," instructed the shaman.

"Where are we going, Wicasa?" asked Simon. "Is it far? What's an Albatross?"

"Sanctum. Yes. A large bird able to travel great distances while expending very little energy," replied the older man. "Now pull that harness behind your headrest over yourself so your head is between the straps. Then put the tab into the slot on your seat cushion until it clicks and fasten your seatbelt tightly."

"That seems a bit much for a boat ride, Wicasa," replied Simon as he followed his mentor's instructions.

The shaman turned to Simon. "Nobody said this was a boat." Then he turned toward the woman and with a sense of urgency commanded, "Go! Go now!"

The command was unnecessary as Simon saw the hatch begin to close overhead and the ladder telescope into the ceiling even as the shaman spoke. He felt movement away from the pier into the water channel concealed beneath the lodge and tightened his grip on the armrests slightly when the nose of the vehicle dipped and he watched water slip over the windscreen.

"A submarine!" exclaimed Simon as he turned to his companion. "I have never been on a submarine before. This is exciting!"

"Neither have I," replied the shaman.

"But you knew all about this craft and how to operate the restraints. Surely you have been on this before."

"Yes. But what makes you think it is a submarine?"

Without warning the vehicle accelerated with incredible speed and both men were pushed back hard into their seats. Simon had been watching a large trout swim by the window next to the shaman but it disappeared in a flash of water and bubbles when the craft sped up. The next thing Simon saw was trees flashing by and then blue sky. Turning forward, he nearly screamed as the face of the mountain opposite the lodge grew rapidly in the windscreen. He felt his stomach drop when it disappeared beneath them.

"I'm going to be sick," Simon moaned. Then he looked down to see a lined bag in the shaman's hand, which he quickly grabbed and vomited into.

"Do not be embarrassed, my young friend," said the shaman as he leaned over to speak into Simon's ear. "It happens to almost everyone on their first ride."

Simon leaned his head back and took deep breaths until the once-submerged aircraft gradually leveled out and settled as it began to cruise above the clouds.

"You may get up and use the restroom in the rear of the cabin," the pilot announced as she turned her seat inward, removed her helmet and set it in the copilot's set, and stood to begin walking down the aisle between the seat rows. "I'm going to grab a chilled coffee from the fridge in the galley. Either of you gents want anything?"

"May I please have a ginger ale?" asked the shaman. "I find the drink settles a queasy stomach somewhat."

"Absolutely," the pilot replied with a friendly smile. "Sorry for the rough and fast exit from the lodge. There was a lot of portal activity showing up on the scanner and a quick exit seemed appropriate." She looked at Simon's face and the bag in his hand. "Let me take that for you, sir. The rest of the ride should be smooth sailing. And thanks for not messing up my cabin."

Simon handed her the bag and replied with a hoarse voice. "Thank you for your kindness," he said looking up at her sheepishly. "Perhaps I also could test the claim my older friend here makes about ginger ale please?"

"Sure. And don't feel bad. A flight instructor back in my Navy days once told me there are two kinds of pilots. Those who've gotten airsick and those who one day will."

The woman moved to the rear of the cabin as the autopilot kept the craft steady and on course.

She opened the door of a square metal box on the wall outside the toilet room and dropped the bag Simon had been holding inside. Upon closing the door she touched a button on the side of the box that flashed red twice before glowing green. The bag and its contents had been reduced to a tiny pile of powder a vacuum system then sucked into the main waste disposal container under the toilet. The pilot stepped over to a small refrigerator to withdraw a bottle of chilled cappuccino and a couple of cans of ginger ale before starting back toward the cockpit.

"Here you are, gentlemen," she said passing the cans to her passengers.

"A question, if I may?" asked Simon. "How fast are we traveling and where are we?"

"Indicated airspeed is 650 miles an hour and we just crossed into northern Utah about 46,000 feet above sea level," the pilot replied.

"The military will see us, won't they?" asked Simon. "We're higher and faster than a commercial jet. Smaller too."

"It's always fun if they do," the woman said with a wink and a smile before heading back to her seat.

The shaman took a sip of soda before turning to Simon. "Not long ago the Navy released video of an encounter two of its fighter planes had back in 2004 with what they called an Anomalous Aerial Vehicle. It went viral on the internet," he remarked. "The UAV went from 60,000 feet to hovering above the ocean in seconds before vanishing from sight. Glad I wasn't on that flight. Not enough ginger ale in the world." It was the first time Simon remembered seeing or hearing the older man laugh.

"Are you telling me the unidentified aircraft that did those amazing things was this one, Wicasa?"

"No, not this one. But a young Navy pilot would not forget the incident or let it go," the shaman nodded toward the cockpit. "Sometimes a person who is remarkably talented and intelligent begins looking into matters best left alone and gets a little too close to the things we must do. Then special recruitment is necessary. We've been fortunate thus far. Those we've recruited have served humanity and The Watch with loyalty and courage."

"But why can't the Air Force see or track us?" asked Simon.

"You have so many questions," the shaman sighed. "Perhaps you noticed the skin of this aircraft was covered with what looked like tiny thin fish scales. Each of those contains a very small camera lens and projection surface. By overlapping them, they simultaneously video what is in front of them while projecting what their counterparts of the other side are seeing. This gives the illusion of invisibility. One could not ask for better camouflage. As to the other elements of stealth technology, I'll defer answering until someone more knowledgeable about it is present. Suffice it to say we cannot be tracked visually, thermally or by radar."

Just when Simon thought he'd seen enough amazing things for one morning, something new appeared in the sky just above and ahead of the craft in which they were flying. It was as if the shape of an airplane was there but it really wasn't. The odd, almost translucent flying object looked similar to the B-1 bombers he'd seen take off and land at Ellsworth Air Force Base east of the Black Hills near Rapid City. But the shape they were approaching was huge, much larger than those bombers.

"Albatross Three, Skyray Five. We are low on your six and moving to docking position for passenger transfer," the pilot spoke.

"Copy Skyray Five. Albatross Three is holding steady. Zero turbulence next 80 miles."

Cleared to dock," came the reply in the pilot's headset and also over a speaker in the wall next to the shaman's window seat.

"Dock? Transfer? Wicasa, please tell me she doesn't mean what I think she means! Are we to walk up a ladder into an invisible airplane thousands of feet in the sky?" Simon's voice had become higher and his knuckles whitened as he clutched his armrests.

"Yes. And try to control yourself, Simon Puking Elk," jested the shaman with a twinkle in his eye and a wry smile. "If you become any more pale, those waiting for us on the Albatross will think you're a white man. Here. Take this and chew it slowly.

Simon accepted what looked like a brown piece of candy from the shaman and started chewing. His mouth tingled with a strong but sweet flavor of spiced ginger and honey. The queasiness in his stomach began to diminish further and he started to feel almost normal.

The Skyray was now beneath the Albatross and inching upward. There was a soft latching noise and Simon saw all the windows go black. A few seconds later the ladder telescoped down and the overhead hatch opened. The face of an older black man peered inside, a large welcoming smile on his face.

"Welcome aboard, gentlemen...and lady," he stuck his head down the hatch to flash and upside-down smile at the pilot.

"Hi Jason," the woman replied. "I won't be staying. Got a call that I'm needed elsewhere. Please greet the Sanctum team for me."

"You got it. Be safe. Gentlemen, please watch your step as you climb up to me and walk down the left wing. Seat yourselves on the bench over there and buckle in," instructed Jason pointing to a place the men inside the Skyray couldn't see. "I'll join you shortly."

Simon and the shaman ascended the ladder and walked along the wing to where it was flush with the floor of the larger aircraft. A row of padded jump seats was along the side of the fuselage in front of them. They sat down and strapped in as told while Jason did a walk-around inspection of the Skyray. He then moved to the front of the craft and gave the pilot a thumbs-up before joining the men on the bench.

"I need each of you to grab an oxygen mask and watch me as I show you how to put them on," Jason instructed. "It's only a precaution. The decompression and re-pressurize cycle will only last a second or two."

Once all the men had their faces covered by what resembled full-coverage scuba masks, Jason touched a button on the side of his. "Everything good gentlemen?" he asked the men next to him. They both nodded and the shaman jutted his thumb upward.

"Skyray Five, you are cleared to depart," Jason said into his mask's integrated communications unit. "Drop when ready."

"Roger that," it was the voice of the pilot in everyone's mask. "And thank you, Jason. We'll see you here, there or in the air."

Simon was about to comment about the Skyray pilot's unique response when the craft they'd been in dropped out the bottom of the larger plane with a loud Whooosh. For a moment there was a sensation of being strongly pulled toward the opening into which the Skyray had docked, but in less than two seconds the opening was sealed by a large, round telescoping hatch that rapidly slid into place horizontally from every direction. Once the docking bay was pressurized again a couple more seconds later, a floor plate appeared over the hatch to blend in with the surrounding floor. No one would suspect that the hatch was there or that the larger plane was capable of docking with smaller craft by just looking. Lights that had been flashing red around the room for the previous minute switched to solid green.

"That's our cue it's okay to take our masks off and unbuckle," said Jason and the three men did so. "Now if you'll follow me, I'll show you around."

Chapter Twenty

Dave and Cindy Birch were celebrating their first wedding anniversary at Roughlock Falls, a beautiful and romantic setting off Spearfish Canyon in the northern Black Hills. Together they had enjoyed a day of viewing the fall colors that adorned the trees of the picturesque canyon, and then gone to the small recreation area at the waterfall for a light picnic dinner of wine, cheese and rolls baked fresh that morning. Lying close to each other on the picnic blanket spread out on the ground, they watched the sky fade from purple to deep blue and stars begin to fade into view one by one. It was idyllic for the occasion.

"Seems like just yesterday we left BHSU with diplomas in hand, wedding bands on our fingers and big plans for the future," said Dave gazing at the sky. "I guess time flies when you're having fun."

"It's been wonderful, hasn't it?" replied Cindy rolling onto her side and placing her hand on her husband's chest as she nuzzled closer. "We were so blessed to be able to stay in the area with jobs waiting for us right after the honeymoon."

"The benefits of being able to code in three languages, huh."

"And have a health education and coaching vacancy open up right on time at the middle school," said Cindy. "Those kids really love you. Almost as much as I do."

"Yeah," acknowledged Dave. "And I really like not having to sit all day long. I don't know how you do it. Staring at strings of code on a screen for hours on end would drive me nuts."

Cindy turned her eyes skyward. "See all those stars? So pretty and always there. We should make more time to enjoy nature like we've done today so we don't take it for granted. Having lived here for five years now, I wouldn't want to go back to Chicago where all the light makes it hard to even see the stars some nights."

"Agreed," said Dave. "We've got it pretty good here. Good jobs, good friends, a great church family and a nice apartment a half-hour from places like this. But lately I've been thinking, Cindy. Is it too early in our life together to put down roots?"

"What do you mean?"

"That house we both think is nice on North 5th Street has a For Sale sign in the yard. It's in a great area, near the park. It'd be a good place to start a family," Dave suggested.

"I thought you didn't want kids until we'd been married for at least three years," noted Cindy turning her gaze back to her husband with a smile on her face. "Have you changed your mind?"

"Well, I think working with some really great kids at the school has made me realize I might like being a dad sooner rather than later. How do you feel?"

"The nice thing about my job is that I can code from anywhere, and they already let us work remotely one day a week. There's no harm in trying."

Cindy leaned over and delivered a passionate kiss to husband and he responded to her affection.

"We really can't try here," Dave observed. "That would be scandalous and we can't have that now, can we?"

"What's scandalous about a headline in the paper tomorrow? … *School health teacher caught giving private instruction to his wife in a public park.* But maybe we should continue schooling one another back at the apartment," Cindy said with a laugh.

The couple gathered their picnic items together and walked back to their silver 2011 Honda Civic hand in hand. Theirs was the last vehicle remaining in the parking area. Dave leaned in for a prolonged kiss and held his wife close.

"Happy anniversary, my love," he whispered in her ear. Cindy responded with a blood-curdling scream.

It loomed behind their car not 50 feet away. Red eyes floating like menacing hot coals as high above the ground as a basketball hoop. The hulking black shape seemed to suck in what pale light remained. It snapped its jaws in anticipation, showing the terrified couple long yellow fangs in the waning dusk.

Dave didn't hesitate. He shoved his wife behind him with one hand as he whipped out his smartphone with the other.

"Cindy get in the car!" he shouted as he began snapping pictures of the monster as fast as he could. The sudden bright flashes had the effect he'd hoped.

The beast stopped in mid-stride and took a step back, waving huge arms in front of its face.

Dave's camera kept flashing and the creature was seeing spots. Cindy picked up on her husband's actions and her quick mind devised a plan of its own. She grabbed the ignition fob off the center console, started the car with one hand and lowered the passenger side window with the other. Dave got more flashes off and the beast was still momentarily blinded.

"I've got this, Dave, get in and drive!" Cindy shouted as she lined her phone's camera up with the side mirror and the monster's head. Then she started taking pictures with her camera's flash as fast as she could. The resulting strobe effect reflecting off the mirror continued to confuse the beast while her husband dove into the driver's seat and floored the gas pedal. A shower of dust and gravel was thrown rearward by the Honda and the creature roared with rage as its intended victims raced off toward the main road.

Overnight camping was not permitted at Roughlock Falls and Conservation Officer Cody Sandberg of South Dakota Game, Fish and Parks was just turning off U.S. Highway 14-A to make sure no one was lingering at the recreation area too long after dark. Suddenly he was blinded by the oncoming headlights of a speeding car and had to swerve hard to the right to miss it. A Honda sedan raced by and drifted into a hard left turn onto the highway before accelerating north toward Spearfish. Sandberg pulled back onto the access road and was about to make a U-turn to pursue when the trunk of a tree slammed through the windshield of his SUV to crush his head and chest.

The monster yanked its improvised blunt spear from the shattered glass and pulled the pulverized remains of the officer through after it. Guttural grunts of satisfaction drifted into the night air as the creature headed back down the road toward the falls, feasting once again on human flesh as it walked along.

"Couldn't we have warned that man?" sobbed Cindy as Dave looked into the Honda's rearview mirror and slowed to cruise just over the speed limit. "He was heading right toward that thing."

"There wasn't time, Hon," replied Dave. "It was coming down the road practically in our trunk and swinging a tree around like a baseball bat. If we'd stopped, we'd be dead. The guy looked like a cop or something and he may have had a gun. I just hope it was enough. We need to warn people that a giant, nasty Bigfoot thing is loose in the canyon. Here, take my phone and see if any of the flash pictures I aimed at its face turned out."

Still shaking, Cindy took Dave's phone and started scrolling through the shots, occasionally gasping at what she saw.

"Dave, this thing was not a Bigfoot. It looks more like a cross between an elephant and a bear with a tapered snout. The teeth are huge! What should we do?"

"My fear is that if we go to the authorities with this first, they'll take our phones to hush this up. We'll end up pressured to sign a paper or something that says we got scared by a big black bear and overreacted. I say we post the images first on social media and then see who shows up at our apartment... if anyone," suggested Dave.

By the time the couple could see the lights of Spearfish ahead, a cryptic account of their frightening experience was spreading across Facebook, Instagram and Twitter. Dave decided they should drive by their apartment building before pulling in. They did minutes later and saw two well-built armed men in forest ranger uniforms heading into their building as they slowly passed by.

"Cindy, I don't like this at all. I've got enough cash for us to spend the night at a hotel. We need some time to think and pray about what our next steps should be."

The young woman agreed and they checked in at the Crow Peak Lodge on West Kansas Street. Dave had told Cindy to turn their phones off before they pulled in, and asked the desk clerk to put the devices inside a security safe set aside for guest valuables in the hotel's office. He explained it was their anniversary and they didn't want to be disturbed. Dave's real motive was a hope that the safe's steel and interior location would act like a Faraday cage to make finding the couple difficult over the next few hours. His instincts proved correct.

◆ ◆ ◆

Dr. Sora Wu stood and entered the "U" of the conference table to stand next to the holographic Yakwawi.

"The Watch has had minimal first-hand contact with this creature, hence its classification as unknown. The specimen in our collection is more than 400-years old and was slain by a group of Mohican warriors in the company of a lone member of The Watch near the banks of the Hudson River in the Adirondack Mountains of what is now eastern New York. The fight was fierce. Of the twenty-three who engaged the beast with obsidian-tipped arrows, spears and knives, eleven were killed and six others seriously injured."

Dr. Wu touched a display and dozens of red marks appeared on the hologram. Each mark took the shape of an arrowhead, spear tip, knife or question mark. She then continued, "These marks map out injuries sustained by our Yakwawi on display and show us the kind of weapons used to inflict them. Notice that there are sixteen arrow hits and four knife slashes in the creature's hind legs alone, the majority of which are concentrated in the lower back hemisphere above the feet. On humans, the targeted area would contain our Achilles tendon. There are 19 arrow hits in the front torso and chest, but only seven in the back. The chest area also has six spear thrusts but we believe the killing blow was the spear thrust angled upward through the bottom of the jaw and presumably into the beast's brain. There were multiple areas impacted by blunt trauma of considerable force, perhaps war clubs or slung stones, and a key blow delivered to the base of the skull where it met the upper neck vertebrae. On humans and other large mammals, that's the vicinity of the brain stem. Analysis of the wound pattern would seem to indicate a plan of attack that involved first trying to immobilize or slow the creature by focusing on the lower part of the legs, then knock it down and finish it off on the ground. The Watch operative left a written account, in Latin, which supports this conclusion. Our translation states one of the combatants stood in front of the creature as it eventually fell forward with the butt of his spear planted in the ground. The spear is said to have pierced the head when it fell and the warrior leapt aside before smiting the beast with several blows using a stone-equipped club."

"So what's your take on how we kill the one on the loose now, Doctor?" asked Dom. "Do you think we could tip it over with high-velocity, armor-piercing bullets from fully automatic rifle fire to the lower legs and then clobber it in the head with a Barrett .50-cal at close range?"

"Engaging with firearms may be problematic for a couple of reasons," Dr. Wu replied. "Both have to do with the creature's anatomy. First, the Yakwawi appears to be a mammalian tank with some of the most impressive natural armor The Watch has ever encountered."

The hologram of the creature changed to allow Dr. Wu to manipulate layers of anatomical structure as she continued her briefing.

"The dark black hair was incredibly dense and its root structure leads us to believe it was permanently anchored in the skin and not periodically shed. The density of the hair and thickness of the skin beneath would likely cause premature expansion of hollow-point bullets. Our operative present when the Yakwawi was skinned wrote the process took considerable effort because the hide thickness beneath the hair ranged from two to three finger widths, or about two inches – more or less."

"That would explain why your .45 had little effect, Julie," Tol noted. "Your big, slow-moving bullets would have likely stopped in the skin or the muscle just beneath it before even getting to bone, let alone vital organs. It doesn't mean you didn't hurt it. Each shot would have hit with about 400 foot-pounds of energy and that's gotta sting no matter how big the beast."

"That's about all her shots likely did," Dr. Wu remarked. "Which leads me to the next layer of natural armor. The Watch operative noted a unique bone structure in place of the standard mammalian ribcage. Most land animals similar to primates or bears have ribs separated by strips of muscle and the rib bones form a semi-flexible cage connecting a sternum to the spine that surrounds vital organs such as the heart and lungs. The Yakwawi reportedly had overlapping slats of bone as thick as a man's thumb from a wide collarbone-like structure around the lower neck to just above the large pelvic bone. In appearance the overlapping bones resembled a type of armor used by soldiers in ancient Rome called lorica segmentata. Such an arrangement of bone would afford flexibility and optimal protection for the entire torso. Also, the near cylindrical shape of this bone arrangement presents attackers with no right angles to impact. What got through the hair and hide would have faced some degree of deflection, similar to the sloping armor of modern combat vehicles."

"So if I understand correctly," clarified Cora, "Any kind of projectile fired at this thing, be it arrow or bullet, would have to penetrate a layer of dense hair and a couple of inches of basically leather before encountering an inch of solid bone at an angle. And since this creature will likely be both moving and enraged, there might be danger to the team from bullets deflecting off the sides or chest and going God knows where. What about attack from behind?"

"Even more of a challenge," answered Dr. Wu as she rotated the hologram and highlighted the large shoulder blades. "Large scapulae cover most of the upper back with yet another inch or so of bone."

"How about head shots with large-caliber bullets?" suggested Tol.

"Again a problem," Dr. Wu replied highlighting the skull on the hologram gram. "You're all seeing the second challenge we face in the form of highly angular bone structure that includes the skull. Notice the football-shaped configuration from a highly sloped forehead in front to an elongated sagittal crest extending rearward a considerable distance. Not only would projectile deflection be potentially problematic unless the shot were placed precisely into an eye socket or ear, but the presence of such a crest in that configuration usually indicates exceptional jaw muscles and biting power. Such precise shot placement on a moving target would be a formidable challenge."

Dr. Smythe cleared his throat and all eyes in the room turned in his direction. "Your analysis is thorough and not entirely encouraging, Dr. Wu. Nonetheless, these beasts were killed off by tribes equipped with less formidable weaponry than we have at our disposal. We don't have the man-power to overwhelm the creature with numbers as the natives of this continent did hundreds of years ago, nor can The Watch sustain the kinds of casualties those brave warriors did. So let us open the floor for constructive ideas on engagement."

Jake Sanders was the first to speak. "This is an impressive animal unlike anything I've ever even contemplated. Nonetheless, it seems to breathe our atmosphere just fine. Therefore, oxygen, nitrogen, argon and carbon dioxide in proportions present here do not seem to have any negative effect. Is there anything we know of that could be toxic to this creature in either a gas or in liquid form? Something that could be delivered to it without harming the team members and anything or anyone else in the vicinity?"

Several seconds of thoughtful silence followed Jake's question before Dr. Wu answered, "We just don't know the answer to that question. What we can speculate is that we would have to determine what such a substance would be and then get a dosage right the first time or face potentially catastrophic results for the team members. Your suggestion has merit, Dr. Sanders, and is a good one. I've also thought about various drugs that might work if injected using a robust tranquilizer dart with a very long needle. But what if we introduce what we think would sedate it, only to discover the drug makes it stronger? There are so many unknowns. While our specimen and the operative's notes provided great insight into skeletal arrangement and positions of key organs, we are limited in what we know about its blood chemistry and metabolism."

"Fire," Ibutho said. "All animals fear flames. Can the monster burn?"

"There ya go mate," responded Jeff eagerly. "Light it up with a flamethrower, I say."

"Seriously?" Julie turned to the Aussie. "You want a large and angry predator running through a National Forest on fire? There's a lot of dead timber in the hills around that area and if this beast is as tough as I think it is, even fire won't bring it down quickly. A mistake made using that approach could result in a huge wildfire, a ton of collateral damage and a lot of embarrassing questions afterward."

"I sense you have another idea, Ms. Reed," observed Smythe. "Please enlighten us."

"Okay," Julie began. "Problems include taking this thing out while minimizing danger to the team, and doing it in a way that doesn't attract a lot of attention. We need a weapon that penetrates deep in order to at least slow down this thing enough for us to get close so we can finish it using more conventional means, right?"

The young woman turned in her chair to look at Moses, who had been listening intently but saying little throughout the meeting. "Time to turn to the tech-commander guy. Have you ever heard of an Airbow?"

"Indeed, my dear girl," the older man replied and corrected his statement to "Deputy Reed" as he saw Julie's eyes bore into him when he referred to her as a girl. "Forgive me. I don't get out much. But the weapon you refer to is gaining acceptance in the global hunting community as a means of harvesting big game. It shoots an arrow propelled by highly compressed air, allowing the projectile to attain speeds and penetrating power that far exceeds those of powerful crossbows widely in use. It looks like a cross between a spear gun and an assault rifle, and is both user-friendly and lethal. And it's exceptionally accurate at ranges out to 75 yards or more. But it's a single-shot weapon. The user, like an archer, must lower the Airbow in order to remove a second projectile from a quiver and put it down the barrel before shooting again."

Julie had been sketching on a notepad while Moses was speaking about the weapon to the group. When he'd finished, she slid the drawing down the desk to Moses. "Can you do that?" Julie asked looking a bit pleased with herself.

"Inspired!" replied Moses as he examined the drawing before lifting his head to address the rest of the group. "Deputy Reed has suggested in a sketch that we modify the Airbow concept with a rotating cylinder containing pre-loaded shorter and thicker arrows or bolts. Between seven and eight, I should imagine. We could configure automatic fore and aft sealing sleeves to engage and disengage during the rotation cycle of the cylinder between shots. In theory, the result would be a powerful semiautomatic spear gun revolver able to launch multiple crossbow bolts in rapid succession."

"How long before you can make field-ready versions to equip the team?" asked Smythe.

"It's a significant redesign of an existing weapon," answered Moses. "But with our advanced computer modeling capabilities and the accelerated 3-D printers in the lab, I should think we could have two or three prototypes ready in a few hours."

"Do it immediately," ordered Smythe, and Moses rose to leave the meeting. He had just reached the door when it opened. Two men with Native American features stood in the doorway. The younger wore jeans, cowboy boots, a denim jacket over a black tee shirt and would have looked middle-aged if not for his flowing mane of snow-white shoulder-length hair. The older man was shorter with tanned, weathered skin, long gray hair, and wore a traditional beaded leather shirt over which lay a strap attached to a leather satchel at his right hip. The shaman quickly scanned the room until his eyes locked on Dr. Smythe.

"Please excuse our rude intrusion," said the shaman. "The matter about which you're meeting has become more complicated. It is imperative Dr. Smythe and I speak alone."

All eyes locked on the two men who had just entered but no one moved.

"NOW!" shouted the shaman sternly, and instantly everyone stood and quickly filed out of the room. As Julie passed Simon, a flicker of recognition altered the expression on her face but she wasn't certain. The old man took Simon's arm in a gesture that he should stay, closed the door after all the others had left and turned to Smythe. "We have other interested parties in play," he said with concern in his voice.

Chapter Twenty-One

Those who had been in the meeting dispersed in the hallway outside the conference room, each going their separate ways except for Jake and Julie.

"Looks like we have our first opportunity to talk without a chaperone since we got here," said Julie. "Want to take a walk?"

"Yeah," Jake replied and the two started down the hallway in the direction of the cafeteria. "I think we should assume we're being watched and likely listened to, though."

"Agreed. Let's step into the cafeteria for a mid-morning snack."

Julie's suggestion was a tactical one. The cafeteria was an open area with circular tables and chairs arranged to seat up to eight people each. Some smaller square tables were located along one wall that was covered with windows from floor to ceiling. Those tables were meant for two or three people and afforded a spectacular view of the ocean. Unlike the beachside rooms in which they slept, the cafeteria was in a part of the complex that sat on a cliff. The window screens were made of the same sturdy material as the sliding door screens in their quarters with glass panels that would slide down to cover them if wind or rain threatened to disturb diners.

Julie led Jake to a table where the sounds of seagulls and waves crashing against the base of the cliff might prove problematic for anyone trying to listen in on their conversation.

"Smart," noted Jake.

"Cautiously paranoid," replied Julie. "Look, Jake, I was trained to deal with death and have done so a few times as a law enforcement officer. We met under some gruesome circumstances. The next thing we know, we're drafted into some covert international group and forced to take in a ton of information fast. You've had no time to grieve, and neither of us was prepared psychologically for what all of this means. I'm not going to ask if you're okay because I can't imagine any sane person would be. You and I got thrown into this together and I don't know about you, but I feel like we need to see this through together."

"What do you mean by see this through?" asked Jake.

"The Watch knows a heck of a lot more about us than I'm comfortable with. While I have to admit this place has amazing technology, incredible capabilities and real esprit de corps among those who seem to have been here a while, there are things I have serious reservations about."

A waiter approached their table. Julie ordered green tea and a bagel with cream cheese. Jake opted for a bowl of mixed tropical fruit and a glass of pineapple juice. The waiter returned in less than a minute with the food, drinks and extra napkins. Jake was about to speak when Julie abruptly snatched the bottom napkin from the small pile the server had placed on the edge of the table and sneezed into it twice.

"Bless you," said Jake.

"Someone better bless us both," replied Julie as she opened the napkin she'd pretended to sneeze into and showed Jake a tiny circular object about 4 millimeters across. Then she folded the napkin over the object and applied pressure with her thumb until she felt it crack. "Seems to be a bit of a bug problem in this establishment," she noted.

"How'd you know?" Jake asked.

"Wanted to see if they'd try something when the newbies ended up talking and they couldn't hear clearly what was being said," responded Julie. "Besides, it's what I'd have done if I ran this place. The thing about covert operations is that they are covert only as long as the people involved can either trust each other and their devotion to the organization is complete, or tight control is maintained over everyone. Usually it's both."

"Julie, if everything we've heard and seen is legit, you and I have stumbled into something impossibly huge in its implications for not just us, but for the world. I'm a scientist. Maybe I look at things differently because of that. You're absolutely right that I'm struggling right now, and you're astute to see it. It's like the two halves of my brain are at war with each other. Half of me is heartbroken. I miss Gail. She and I had something so special that I can't put it into words. A connection that was...was..."

"Spiritual?" suggested Julie.

"Yeah, I guess that's as good a word as any. A connection at the level of the soul. But I feel so guilty because this place...what it does...or says it does...and those creatures we saw. That really revs up my scientific curiosity. The possibilities are endless. There's an excitement of discovery, the thrill of seeing and studying what few if any other people ever will. I know it sounds selfish but the chance to be a part of that kind of thing isn't just appealing, it's compelling."

"At what cost, Jake?" Julie turned slightly to look out at the view. "I spent a few years in the Far East. Over there the dominant spiritual teaching is about yin and yang. A balance to the universe between light and dark, positive and negative. The ongoing battle for equilibrium between forces that oppose, yet need each other to exist. I never bought into that philosophy because there's no winner in the end. Good and evil are opposites but they are not equals, not in my book anyway. If the universe is destined to always ultimately end in a draw, what's the point of picking a side and fighting for it? I have to believe that good wins in the end, but it won't if good people don't stand up to evil. It's good to pursue goals and dreams but we always have to, as magicians put it, watch the other hand. Right now The Watch has dangled some hefty temptation in front of us both. For you an opportunity to avenge your wife's death and work in areas of science and biology you never even knew existed. For me, a fighter for good and justice, it's a chance to be a protector of the innocent not just in Crook County, but everywhere. I also get suspicious when someone knows what buttons to push to get people to do their bidding, and you and I have someone somewhere pushing all the right buttons where we're concerned."

"We don't know each other very well, in spite of what we've been through," Jake said trying to change the subject. "I haven't had the chance to thank you for what you did by risking your life to try to save Gail and me. That took serious courage. But I'm not sure where you're going with this conversation?"

"Okay," Julie replied. "I'm sorry. I don't know how much they'll let us talk so I'm throwing a lot at you myself while I can. I look at things as a tactician, a strategist and a fighter. Certain people develop non-linear ways of thinking to help them do what they do."

"You're losing me, Julie."

"Try this. Why do most land predators have eyes side by side in the front of their heads?"

"Easy. Depth perception. That's essential for predators to be able to gauge distance to prey and measure the strike zone for optimal effect," Jake replied.

"And prey animals such as deer, antelope and rabbits have eyes on the sides of their skulls because...?"

"It gives them better peripheral vision and enhanced abilities to identify approaching threats."

"Right," said Julie. "Most people these days behave like prey animals in the sense that they think in linear terms. Yesterday, today, tomorrow. Forward, backward, right and left. Life is lived on a flat, horizontal plane. But some of us...soldiers, cops, fighter pilots, submariners, meteorologists, astronomers and such...to be good at what we do, we have to think spherically in three dimensions all the time. Why do hunters often use tree stands or elevated blinds? Why do mountain lions look for sturdy branches or elevated ledges of rock?"

"Because deer and other prey animals aren't accustomed to looking up. Elevated positions provide a vertical ambush attack vector," answered Jake.

"Now let me wrap this up for you concerning The Watch and what I see happening," stated Julie. "I'm thinking short-term, mid-term and long-term as far as what happens to you and me. First, in the short-term we have to find the creature that killed Gail and take it out. More on that in a moment. Second, what happens after we kill the Yakwawi or whatever it is – if we survive? Why would The Watch want to keep us around? You're a good scientist and I'm a good cop, but in skill and brain power we're not at the top of the totem pole here. And then there's the long-term, Jake. Have you seen any families since we got here? Any kids? Anything resembling a couple? Humans have basic needs, not the least of which is to love and be loved. I may seem cold-hearted and snarky, but deep down, one day I'd hoped to find the right guy, settle down and maybe have a family of my own. How am I supposed to do that if everything I do and say is being monitored 24/7? Is that even an option here?"

"I'm a bit surprised," answered Jake. "You're thinking way beyond what I have. My focus has been on this place and the Yakwawi. I've honestly given no thought to anything much else. But now that you point these things out,

I can see where some of your concerns may have merit. Perhaps we should talk to Dr. Smythe and…"

"NO!" Julie responded a bit more loudly than she wished she had. Fortunately, no one else in the cafeteria seemed to take notice. "Call it my gut or my intuition, Jake, but there's a ton of stuff we're not being told. Stuff that's being hidden from us on purpose. I don't trust anyone here. At least not yet, and remember what I said is essential for covert groups to stay covert?"

"Mutual trust," answered Jake. "Do you trust me, Julie?"

"Not fully," her answer was honest. "But I do enough to share what I have already and if Smythe or whoever runs this place finds out what I'm thinking, my guess is things could go badly for me. Trust is something that is built, Jake. It's built by mutual experiences between individuals over time, and no one here has earned my trust yet."

"Then I will do my utmost to do so," said Jake. "But you mentioned you had more to say about the short-term goal of bagging the beast."

"Yes and you may not like it," replied Julie turning to aim her deep blue eyes into Jake's like a pair of penetrating lasers. "It sounds like we're going into battle with that beast soon and I don't think you're ready."

"Julie, we heard about the battles Native Americans had with these things and the outcome. Are any of us ready?"

"You ever been in combat, Dr. Sanders? Ever been shot at? Have you ever even been in a serious fight since playground duels in elementary school?"

"I was on the high school wrestling team," was all Jake could offer as he suspected where Julie was going. "But before you underestimate me based on the meltdown of a man who'd just seen the love of his life mutilated and impaled on a tree when you first met him, it might interest you to know that I've faced down some nasty critters doing my job."

"I'm told your specialty is the study of predators," said Julie. "Doubtlessly, you've encountered a few on their turf."

"Indeed I have. I got between a wounded Kodiak bear and her cubs once. She'd been injured, likely by another bear, and had festering wounds across her right flank. I was brought in by Alaskan game officials to assess if she'd heal or needed to be put down. The wind shifted, she smelled me, charged

117

and had a close encounter with the .45-70 lever-action rifle I was carrying. The bear fell less than two feet from my boots, a 400-grain slug through her eye. I was lucky the cubs didn't attack. They're now safely in a zoo."

"Sounds scary," said Julie. "But that's not the kind of pitched battle free-for-all I was referring to. The kind when you're faced with multiple attack vectors and people are being killed or wounded all around you."

"I'm sorry you're unimpressed, Julie," said Jake with some irritation. "I could tell you about evading a pride of lions in Zimbabwe, outsmarting a pack of wolves in Russia, or a certain jaguar in Guatemala whose nose is probably still sore from me having to go all Babe Ruth on him with a very sturdy walking staff I was glad to have, but I guess nothing short of knocking off a group of terrorists or pulverizing a gang of human traffickers would rise to the level of prowess you're looking for."

"Jake, I'm sorry," Julie reached out her hand across the table to touch his but he pulled it away. "I can tell by looking at you that you' re fit, strong and can likely handle yourself. Please understand that I wasn't questioning you in that way. It's just that things can get real crazy real fast in combat."

"And have you been in combat, Julie?"

"Your question is a fair one. I'm not a veteran of the military and have never been in a war zone. But I have been in a couple of firefights with drug dealers and some hand-to-hand engagements with criminal scum that didn't know when to give up. I also trained a lot in martial arts, earned a few black belts and won a few tournaments. But we're going up against a super-human monster, one that took the dearest thing in your world away from you. My basic question is this. How are you preparing and conditioning yourself emotionally and mentally for the coming encounter?"

"I'm sorry I was short with you," Jake apologized. "I get what you're trying to do and see you're trying to protect me. The sentiment is appreciated but unnecessary. It may not seem like it, but I do understand the concept of a team takedown. I've seen wolves, lions, orcas and hyenas work together as a team to take down prey that was often far larger and more powerful than they were. I get that everyone will have a role to play and we'll all need to do our part to succeed. But I need you to have a little faith in me. You saw me at my worst in a deeply emotional and traumatic crisis. Give me the chance to show you what I can do when I'm at my best. That's all I ask. And all I'm really focused on now is the short term – avenging Gail."

"Glad you see my heart is in the right place, even if I don't always articulate things well," said Julie as the waiter returned and refilled their drinks. "Now that we've established that we find one another smokin' hot, what do you say we head back to my room and indulge in some mind-blowing sex?"

Jake's eyes looked like they were about to pop out of his head until he realized Julie's were darting between his and the edge of the table where a new napkin had appeared that wasn't there before their drinks were topped off. Then he put on a devious smile and said, "That's the best idea you've had all morning, Miss Reed."

Julie laughed out loud and cocked her head toward the exit. She and Jake rose and he offered her his arm. She took it as they walked past the waiter whose look of complete shock made them both laugh when they got to the hallway.

"Well played, Julie," said Jake with a smile. "We've likely created all manner of consternation in the surveillance room."

"We have to remember to laugh a little now and then," Julie responded, disengaging her arm from Jake's.

"Look," said Jake as they continued down the hallway. "We do think differently. I'm a glass half-full kinda guy, and you're a glass half-empty kinda gal but that's okay."

"Yup," said Julie. "And that means as long as we stick together we'll have a full glass between us. I will, of course, be watching all the bottles behind the bar to make certain there's enough stuff there to refill our glass if need be."

"Even as I make sure there's an ample supply of clean glasses to replace ours if someone knocks it over." They both laughed again.

Jeff came bounding around the corner from the direction of Julie's room, his face showing obvious relief at finding them together in the hall, which made Jake and Julie laugh even harder.

"Oh…um…hi…err, there you two are," stammered Jeff, unable to hide the red in his blushing face. "Julie, I mean Miss Reed… deputy…"

"Jeff, please call me Julie. It's okay. What's got you so worked up?"

119

"Sorry. Moses asks that you join him in R&D to have a look at a prototype of that weapon you sketched in the meeting. And Dr. Sanders..."

"I'm Jake, Jeff."

"Right, well Dr. Smythe was hoping you'd meet Ibutho in the gym for an evaluation of your basic fighting skills."

"Let them know we'll be right there," said Julie.

"Actually, I've been asked to go with you, sheila," Jeff responded as he glanced down at his feet in apparent embarrassment.

Jake and Julie exchanged knowing looks by which they confirmed their earlier suspicions about being closely monitored. Julie decided to mess with Jeff's mind by standing on her tiptoes and planting a kiss on Jake's cheek.

"Another time, love," she said playfully as Jake grinned, understanding the joke. She turned to Jeff. "Well, let's not keep Moses waiting. Wouldn't want him to drop a stone tablet or something. Off we go, mate."

Jeff looked mortified and blushed again as Julie put her hands on his shoulders and turned him in the direction of the R&D lab. Jake constrained himself until the pair had turned the corner and then started laughing again before heading in the opposite direction toward the gym.

It was then it occurred to him it was the first time he'd laughed since his wife was killed, and he felt grateful to Julie for making that happen.

Chapter Twenty-Two

"You're certain?" Dr. Smythe addressed the older of the two men standing before him in the conference room.

"Absolutely," the older man replied.

"Well that does complicate things, doesn't it old friend? Oh dear. Where are my manners?" Smythe turned to the younger of the two men and extended his right hand saying, "I am Dr. Jonathan Smythe. You must be Simon Standing Elk. Welcome to The Watch base of operations we call Sanctum."

"Thank you doctor," Simon replied. "I've seen this place before. The island I mean."

"Ah, yes. I was told you may be one of the gifted. Please sit down. Share with me what you've seen in your visions. And spare no detail, however small or insignificant it may seem."

Smythe gestured to the nearest chairs at the end of the U-shaped conference room table and the three men were seated. Simon then recounted the vision he'd had just before he and the shaman fled the lodge.

He spoke of the flash of light, the complex of buildings on a tropical island and deep blackness. The recounting included faces of people frozen in terror, gory remains of two elk, the Yakwawi turning to look at him and the flash of a flaming sword.

At the mention of the sword, Dr. Smythe rose suddenly. He looked shaken but quickly composed himself. "We have fruit, coffee, tea and pastries over here," he said walking to the nearest refreshment table to pour a cup of tea. Simon noticed a slight tremble in his hands. "Please come help yourselves. Simon, I ask that you think carefully. Is there any element of your vision you may have left out?"

Simon thought for a moment. "A man and a woman. Both white. The man was tall with sandy hair. The woman a very pretty blonde."

The shaman listened as he munched on a glazed donut. Smythe nodded, his expression tense. "What else?" Smythe leaned forward putting his cup on the table.

"The woman. Her hands were bloody," said Simon staring toward the wall at nothing in particular as he searched his memory. "And the ring finger of the man's left hand was missing. No scar, no blood, just not there."

"What were this man and woman doing?" asked the shaman.

"I only saw them for a moment," answered Simon. "In a garden, walking together."

Smythe reached for a tablet on the table and poked at it a few times with his finger. A zoomed-in picture of Jake and Julie walking together in a hallway appeared on the screen. "Are these the people you saw?" asked Smythe.

Simon took the tablet handed to him and looked at it carefully. Recognition flashed across his face. "It is them. Who are they? The woman looks familiar. Did she walk by me into the hall earlier?"

"Dr. Jake Sanders is a world-renown scientist specializing in the study of predators. And the woman is a deputy from Crook County in Wyoming named Julie Reed," answered Smythe.

Now it was Simon's turn to show unease. "Julie Reed? From near Sundance in Wyoming?"

"Yes," answered Smythe. "Do you know her?"

"We've met. At the Crook County courthouse. At a trial and later in the jail," replied Simon. "My nephew killed her father."

Dr. Smythe and the shaman exchanged looks of astonishment. A second later the conference room door burst open and Cora rushed in.

"I'm really sorry, gentlemen, but we've got a new situation involving the Yakwawi." The woman grabbed a remote control off the table and aimed it at the large monitor on the wall as she pressed a few buttons. The screen came to life with a young couple standing next to a TV news reporter from a Rapid City television station. The banner at the bottom of the screen read *Monster terrorizes Spearfish couple, state employee killed*. Dave and Cindy Birch recounted the story of their encounter with the beast at Roughlock Falls, then the camera cut to images of crime scene tape around a damaged state Game, Fish and Parks SUV. A crystal-clear picture of the Yakwawi's face with fangs bared went from a box in the upper left corner to a full-screen close-up. Cora clicked off the monitor at the end of the report.

"The situation has escaped any hope of containment. Assemble your team, Cora," ordered Smythe. "Dr. Sanders, Miss Reed and Simon Standing Elk here will accompany you," he gestured to the man with the long, white hair. "I'll remain at Sanctum with Moses and our other guest to advise and coordinate. Wheels up in twenty minutes. We're out of time."

◆ ◆ ◆

Julie and Jeff were in the R&D lab with Moses handling two of the new compressed-air bolt guns based on the sketch from the team meeting. A technician was explaining how to swap out empty bolt cylinders for fresh ones.

"Capacity was limited to seven bolts preloaded into each cylinder in order to facilitate optimal weight and balance of the weapon," explained the middle-aged balding man in a lab coat. "The green dot in the optical sighting system will turn red when the last bolt in the cylinder is aligned and ready to shoot. If fired, the red dot will flash to indicate a reload is necessary at which point you must reach two fingers into the front stock – like so – and then pull downward to release the empty cylinder. Once it drops clear, slap the next one into position and push the loading lever back up into the front stock until it snaps into place. Your sight's dot will turn solid green and you're ready to engage targets again."

Jeff and Julie both practiced the reloading procedure a few times to get a feel for the process. Then, at the invitation of the technician, they stepped up to a firing line in the lab. A cylinder of ballistic gel four feet thick and equally tall sat atop a platform 15 yards downrange.

"Ladies first," said Jeff indicating Julie should take the first shot. "After all, this bolt-shooting gun was your idea."

"Not really," replied Julie shouldering the weapon and taking aim. "I just took an existing concept and changed it up a bit. Man, this thing is lighter than an M4 rifle and handles kind of like a P90. Here we go."

Julie squeezed the trigger and the weapon made a soft popping sound. Then there was a much louder noise behind the target where the carbon-reinforced aluminum bolt smashed into a concrete wall and shattered.

"Oh... my..."

"Goodness," interrupted Jeff before Julie could complete the expression. "The gel didn't even seem to slow the bolt down. Let's look at our high-speed camera footage of the shot."

The technician grabbed a remote control off a nearby table where extra cylinders sat and aimed it at a flat screen monitor on the wall next to the shooters.

"This camera is one of our older models and shoots only 900-million frames per second," the technician said in an apologetic tone. "Our newest ones capture 10-trillion frames per second and are the fastest in the world, though the Japanese are catching up. Still, this will serve nicely for our analysis. Look."

The scientist zoomed in on Julie and the weapon at the moment of the shot and began his analysis. "We see the shooter has a good form, amazingly good form actually, and superb trigger control with an even squeeze to touch off the shot. The recoil-dampening stock appears to have been effective. Her form is truly exceptional."

"Hardly kicked at all," interjected Julie. "And if you mention my form again, I WILL deck you."

The technician turned beet red, glanced down, composed himself and continued. "Yes. Well." he paused to clear his throat. "Then we see the bolt clearing the muzzle, balanced and rotating on its horizontal axis perfectly." The man manipulated the images to keep the bolt in the center of the frame all the way to the target. "Miss Reed's shot is perfect, piercing the gel dead center. Interesting. The bolt's carbon-iron tip guides the projectile straight through the gel with minimal energy transference to the target. We're left with a straight hole roughly 12 millimeters in diameter through the gel. According to the camera's sensors, a deceleration of only 25 feet-per-second took place from the time it entered the target at 455 to its complete exit at 430. Impressive penetrating power indeed!"

"Yes, but that could be a problem. A big problem," declared Julie. "With little or no kinetic energy being transferred into the target, all we're really doing is punching half-inch holes through the monster. There's no real stopping power."

"Not necessarily so Miss Reed," Moses observed. "You shot a blob of gel with no bone or organs of various density inside it." He picked a bolt up off the table and showed the tip to Jeff and Julie. "The tips of these bolts are narrow but very hard. Solid and triangular with sharply serrated edges. The effect on internal organs will be to initiate blood loss, and contact with hard bone should have a shattering effect on both bone and projectile. Perhaps like what happened when Miss Reed's shot hit the wall. The objective is to break the beast down with these. I'd imagine a hit on a major limb bone, the pelvis or a shoulder blade should have considerable impact on its mobility and fighting capabilities."

"Still, I think I have an idea to improve the design," said Julie.

"No time!" It was Cora on the walkway over the lab area shouting down to them. "Jeff and Julie grab what you've got and get to landing bay two. We leave ASAP."

◆ ◆ ◆

"This was not expected," said Ibutho lying on his back with Jake on his chest pinning him to the mat.

"What? That I could fight?" Jake responded with a hint of smug satisfaction. "Or did you think a science nerd was incapable of handling himself?"

Jake sat back just a bit when he felt his opponent relax. It was a mistake. In a fast move, the big African brought his left leg up and around front of Jake's face to peel him off backwards before rolling forward intending to reverse the initial position. But Jake surprised him again by continuing to roll back and both men ended in a crouched position facing one another.

"You are clever and quick, Dr. Sanders."

"One has to be in order to wrestle problem pythons in the Everglades or renegade crocs in northern Australia. And please call me Jake."

Ibutho rocketed forward, head down, and got his shoulder into Jake's midsection before pushing up and tossing the scientist over his back. Jake landed hard on the mat, flat on his back with Ibutho standing over him extending a hand.

"One also must be focused when wrestling the rhino in the Sanctum gym," the big man said with a wide grin.

"So I see," Jake groaned as he accepted the helping hand up. "I' m going to feel that in the morning."

"Playtime's over guys," Cora shouted from the doorway. "The situation we've been working on needs to be resolved fast. We need to get to the hanger for immediate departure."

The two men took off at a run after Cora. She held the door of the elevator open for them at the end of the hall and instructed AVADSA to take them to the flight deck. The lift's doors opened to reveal a huge aircraft hangar containing three massive swept-wing airplanes and several smaller craft Jake thought resembled stingrays he'd seen when scuba diving. A rear ramp was down on one of the larger aircraft. Cora led the way as the three ran toward the ramp. It was a longer run than Jake had realized because the size of the aircraft made it look closer than it actually was. He noticed as he drew near that one of the smaller planes was mounted almost flush with the bigger craft's lower fuselage. Racing up the ramp, the trio found Julie, Jeff, the rest of Cora's team and a white-haired newcomer at the top. And Julie had the new guy backed against a wall with Tol and Dom struggling to hold her back.

"I told you the last time I saw your drunk sorry butt what I'd do to you if our paths ever crossed again, Standing Elk, and if you thought dyeing your hair would fool anyone, you've sorely underestimated me mister," Julie shouted.

"Julie, what's got into you?" pleaded Jeff. "How do you know this guy? What did he do to you?"

"Please, Miss Reed," begged Simon. "I'm a different man now. I have learned from my nephew's misdeeds, as well as my own."

"Misdeeds!?" Julie retorted. "Jaywalking is a misdeed. Ambushing and shooting my father nine times is cold-blooded murder! And then you have the gall to show up in court reeking of alcohol and demanding your nephew be released because you claimed he was arrested by racist cops? How did you even get here? I need someone to start explaining things NOW!"

The ramp to the airplane started to rise and those aboard felt the craft begin to move forward, despite the absence of engine noise. Cora spoke up, "We all need to sit down and COOL DOWN immediately! Then we can get to the bottom of this."

Everyone took a seat. Cora, her team and Simon on one side of the aircraft, Jake, Jeff, Julie and Ibutho across from them on the other. Julie's glaring eyes were burning holes in Simon, who sat looking oddly peaceful as he stared back. There were no windows in that section of the aircraft. The pilot announced cruising altitude had been reached a few minutes later. Straps were undone and the parties opposite each other moved toward the center of the cargo hold like cautious prize fighters approaching center ring. Cora spoke first.

"Here's the deal. The Yakwawi's picture is all over the media. It terrified a young couple but they got away with digital images that are now viral. Then it killed a state employee. We know what area it's in and we're going to kill it. But I can't take a divided team into what's bound to be a challenging fight so we need to get on the same page fast. I'll start by introducing Simon Standing Elk here. He's apparently got some special abilities that could help us locate the creature. But it seems he has a history with Julie we need to sort out." Cora pulled a Taser from her tactical vest and continued. "I will use this on the first person I think is getting out of line. Now I want to hear from Mr. Standing Elk what the problem is here."

"I am the problem," Simon began. "And I was a much bigger problem five years ago. My nephew ran away from home and came to live with me and my wife when he was 14. I was… I am, an alcoholic. Sober now, but not then. I… I was verbally and physically abusive to my wife and the boy. They left me. They had to. Then the boy fell in with the wrong crowd. By his late teens he was involved with drugs and a gang. Like many alcoholics, I blamed everything and everyone else for my problems. I especially hated white people. I was a racist in that regard but thought the reverse to be true as well. Much happened in a short time. My wife was killed in an accident. She hit a deer on the way home from her job at a truck stop near Hot Springs late one night. It wasn't even a week later that I got news of my nephew's arrest in Wyoming. He and three other gang members were at a meth lab in a remote area when a white man hunting antelope came across them. That man was Julie's father. His hunting rifle was no match for the gang's fully automatic weapons and they killed him. The whole thing was caught on video by a pair of DEA agents who had the lab under surveillance using high-powered cameras more than a mile away and a drone high overhead. They were too far away to warn Mr. Reed before it was too late, but did call in a helicopter with armed backup. Agents shot two of the gang members when they fired on the chopper. My nephew was one of the two survivors taken into custody."

The cargo hold was silent. Julie stood ramrod straight facing Simon, her hands balled into fists. Her face showed an anger no one present had yet seen. Some silently prayed things wouldn't explode into a physical altercation at any second. Cora turned the Taser in her right hand toward Julie as her left discretely slid down to the Glock on her hip, unsnapping the holster's retaining strap while everyone's focus was locked on Julie and Simon.

"I was filled with rage," Simon continued. "I was angry at my nephew, at the cops, at Mr. Reed for being in the wrong place at the wrong time, at everyone but the person who really was to blame. Myself."

Simon took his eyes off Julie and looked one by one at the others now standing around them in a loose circle. He continued, "Overwhelming evidence moved the case to court quickly. My nephew was encouraged by a white public defender to admit his guilt in hopes of a plea agreement. Life without parole instead of the death penalty. Miss Reed is correct. I arrived at the courthouse as the plea and sentencing were to take place and I had been drinking. I made a scene, shouting obscenities as the court officers tried to restrain me. And then I did the unthinkable. I saw Miss Reed in the courtroom and shouted vulgarities at her, blaming her and her father for trespassing on the sacred lands of my people, killing our animals and wrecking the life of my nephew. They dragged me from the courtroom and I ended up spending 90 days in jail with a year of probation for my condition and actions that day. A man has a lot of time to think in a jail cell."

"More time than my dad had to think when he was gunned down," Julie growled. "In all the years I knew him, my father never uttered a racial slur of any kind. In fact, he encouraged my study of Indian culture in high school. You had no right to say those things about him and if you'd been even half a man, you could have turned that boy's life around and saved your marriage instead of sacrificing your liver and brain cells on the altar of fire water you disgusting boozer! Do you remember when I came by your cell after you were locked up and your nephew's plea deal was denied? Do you recall what I told you Mister Standing Elk?"

128

Simon looked into Julie's eyes as tears began to form in his own. "You told me that you hoped my nephew's execution went slowly, that he would suffer. Then you said I'd better pray to The Great Spirit that our paths never crossed again or it would be I who would know suffering."

No one was prepared for what happened next. With almost superhuman speed, Simon Standing Elk snatched Cora's Glock from its holster, shoving the soldier aside. He flipped the pistol around so it pointed at himself and handed it to Julie, who quickly took it and leveled the muzzle inches from Simon's face. No one moved and hardly dared even breathe.

"Before I die, a few last words please," Simon pleaded.

"Make your peace," said Julie.

"After your visit to my cell, I understood the gravity of my sins. I was confronted by the weight of my failed existence and wrote a letter to my father, a man I'd not spoken to in years. In the letter, I begged his forgiveness for the disgrace I'd brought on our family and to him. There was no reply until the day I was released from jail and found him waiting outside next to his pickup truck. A process began that day that continues to this moment. With my father's help and guidance, I went through rehab and joined AA. I reconnected spiritually with the ways of our people and The Great Spirit. A cleansing of my mind, body and spirit changed the man I was. A year later I was working to help others trapped by the chains of drug and alcohol addiction get clean and sober. I joined a Big Brothers program a year after that and mentored three boys, helped them with school work, took them fishing and hiking. I gradually made amends with all who my actions had hurt. All but three. The three that mattered the most. My late wife. My nephew on death row who refuses to see me. And you Miss Reed. There is nothing I can do to bring your father back or erase the hurtful things I said to you in the past. I just want you to understand the man you knew four years ago is dead already. He died in that jail cell. The man before you is a different man. A man who begs your forgiveness, regrets his past actions, has been sober four years now and desires to enter the spirit realm with a clean conscience. Please, Miss Reed, forgive this foolish man for his sins."

Julie's icy stare was unchanged, her countenance unmoved by Simon's confession.

"BANG!"

Chapter Twenty-Three

It sat on a rocky ledge overlooking the scene in the canyon below, unafraid and unconcerned. With its back against the cliff's face and the sun behind it, the monster appeared as a dark indentation among many against the stones. So long as it didn't move, no one would notice it. It understood the value of patience.

Law enforcement teams had assembled and dispersed throughout the day, gathering at the scene of Officer Sandberg's wrecked SUV and fanning out across the forest surrounding it below the cliffs. The creature was somewhat amused by the two-dimensional thinking of its pursuers. They hadn't realized its powerful forelimbs gave it exceptional climbing skills and were oblivious that it was right above them.

Three teams of tracking dogs had been brought in, but one whiff of what remained of Sandberg's shirt sent them howling back into the trucks they'd arrived in. The humans were on their own. Steady thumping of helicopter rotors rose and fell in volume up and down the canyon as it had been doing since morning. The monster knew it was best to stay hidden during daylight. It had planned to make its next move when dusk settled across the area. But circumstances would alter the beast's plans.

A different noise from that of the helicopter it had been hearing all day came to the creature's ears. It was somewhat similar, but unique in its rhythm and getting louder. The sound became a roar as a modified MH-60G Pave Hawk helicopter from Ellsworth Air Force Base swept over the rim of the canyon where the monster had spent the day resting. It stopped to hover over the trees surrounding the crime scene below. The beast saw humans sitting in big openings on the sides of the insect-like aircraft astride what looked like large weapons. The helicopter started to creep forward, advancing up the canyon. Instinct told the creature it was no longer safe to remain in the area.

The Pave Hawk had forward-looking infrared cameras with sensors that scanned for thermal heat signatures and converted them into video images. Temperatures had fallen since the early afternoon and heat typically collected by the dark trees and rocks in the Black Hills during a sunny day was rapidly radiating away, allowing the cameras to scan more effectively for warm-blooded creatures in the area.

Members of the armed search parties showed up clearly on the thermal imagery as the chopper made its way through the canyon. The first pass also revealed six deer, a coyote and many smaller mammals. The Pave Hawk made a 180-degree turn and began to scan back toward the trailhead in the direction of a beast that had no way of knowing about the new capabilities the helicopter had given the searchers. The chopper cruised by the creature, halted abruptly and turned around. It began to crawl through the air toward the monster's location, investigating an anomaly that had appeared in the imagery as it had passed.

The creature waited until it could see helmeted figures through the windscreen of the Pave Hawk pointing in its direction. Then the beast rose to full height and the helicopter pulled away slightly, rotating to turn its port side door gunner toward the monster. The creature turned, jumped upward and began to scale the side of the cliff just as the gunner opened fire with a GAU-18 .50-caliber machine gun. Heavy bullets slammed into the face of the cliff beneath the rapidly climbing monster. The gunner initially had difficulty directing his fire upward. The helicopter's door armaments were intended to engage targets below or alongside the craft and the big gun's ability to be aimed upward was limited. The creature continued to climb, gaining critical seconds as the Pave Hawk crew coordinated and helicopter started to rise.

The aircraft emerged from the shaded canyon with its nose pointed northwest and the gunner's open door facing southwest. As soon as it cleared the rim, the crew was momentarily blinded by the bright disc of the low-hanging sun. Blinding sunlight was obliterated by shade for the door gunner when a 250-pound boulder blocked the solar disc a second before it crushed his chest and continued across the Pave Hawk's interior, breaking the legs of the gunner on the starboard side of the aircraft before crashing into his machine gun. Searchers at the trailhead watched helplessly as an airman, machine gun and boulder flew out of the aircraft's starboard side and plummeted to the canyon floor. With one crew member dead and another hurt, the disarmed and crippled Pave Hawk pulled up and away from the beast on the canyon rim. It then dipped its nose eastward to return to base where damage could be assessed and the injured remaining gunner could get medical attention.

The beast watched the helicopter retreat into darkening blue and purple hues of dusk gathering on the eastern horizon. It looked down into the canyon and saw a group of people arriving at the airman's shattered corpse. Prudence would have dictated a hasty retreat from the area, but the monster was hungry and night was coming on fast. It was time to hunt and feed.

◆ ◆ ◆

Dr. Jonathan Smythe knelt before the altar in Sanctum's chapel. He was in prayer. Moses prayed beside him. The shaman stood behind them at a distance, arms extended toward the heavens as he quietly chanted in the tongue of his people. The men were offering intercessory supplications on behalf of the team they'd sent to battle the Yakwawi. But of more immediate concern was what they knew would be a confrontation between Simon and Julie, especially when they'd learned details concerning the last time the two had spoken.

A disc of glowing white mist began to grow between the men and the altar. None of them looked directly at it as it grew in size and brightness. Soon it was a blinding glowing orb hovering in place, illuminating the entire chapel. A voice came from within it, a voice unique in its ability to convey affection, compassion and ultimate authority simultaneously.

"Jon... Moses... one now called Wicasa... You have been heard. Zadkiel has dispatched a sentinel of his order. Be at peace and trouble yourselves no longer with this matter of conflict among your team's members."

The orb of white mist dissipated seconds after the voice had spoken. The kneeling men rose and raised their arms with the shaman, offering prayers of thanks and praise. Several minutes passed, then the trio silently filed down the aisle and headed for the operations center.

◆ ◆ ◆

"BANG! ... BANG, BANG, BANG!" screamed Julie holding the Glock inches from Simon's face, a lone tear sliding down her left cheek.

"*Forgive us our sins as we forgive those who sin against us,*" the voice in her head spoke clearly and firmly but in a compassionate tone.

Even as one voice in her head repeated the orison, another screamed, "*Why now? Why at the moment of my longed-for retribution is THAT line from a prayer I learned as a child in Sunday school haunting me? Why can't I pull the trigger?*"

The sentinel was cloaked from sight, invisible to the team members. Its form was that of tall and slender woman with Middle-Eastern features embracing Julie's shoulders with one arm as the hand of her other grasped the pistol's slide and Julie's trigger hand. Her face, one of exquisite beauty with smooth, olive skin, was framed by long, straight, black hair and pressed against Julie's as she spoke the words into her ear over and over again.

The others present in the cargo hold had been startled by Julie's sudden shouts. They stood frozen in place, daring not make a move for fear of provoking a tragedy. Cora couldn't use the Taser, knowing the jolt of electricity could cause Julie's trigger finger to contract and fire the pistol. Jake quietly stepped forward to stand closely behind Julie. He chose his words carefully, his voice barely more than a whisper.

"Remember what you said this morning in the cafeteria? You told me you were convinced that good and evil aren't equal, that you believe good wins. Justice meted out in the absence of mercy for the truly repentant is only revenge, Julie. I believe what you said earlier today. That good wins. And I believe you're good, Julie. Please. Show everyone else what I know to be true about you."

Julie looked beyond the front sight of the pistol into Simon's eyes. For the first time, she saw the sincerity of his regret. She also saw something else. At first she thought it was hallucination. Was Simon beginning to glow? The others were quietly murmuring as Simon's countenance brightened. Julie tripped the magazine release with her thumb, jettisoning the cartridges to the floor of the aircraft. She racked the slide to eject the chambered round, tossed the pistol to Cora, and turned sobbing to bury her head in Jake's chest. Jake gently embraced her, offering quiet words of comfort and encouragement as years of pent-up anger and hurt poured out in tears.

The sentinel stepped back, a beautiful smile on her face, a smile that waned a bit when she turned to Simon and saw him staring at her with a knowing look. *Could he see her?* She nodded at Simon. He closed his eyes for a moment and gave a barely perceptible nod of acknowledgment in return. He'd known she was there the entire time. She would report the encounter with this human who had at least some ability to see across a dimensional plane. Such people were rare. Then the sentinel vanished, her mission complete.

All relaxed a bit and moved away, leaving Jake and Julie in the center of the cargo hold. Cora beckoned to the others and they followed her. Once out of expected earshot of the two, a quiet conversation began.

"Are you okay Mr. Standing Elk?" Cora whispered.

"Yes, and please call me Simon."

"I need to understand why you're here sir," Cora continued. "We're about to go into battle with a bloodthirsty creature possessing lethal fighting skills. Then I find you unexpectedly joining us, instigating a potentially team-busting and nearly fatal incident by your mere presence, and next thing I know you go all incandescent on us. Who are you and what exactly do you bring to this party?"

Simon recounted his story, beginning at the sweat lodge and ending with him at Sanctum. He explained his apparent ability to sense the presence of the Yakwawi and the shaman's hope he could be of help by either locating it or drawing it to them. He expected a deluge of mockery and derision when he finished. Instead, a question was posed. It was the last he'd anticipated.

"Can you fight, mate?" asked Jeff. "Any special weapons skills or training? Military or law enforcement background? Anything like that?"

"I have never been in anything other than drunken brawls at which I fared poorly," replied Simon. "As to weapons, I did go hunting with my father and the shaman when I was young. If you happen to have a lever-action .30- 30 deer rifle aboard, I believe you'll find me to be a good shot."

"No offense, Simon, but I'm not confident a deer rifle will be effective against what we're going up against," said Tol. "There's a .450 Marlin Guide Gun in the armory but I think Dr. Sanders has dibs on it, though I'm not sure even that shoulder canon will take out a Yakwawi."

135

"No offense taken, sir. I viewed my role on this assignment as more of a guide or perhaps bait. Not a direct combatant. I do have Red Cross certification in advanced first aid. I presume you have a med kit aboard?"

"Well, that's something," said Dom. "Let's hope we won't need that particular skill set."

"Now I think we need to address the elephant in the room," said Cora nodding toward Julie and Jake. "What do we do with her?"

"There's no need to change whatever role you'd intended for her to play," said Simon. "I believe our situation is resolved and behind us. I sensed the anger that had built up inside of her dissipating. And I have no reservations about her presence on this assignment."

"Well that's mighty big of you," said Cora. "But I'm reluctant to arm up a woman who almost killed you a few minutes ago. What if she snaps in the heat of the moment and puts a bullet in your back?"

"Then I go to The Great Spirit and rest with my ancestors beyond this life having done all I can to right what wrongs I've done," replied Simon. "I have no fear of Julie. No fear of death at all."

"You have a big heart, my brother," said Ibutho. "And I sense great courage in you."

"Thank you, my large new friend."

"Just to be certain, I want everyone to weigh in on this," said Cora. "Does anyone here have reservations about Julie's participation as an armed combatant on this mission? This is your last chance to speak up."

All present shook their heads so Cora left them. She walked toward the plane's ramp where Julie had stopped crying and was wiping her eyes with a handkerchief Jake had offered her.

Before Cora could say anything, Jake intervened. "She's not the one who grabbed your gun. He put it in her hand. If there's any blame for what happened, it lies with him for escalating the situation from serious to dangerous."

Cora sighed heavily. "I know. If I'd had any idea about the past Julie had with Simon, I wouldn't have signed off on having him with us. But Dr. Smythe seems to think he's an asset. We're about ninety minutes from our LZ and I've got to make a decision. Julie, look at me."

136

The younger woman turned to face the soldier. Julie had regained her composure. The women locked eyes.

"Can you assure me you are not a threat to anyone on this team or yourself?" Cora asked.

"Yes ma'am," Julie replied.

"Give me your word by the oath you took as a law enforcement officer that you will not harm or abuse Simon Standing Elk in any way whatsoever."

"You have my word," Julie promised. "And my sincere apology for my actions. I let emotions I didn't even know were bottled up inside get the better of me. It won't happen again."

"Correct. It won't," said Cora sternly and then moved to put her face close to Julie's before quietly giving a warning. "I've seen you fight. I know what you're capable of. And if I even suspect you pose a danger to anyone else on this team, I will take action up to and including the use of deadly force to protect them if necessary. Do you understand me?"

"Completely," replied Julie.

"Good. Now we've got just more than an hour to get ready to engage this monster so let's get to it." Cora moved away from Jake and Julie toward the others, whistled to get everyone's attention and motioned for them all to follow her out of the cargo hold deeper into the big aircraft.

Chapter Twenty-Four

The armory on the aircraft was impressive. Located just forward of the cargo bay, the room was roughly a 20-foot square with weapons of various types lining all four walls from floor to ceiling. A rectangular island in the center of the room afforded space for assembling, cleaning, maintaining and modifying or configuring weapons. Members of Cora's team fanned out, each selecting arms they were proficient with.

"The new bolt guns are back in the yellow crate in the cargo bay," said Cora. "Since Julie and Jeff are the only ones who've been trained in their operation, those go to them. Everyone else select what you think will work best against this thing. And everyone take backups as well. Dom, Tol and I are already in uniform. Somehow, I don't think camo is going to matter much against this creature so suit up for speed and mobility. And don't forget to use garments with body armor."

"Body armor tends to be restrictive," noted Julie. "And I don't think this monster is packing anything other than raw power."

"We know it can throw things," replied Jake. "I took a rock dead center that sent me flying and did a number on my ribs. Some level of protection would be prudent."

"You'll find our armor unique, sheila," Jeff told Julie. "Give a touch to Tol's BDUs."

The big Russian was standing closest to Julie so she took a looser portion of his shirt between her thumb and forefinger, rubbing the material between them as Jake did the same to Dom, who was next to him.

"Huh," said Jake. "It feels light and smooth like silk but is thicker. And almost a bit squishy."

"Don't tell me you guys have perfected reactive body armor!" exclaimed Julie.

"We didn't," replied Dom with a grin. "Our R&D people did. Not much noticeable added weight, but able to stop most handgun rounds, rifle bullets up to .30-caliber, and it dampens the effects of blunt-force impact to some extent too."

"How is this possible?" asked Jake.

"Moses can explain all the science details when we get back," said Dom. "The short version is that we have ultrathin layers of a fabric similar to Kevlar but stronger, and between them is a layer of a substance that's something between a liquid and soft plastic in its neutral state like it is now. When a sudden sharp force impacts it, the tiny particles that make it up instantly flow to the place hit and solidify stronger than steel until the force is dissipated across the garment. Then it returns to its original state."

"I read about ongoing research into something like that," said Julie. "But from what I understood, field deployment on a wide scale was more than a decade away."

"Yeah, well we've been using it for more than a decade already," remarked Jeff. "And on more than a few occasions it saved lives of our operatives. But physics is still physics and when something big hits you hard, reactive armor or not, you're going to get banged up. A bullet may not get through, but you'll get knocked on your rear."

Jake and Jeff went into an adjacent dressing area first and emerged in the same camo BDUs Cora's team had on, complete with integrated body armor. Then they selected their weapons. Jake spotted a Marlin lever-action carbine in .450-caliber with a black elastic holder for ten extra rounds on the stock. The rifle was outfitted with a ghost-ring rear sight, a type preferred by guides in areas with dangerous game because it allowed a shooter to acquire the target quickly and reacquire it just as fast for follow-up shots. Jeff took a box of ammunition for the gun from a drawer on the center island and Jake nodded approvingly at the 430-grain penetrator bullets inside, though their odd coloration confused him a bit.

"These would kill the biggest bear in the world," Jake said. "Let's hope they can do some damage to a Yakwawi."

Jeff went to a wall to retrieve a Magnum Research Desert Eagle semiautomatic pistol in .50 Action Express, along with a pair of extra magazines, sliding the massive handgun into a tactical holster on his right thigh. Cora cast him a questioning look.

"Hey, if I'm going to be throwing pointy sticks at the thing, I at least want something that has a chance of making enough noise to scare it if the arrows don't work," the Aussie explained.

Tol and Ibutho were assembling a pair of DRD Tactical Kivaari .338 Lapua Magnum rifles in the center of the room. Thermal imaging tactical scopes sat nearby, along with special magazines that doubled capacity from ten to twenty rounds each. Ibutho also had a pair of short spears in special sheaths slung across his back to form an X underneath a teardrop-shaped shield.

The door to the dressing room opened and all heads turned as Julie entered the room. She was clad neck to combat boots in a form-fitting outfit made from the reactive armor material and had opted for complete ultra-black in place of camo. She also wore special black fighting gloves outfitted with polymer-reinforced knuckles. Dual holster belts held Glock 40 MOS semiautomatic 10 mm long-slide pistols against each of her hips. Strapped above her boots on each calf was a Gerber Mark II fighting dagger. A pair of round grenades, one on each holster belt, appeared to complete her choice of weaponry. But what gave her the look of an angel of death were the streaks of black face paint she'd applied. She'd also put her hair back in a ponytail.

"Whoa," remarked Jeff.

"What?" asked Julie, "Are we going into combat or not?"

"That's a different look for you," said Jake with a smile.

"It, ah, suits you," Dom stated. "But it also scares the heck out of me."

"Enough gawking, boys," said Cora. "Everyone's geared up except for you, Simon."

Simon had watched the preparations silently from a corner of the room. He'd not changed his clothes, nor had he selected a weapon. Sensing the strange inner peace he'd had in the presence of the sentinel in the cargo bay, he simply said, "I have what I need." Then he left the room.

The others followed.

Once back in the cargo bay, the crate containing the bolt guns was opened. Julie and Jeff each took one, along with two replacement cylinders.

"Between us we've got 42 shots with these," stated Jeff. "Let's pray that's enough to take this thing down."

"We've got enough firepower here to slay a herd of elephants," said Jake. "I don't like killing animals, though I've done my fair share of it in defense of myself and others. There's nothing alive on this planet that could withstand what this group is capable of unleashing."

Simon finally spoke up. "You've made an assumption, Dr. Sanders. One that I hope is correct but has a flaw we must not forget. The beast we're about to battle did not originate on this planet."

"Your point being?" asked Cora.

"All these preparations. The weapons. The armor. Centuries ago the tribes of this continent prepared with the best of such things they had. My understanding is that some of those weapons were also advanced for the time. They prevailed, but at terrible cost. Be cautious, my new friends. The beast we face may have capabilities we do not yet know of. And it may have allies."

"Wait, what?! Allies? Explain, Simon." Cora seemed alarmed.

"We see what we can see. We know what we know. The Watch exists, from what I understand, precisely because there is much we cannot see and still do not know in this universe. But this I do know. We must fight together. If we're to prevail, it must be as a team. You each chose weapons you know and dressed for battle as you saw fit. Your decisions are based on training and past experiences as individuals. Ms. Cora is in command. Who commands if she falls? The plan, as I've heard it, is to find Yakwawi and kill him. That is a plan but not a strategy. Because once we're on the ground, be assured the beast will have a plan identical to ours. Find us and kill us. I am not a warrior. But I strongly suggest we spend now until we begin our descent discussing tactics. And once we start down, devote ourselves to prayers for protection. They'll be needed."

Jake felt the hair on the back of his neck stand up and a chill run down his spine as Simon finished his remarks. As he looked at other faces around him, he saw something for the first time. There was doubt. A hint of uncertainty on every face but two – Simon's and Julie's. The apparent holy man and the tigress. But Simon's words had struck home in the hearts of everyone else. There was a realization that some of the team may not come back from this fight. As the predator expert, Jake used his scientific mind to begin assembling relevant facts based on his extensive knowledge of animal behavior. He focused his thoughts specifically on how predators competed with one another in an ecosystem, and what happened when smaller predators encountered a bigger and more powerful foe. Wolves versus grizzly. Dolphins versus shark. Hyenas versus lion. Rolling actual scenarios over in his head, a true strategy emerged and he shared a tactical solution with the team, one he hoped would defeat the Yakwawi and bring everyone back safely.

◆ ◆ ◆

It had waited until darkness filled the canyon, the tiny sliver of a moon unable to cast even minimal light to where a team below worked to recover the shattered remains of the fallen airman. A half-dozen men struggled to maneuver the stretcher carrying the corpse down a steep and brush-filled incline to an ambulance on the access road across a stream 90 yards away. They had only headlamps to illuminate their steps, the emergency vehicles having dimmed their spotlights to keep from blinding the recovery team as it approached. Moments after the bright spotlights winked out, it leapt off the canyon rim.

The only warning those carrying the stretcher had was a loud crash near the base of the cliff behind them. The monster landed on thick, powerful legs, crouched and then sprang horizontally at the team. At the last moment, it stretched its front limbs wide and took down all six of the men at once. The two closest to the cliff died instantly as their necks and spines snapped on impact. The other four fell before they could even cry out a warning. Powerful jaws and knife-like claws combined with incredible speed to dispatch every member of the team in seconds.

Police, rangers, game officers and a team of Air Force recovery personnel on the road heard only a brief commotion caused by rustling brush and snapping branches. When there was no response to shouts or radio hails. An intense foul odor suddenly swept over the assembly. Emergency vehicle spotlights flipped back on only to have their beams soaked up by the black coat of the monster already among them.

Shouts and gunshots shattered the otherwise still night air as nearly two-dozen law enforcement professionals engaged the beast in sudden and violent close-quarters combat. But the creature had initiative with the element of surprise. Those present were in the process of recovering a body and had last seen the monster fleeing over the canyon rim. The last thing they expected was its return to battle so many armed men and women. Bodies and limbs flew in all directions as bloodlust-induced rage fueled the beast's attack. Multiple shots from 9 mm service pistols hit the monster with little effect. A couple of officers scored hits with AR15 rifles. Their 5.56 mm bullets penetrated more deeply than the pistol rounds, even enough to touch internal organs, but their damage was ineffective in stopping the onslaught. A SUV behind which three officers had taken cover was flipped, crushing them before bursting into flames. Another vehicle tried to speed away to get help but a side kick from the monster sent it crashing down an embankment, rolling onto its roof in the creek below.

Lawrence County Deputy Robert Jensen huddled with USFS Ranger Beth Merlino behind the last undamaged vehicle in the canyon, each slapping fresh magazines into their service Glocks. They were the only people left alive without major injuries. Both were veteran law enforcement professionals and understood they'd be making their last stand against an unstoppable foe in the seconds that followed. The ranger said a quick prayer for her husband and two children before turning to the deputy and giving a nod. The pair rose as one, pivoting to rest their pistols on the hood of the SUV and take aim. They never got off a shot.

Chapter Twenty-Five

Darkness was abruptly annihilated by a blinding strobe of alternating red and white light from above aimed right at the monster's face. It rose to full height, swinging its front limbs violently before its eyes. The black silhouette of a woman dropped from the sky, landing between the desperate officers and the monster. She held a strange-looking weapon and wore a pistol on each hip.

Deputy Jensen and Ranger Merlino each felt a strong hand grip a shoulder and something clip to their duty belts. They whirled to look up into the face of an enormous black man clad in unique 3-D camo. A voice came from the woman in front of the creature. They spun to look at her.

"Hi," they heard her say to the beast. "Remember me?"

It responded with a furious roar. They turned again, speechless, to face the man behind them.

"You may go now," Ibutho told the two officers, his deep voice rich with authority. Immediately they were pulled upward into the Skyray silently hovering above.

A moment later the pair was staring into the face of a white-haired Native American who unhitched winch ropes from their belts and gently pushed them backward into padded seats behind them. The deputy drew his Glock, aimed at the head of the man who'd pushed him before noticing the fellow was holding a can of soda.

Simon sighed heavily, shaking his head as he spoke. "Two questions trouble me this night. Why does my face seem to attract pistol muzzles, and why does the white man always want to trade with the Indian?" Simon swiftly snatched the gun from the dumbfounded man's hand and replaced it with the pop can before tossing the gun down the open floor hatch beside him. "I highly recommend the ginger ale for stomach upset. Goodnight."

With that, Simon disappeared down through the hatch using one of the ropes that had hoisted the officers aboard.

Julie engaged the beast head-on and had already put ten bolts into its torso. She was meticulous in following a cardinal rule of close-quarters combat – keep moving. Every second shot, she'd roll to one side, backpedal or advance. With the strobe in full effect, she was never where the monster expected her to be as it lashed out blindly, always a split-second late.

Jeff was prone on the side of the road with the embankment but had fired only two bolts, having taken precious time to drag two officers from the upside-down vehicle in the creek so they didn't drown. Both were unconscious but breathing. His bolts flew true and penetrated deep.

The monster began to stagger backwards, hammered by shot after shot from Tol and Ibutho's .338 magnum rifles. The pair had replaced the deputy and ranger at the SUV, their guns rested across its hood. The steep slope of the creature's head from front to back made frontal headshots ineffective, though the pair could see deep gashes in its forehead and cheeks where their initial volley of bullets had hit and torn skin. Now they were repeatedly slamming 250-grain bullets, each delivering more than 4,800 foot-pounds of impact energy, into the center of the monster's torso.

There was the unmistakable *THWAP* of a big bullet solidly connecting. The beast's head snapped sharply left, causing it to stagger. Jake had scored a solid headshot from its right side with a heavy slug from his big-bore lever-action rifle. The Watch attack team started to feel a rush of excitement. They were drawing blood by employing coordinated attacks from multiple angles, a strategy Jake had recommended in the plane based on how pack animals take down big opponents. The strobe kept the creature disoriented but special eyewear resembling swimming goggles made The Watch team immune to the effect. The strobe was also Jake's idea, one he'd recommended after learning how the young Spearfish couple had used camera flashes to escape the monster. The Yakwawi was blinded, disoriented and staggering against the onslaught of bullets and bolts.

"Time to play our ace!" Jeff shouted from the roadside.

Cora and Dom stepped into the road behind the hulking, roaring, bloody mass of rage.

"Forward units CLEAR!" Cora shouted into her com unit.

That was the cue for Julie, Tol and Ibutho to move to the sides of the road and get down as she and Dom played their part. The pair brought up their FN P90 assault rifles set for fully automatic fire and each began to empty a 50-round magazine into the monster's rear ankles. The P90s were loaded with small high-velocity 5.7 mm rounds specifically engineered to defeat body armor and deliver maximum penetration. The beast screamed in pain as the soldiers delivered their payloads on target before rolling sideways into opposite road ditches to reload.

"Everybody FIRE!" Cora commanded.

A devastating fusillade of bolts and bullets raked the Yakwawi. It staggered heavily. First left, then right, and finally looked as though it would fall backwards. Julie, having expended all of her bolts, dropped the bolt gun and drew her twin Glocks. She advanced on the beast, firing bullet after bullet into its chest.

It started small, but rapidly swirled into a massive opening. Light from the Skyray disappeared into its blackness. A dimensional rift appeared directly behind what the team hoped was a mortally wounded Yakwawi and it fell backward into the opening with only its legs remaining on the road. Four large demonic entities with both canine and human characteristics emerged from the rift and began to drag the Yakwawi the rest of the way back into the portal.

"NOOOOOO!" screamed Julie. She rushed the rift, firing at the new invaders. Two shots caught one, knocking it back into the portal. Another dropped one of the new intruders to its knees. Almost there, she holstered her empty pistols on the run, yanked the grenades from her sides and popped the pins. The entities and Yakwawi were just disappearing from view less than 20 feet away as she tossed the grenades into the rift, oblivious that her forward momentum would carry her into it after them.

He hit her hard from the side with a tackle worthy of a professional linebacker. Momentum carried both he and Julie to the side of the rift just as the flash and boom of the grenades appeared in the collapsing portal. Simon rolled off Julie and they lay side-by-side on the edge of the gravel road, breathing hard.

"I could not... let you go... in there...Miss Reed...I'm sorry. We just can't... afford to lose you," panted Simon.

"We had him! WE HAD HIM!" Julie shouted into the night as the rest of the team gathered around her and Simon. "What was THAT? What were those...those things? It's not fair! WE HAD HIM!"

Julie jumped up in rage, stomped onto the gravel road and kicked up a cloud of dirt and stone in frustration. Simon sat up and crossed his legs.

"A cross-dimensional portal?" suggested Cora.

"Awfully convenient timing and location, don't you think?" Jake noted with a definite tone of frustration in his own voice. He shared Julie's anger at not being able to see a definitive end to the beast that had murdered his wife. His tactics had been working.

"This is not coincidence," said Ibutho, stepping forward with his two spears in hand.

"I can't recall anything like it," said Dom. "I mean we know there are those with some level of control over cross-dimensional travel, but..."

"DOM!" scolded Cora.

"Wait just a minute here," said Jake with alarm. "What do you mean, Dom? Who can control travel across dimensions?"

"SILENCE!"

Everyone froze and looked at Simon. He now stood among them. No one present had ever heard him raise his voice. At least not since he'd given up alcohol.

"There is much we must know, but not here and not now. Look around you. We feel robbed of a victory. See the bodies of the fallen, the maimed and injured. Before dawn there will be wives, husbands, parents and children learning the terrible fate of a loved one. And what of this mess? We must leave here quickly. Think of what will be on the news networks and conspiracy Internet sites when word of what happened here gets out. No, my friends. Now is not the time to lick our wounds. Now is the time to swiftly care for those wounded and get out of here."

Moments of silence followed Simon's admonishment. Then Cora spoke into her com unit.

"Skyray seven, this is Gladius. We need extraction. State 20 and ETA please."

"Gladius, Skyray seven. We're overhead. Able to set down at trailhead on highway at your call."

"Copy Skyray seven. Give us ten minutes and stand by for fast exfil. Notify all local authorities that large-scale medical aid is needed at my location upon exfil."

147

"Copy Gladius. Skyray out."

"Okay everyone," Cora commanded. "We need any and all evidence that can help us. Blood, hair and tissue samples of anything non-human. We have eight minutes to gather what we can and two to get to the exfiltration point and away. Make sure we don't leave any weapons unsecured or other Sanctum gear behind. Now let's get to it."

"Miss Reed," it was Simon motioning to Julie that he wanted to speak to her as the others fanned out to gather what evidence they could. "I hope I did not injure you but I could not let you pursue into the portal."

"No. I'm okay. A bit embarrassed I didn't see you coming at me in time to dodge, but I guess I had combat tunnel vision. My body armor hardened the moment you hit me. It really works. What do you think would have happened if I'd gone in after them anyway?"

"It's likely we'd have lost you for good. There's no telling what lay beyond the portal, but based on the look and intent of what came out of there to pull the Yakwawi back in, I suspect even someone of your fighting skill would have had a difficult death on the other side," Simon replied.

"Maybe," Julie responded. "But you saw I took out one of the things with my Glocks and I know I winged another. My hope was to confirm the Yakwawi was dead after clearing the area ahead of me with the grenades and then jump back here. Those dog-men aren't immune to lead, we saw that."

"Did we?" asked Simon. "Remove a magazine and look closely at your bullets, Miss Reed."

Julie did so, noticing for the first time that the slugs had unique coloration. "What the...?"

"Specially made at Sanctum using a number of elements in metallic form. Tol told me. There wasn't time for a full explanation beyond something about the bullets triggering adverse reactions in targets. I'd like to know how and why such things are known," said Simon. "But for now, I want you to know that I do sincerely appreciate you not shooting me in the face earlier this evening."

Julie shot a look at Simon with a tinge of warning to it. "Oh, I wanted to Standing Elk. Believe you me, I was a millisecond from sending your brains splattering against the bulkhead. But this voice in my head..."

"Forgive us our sins as we forgive those who sin against us?"

"Wait. How?" Julie was alarmed and suddenly very uncomfortable.

"We have much to talk about," said Simon. "But now we have a task to complete."

The team worked quickly by the light of red LED headlamps they'd brought along so as not to impair their night vision. Simon moved among the fallen, tending to the wounded as best he could with the limited time he had available. Only six of the original complement of first responders were still alive, excluding the pair on the Skyray. Two of the wounded were semi-conscious, neither was coherent. Simon was certain three of the other four wouldn't survive given the severity of their wounds. Jeff had somehow donned a cleric's collar and was moving among them, ministering prayers and last rites for the dying.

The rest of the team worked primarily in areas where the Yakwawi had been. Jake tracked the creature's attack path back to the base of the cliff and bagged some hair samples. Julie and Ibutho concentrated on collecting blood and tissue. Tol was casting some footprints with fast-setting plaster. Dom grabbed what weapons he could find on the scene and put them in a duffle bag to prevent their falling into wrong hands. When his bag got too heavy, Ibutho left Julie to her work and assisted filling a second duffle. Cora stood watch over the operation, her P90 at the ready. At two minutes to pick-up time, she gave the order for the team to make for the trailhead and brought up the rear, leaving on the road a gold medallion about 4 inches wide and an inch high. It was inscribed with a symbol that looked similar to the anchor of a large ship.

The team's newcomers marveled how the Skyray seemed to almost magically appear above the area where the gravel and paved roads met. There was no noise and minimal disturbance of dirt or nearby vegetation as the craft gently set down while deploying a stairway from the rear fuselage. They lost no time boarding the craft, which lifted into the night sky less than a minute after touching down as sirens of approaching emergency vehicles grew louder.

It was cramped inside the Skyray, largely due to the presence of a deputy and forest ranger in addition to the large bags of equipment Dom and Ibutho hauled aboard. Cora stood at the front of the cabin to address the two law enforcement officers seated before her.

"I'm pleased the two of you made it out of there alive," Cora began.

"But you've seen things we cannot allow you to share with others in the interests of national and global security. I hope you understand that."

"Who are you people?" Ranger Merlino asked. "What do you intend to do with us?"

"You're holding law enforcement personnel against our will," said Deputy Jensen. "That's a serious offense, even for military personnel."

"Well, they tend to do that Bob," said Julie stepping around to face the two detainees.

"Julie! Julie Reed? I thought you were dead! How are you mixed up in all of this? I haven't seen you since the bar fight we backed you up on a couple weeks back," the astonished deputy noted.

"Thanks again for that, Bob. Picking up the prisoners and taking them to Spearfish Hospital for me was kind of you. Now I'll return the kindness. You and Ranger Merlino here, through no fault of your own, are smack dab in the middle of some seriously secret stuff and the ramifications would be huge if any of it leaked. Believe me, what's about to happen is best for both of you and your families."

"What are your intentions?" asked the ranger nervously.

"You're both going to be injected with a safe but effective drug," explained Julie. "It causes short-term amnesia, basically giving you no memory of past events over a designated period of time based on the dosage. I understand these people have this down pretty well, and in a moment we're going to wipe your minds of everything that happened tonight. You'll be unconscious for a while and have major headaches when you wake up. Each of you will be found by search and rescue personnel not far from the trailhead to Roughlock Falls. The drug won't show up in any of the conventional screens they'll do on you so the memory loss will likely be attributed to severe PTSD. You'll both be off-duty with pay during the standard post-shooting investigations, and ultimately be allowed to return to your jobs if you so desire. I know you might not like this, but look on the bright side. You'll be with your families again by sunrise and the same can't be said for most of those who were in that canyon with you."

"What's the other option?" Deputy Jensen asked.

"I didn't give you one," Julie replied.

At that moment the ranger and deputy both felt brief sharp pricks in the sides of their necks as Dom and Tol used compact jet injectors to administer the drug. The detainees were unconscious in seconds. Even as emergency medical vehicles and personnel swarmed the site of the battle, the Skyray's pilot skillfully maneuvered quietly overhead to deposit the ranger and deputy a couple hundred yards apart nearby. Though Cora's team hated to do it, each of the temporary guests had been administered bruises consistent with those they'd have received had they been thrown violently into the brush. Dom had located Deputy Jensen's Glock near the spot where Simon had touched down during the fight and slid it back into the unconscious man's hand. Ranger Merlino's was already in hers. Tol had put powder residue in the gun barrels and removed some cartridges from their magazines to give evidence of the Glocks having been fired. Dom also dropped spent shell casings near where they were lowered. Julie, Jake and Simon looked on soberly, impressed by the ability of the rest of the team to stage a scene to look a certain way, even when done from a cloaked aircraft silently hovering over a gathering crowd of emergency first responders in the canyon. In the end, investigators would have little doubt that Jensen and Merlino fought bravely and were lucky to have escaped the carnage with only cuts and bruises. The Skyray lingered over the area an additional thirty minutes to be sure the pair had been found, then zipped away into the night for a rendezvous with an Albatross waiting for them high over Devil's Tower across the Wyoming state line.

Chapter Twenty-Six

Dr. Jake Sanders was wide awake in one of the window seats, staring out at the ocean stretching to the lightening pre-dawn horizon. Everyone else aboard was asleep except for Simon on the opposite side of the aircraft a row in front of him, sipping a can of soda. The Albatross was a very large aircraft and the rest of the team was napping in private bunk berths behind the row seating. Jake decided he needed to know more about The Watch's newest recruit and made his way over.

"May I please sit with you a while?" he asked.

Simon looked up at Jake. He hadn't slept in nearly two days and the look on his face conveyed a weariness that went beyond the physical. Simon managed a weak smile, "Please do, Dr. Sanders. Your company would be welcome. I'm afraid I've not yet become accustomed to frequent flying, let alone trips back and forth across the globe in record time."

"Thank you," Jake replied, leaving an open seat between them so as not to make their initial substantive conversation too cramped. "And please call me Jake. It seems The Watch has no shortage of people holding doctorates in a wide range of fields. Mine is zoology. Predators to be specific. How about you?"

"That's a very good question, Jake. I'm not sure I have an answer for you. Until recently, I was a recovering alcoholic doing social work with youth on a reservation. Then I had a profound spiritual experience in a sweat lodge involving a vision, a bear and a Yakwawi, my hair turned from black to white, I ran into a shaman, a Bigfoot, a flying submarine, people who wanted to shoot me, and now find myself heading back to a place in the ocean I'd been for less than an hour before I was flown back near the place where it all started to face a real Yakwawi."

"I'm sorry, Simon. May I call you Simon? You lost me between shaman and Bigfoot."

"Indeed you may," Simon responded with a sigh. "I am Simon Standing Elk of the Lakota People. Though experiences of late make me think there may be more to me than I know."

"If you're up for it," Jake prodded, "I'd like to hear your story. I got the background from what you said to Julie on the plane before the mission, but please bring me up to speed on what's happened to you in the last month or so."

Simon took a long drink from his can of soda, crushed it, and placed the remnants in the seatback pouch in front of him. Turning slightly, he leaned into his armrest to face Jake, and recounted all that had happened since his sweat lodge vision. When he'd finished, Jake shared his own story from the field study he was doing with Gail until the moment they'd left on the mission to kill the Yakwawi. When Jake stopped speaking, there were a few seconds of silence as each man looked at the other and reflected on what had been said.

"I know it's just a series of unfortunate coincidences," Jake broke the silence. "But it's strange how the Yakwawi's arrival caused you, Julie and me to have our life paths intersect and bring us together here, isn't it?"

"Do you believe in The Great Spirit, Jake?" Simon asked.

The question took Jake off guard. He reflected for a moment before giving his answer. "I went to a Catholic elementary school and a Jesuit academy for middle school. Then my family moved and I went to a secular private high school for gifted students. I stopped going to Mass when I moved out and went off to college, but I guess you could say I'm Catholic. At least that's how I was raised."

"That is not the question I asked you," said Simon leaning closer to Jake.

"It's a tired cliché these days, but I guess you could put me in the group called spiritual but not religious," Jake replied.

"I asked if you believe in The Great Spirit," asserted Simon, and Jake became a bit frustrated by the persistence of such a personal line of questioning from someone he hardly knew.

"Simon, if you're asking whether I believe in God or not, my answer is yes. But perhaps not in the way He's presented by some church doctrines in organized religion. I spend a lot of my life outdoors. When I see the intricate way nature's elements work together, I see the work of an intelligence behind its design. I was taught as a boy that God is the personification of ultimate intelligence. Your people call Him The Great Spirit. Others might call Him something else. I honestly don't know because I haven't given religion much thought for years and don't see why you're bringing it up now. The bottom line is I think what can be known about the Creator, the Designer, The Great Spirit or whatever, is revealed in the things He made."

"Interesting," remarked Simon, his eyes now staring deep into Jake's.

"What?"

"You claim not to know, yet assign the personal pronoun He."

"Yeah. That's from my upbringing, but I think what can be known about Him is evident in the things He made..." Jake stopped. The color drained from his face. He realized he'd just spoken the phrase Dr. Smythe had used to open the door to the taxidermy display at Sanctum.

Simon began to smile. "An interesting choice of words, Jake. Sound familiar?"

Jake composed himself. "Why? How would you know? Why bring this up now?"

"Because you are a scientist, Jake. You're trained to hypothesize, experiment, observe and theorize. What we'll be dealing with when we get to Sanctum will require us to add new levels of perception to our observations. Spiritual levels. I assume you're up to speed on the intersection of dimensions and the crossover theories at Sanctum. It would seem we had a first-hand experience with such a crossover a few hours ago. And now we'll have to adjust our mindsets to include potential new realities. We saw entities that looked demonic come through what I can only assume was a portal between dimensions to recover the fallen Yakwawi. This raises new and disturbing questions in my mind. Does it not in yours?"

"Yes it does. Demonic or not, my first question instinctively is why? Why would someone or something want to recover what looked to me like a mortally wounded Yakwawi?" answered Jake. "That opens the door, pun intended, for additional questions such as who or what were those wolf-man things? Where did they come from? How did they know what was happening and where? Perhaps most importantly, are we dealing with an intelligent alien species that knows how to open and close interdimensional portals at will? If so, what implications does that have for the sovereignty and stability of our dimension?"

"Questions well worth seeking answers to, Jake," Simon said as he turned to face forward again. "We'll be seeing him again, you know."

"Who?" Jake asked.

"Yakwawi."

"What? How? We killed the thing. You saw it yourself!" exclaimed Jake struggling to keep his voice down.

"Did we?" Simon asked.

"How can you be sure we didn't?"

"Because I still sense him in my spirit," answered Simon. "He will be back. And he will not be alone."

Chapter Twenty-Seven

Julie woke as she sensed the Albatross beginning to descend. A clock on the wall of the berth she'd been sleeping in indicated less than five hours had passed since the team had disembarked from the docked Skyray over Wyoming to enter the Albatross. She rolled out of bed, entered one of the bathrooms across the narrow hallway, and paused to look outside. The position of the rising sun seen out the aircraft's window told her they were traveling south-southwest and the expanse of ocean in every direction she looked caused her to suspect Sanctum was located somewhere in the tropical Pacific. That the aircraft was very gradually losing altitude was indicated by the slow rising of the curved horizon. If she was right, she concluded they had to be traveling at least Mach 3 and were flying higher than any commercial airliner she'd ever been on.

She used the facilities, quickly disrobed and hopped in the shower. For an airplane, the bathrooms on the Albatross were downright spacious. As hot water and soap revived her, Julie mentally pictured a map of the Pacific to make some calculations. No stranger to flights across the world's largest ocean, she'd studied maps of the Pacific before her overseas martial arts training. Her thinking led her to believe Sanctum was somewhere between the Gilbert Islands and French Polynesia. Not that it really mattered. Escape would be impossible due to the amazing surveillance capabilities of The Watch, but the events of the previous night had her wondering what she'd gotten herself into.

Her feelings were reinforced when she emerged from the shower to see a small backpack leaning against the wall just inside the bathroom's door – a door she'd locked for privacy when she'd entered. Inside the pack were navy blue panties with matching socks, bra and leggings, a light blue pocket tee shirt that dropped to her hips, and slip-on shoes in her size that matched the shirt. An interior pocket contained floss, a toothbrush and toothpaste, feminine products, a hairbrush and deodorant.

Though grateful for the fresh clothing and hygiene items, the thought of her every need being so precisely anticipated and provided for made her uneasy. But not so uneasy as to make her forgo the use of the things she'd been given.

Julie opened the door and stepped into the hallway just in time to see Cora dropping her soiled uniform from the previous evening into a hamper near the galley. The woman looked decidedly more ladylike in an outfit identical to the one Julie was wearing. Cora's hair was down.

"Good morning, Julie. How are you feeling?"

"Refreshed, Cora. Do I have you to thank for the outfit?"

"Thought we both could use a change of clothes," answered Cora. "I saw you head into the bathroom as I was coming out of another down the hall so I put the pack together while you were showering. Hope you didn't mind."

"Not at all," Julie replied, hiding her unease about the lack of privacy. "I'm grateful. We seem to be descending so may I assume we'll be landing soon?"

"We're about fifty minutes out," Cora responded. "Put your used clothes here in the hamper, grab some coffee from the galley and let's enjoy a cup together on the way in."

Julie did as Cora suggested and took a seat next to her in the back row, noticing Jake and Simon talking in another row ahead and to the left of them. "How long have you been with The Watch?" Julie asked Cora, hoping to use some small talk to get more intelligence on the group.

"Many years," replied Cora. "I've been a team leader for fifteen now."

"Cora, I look at you and see a fit woman in her mid-thirties tops. That would mean you were leading Sanctum teams when you were around twenty. Forgive me, but I find that a bit hard to believe,' said Julie.

"Everything you've just said is based on assumption, Julie. In time you'll come to understand just how misleading assumptions can be. Though I'm very flattered by your estimate of my age."

"C'mon, Cora. I'm a cop, remember? I can't be too far off. And by your features I'm guessing you're of South American ancestry. Columbian perhaps?" asked Julie.

"Close. I was born in Peru near the Columbia border. As to age, it's nothing but a number. An irrelevant one at that, so long as one can do the job and has the physical stamina to succeed. You'll discover that eventually at Sanctum," Cora responded.

"Is there a man in your life?" Julie asked with a smile, hoping some girl talk would get Cora to open up more.

"There was. My husband was killed by Shining Path rebels. We'd been married three years and had no children," Cora replied. "He was my one and only. There will never be another."

"I'm so sorry, Cora," Julie responded while making some mental calculations. She remembered from DHS training material that the Shining Path was a Maoist rebel group most active in Peru during the 1980s. Though activity associated with the group diminished to almost nothing with the capture of its leader in the early 90s, it was still classified as a terrorist organization. If Cora was married at the height of Shining Path military activity and raids, she'd be closer to 60 than 30. But Julie's assessment of her appearance made that seem impossible.

"How did you get your military training?" Julie persisted, seeking information.

"Peruvian military," Cora replied. "I was a member of the country's first all-female combat unit, a unit given special missions and assignments that often involved infiltrating Columbian drug cartels, counterterrorism ops and sting operations against corrupt officials in Peru's local and national governments. Then one day we were sent to a village on the Brazilian border to deal with what we assumed were bandits or Shining Path leftovers abducting children and stealing livestock. Four kids and twice as many goats had gone missing the week before we got there. The problem wasn't criminals or terrorists."

"Go on," encouraged Julie. "What happened?"

"It's still hard for me to talk about," said Cora. "The villagers said a monster had dragged the children and livestock into the jungle. We were, of course, skeptical, but did find strange footprints along a path of broken vegetation leading into the rainforest. We didn't have to go far to find traces of blood. Then more blood. About three klicks into the forest we found bones, both human and animal. It became clear whatever had taken the children and goats had eaten them."

"That's awful," remarked Julie. "What was it? A jaguar or puma?"

"I wish," Cora remarked. "That was the assumption our team leader made as well."

The woman sighed and took a sip of coffee.

"Suspecting we were dealing with a man-eating jaguar, and with the sun getting low, the team split up. Six headed back to the village to stand watch during the night there, and the other six of us divided into pairs to hunker down and watch the feeding area in case the animal returned. Our orders were to shoot it on sight. A jaguar did show up just before midnight and the C/O took it out with her rifle. We got some pictures of the cat and the area, but then made the mistake of relaxing, planning to head back to the village at first light."

"I'm guessing the jaguar you shot wasn't the one raiding the village?" asked Julie.

"Gunshots came from the direction of the village around 0300," continued Cora. "And we could hear screams even as far out as we were. Then we lost coms with our team in the village. The last thing we heard was a villager on one of our radios screaming `Mapinguari is here'. The six of us took off for the village moving as fast as we could through the jungle at night using our headlamps and weapons lights. The thing hit us about halfway there."

"What was it?"

"Apparently, a Mapinguari. Huge. Maybe nine feet tall, covered in reddish fur, thick-skinned and quick. Our M16s and Browning Hi-Powers had no effect. Its claws were like Bowie knives and its stench nearly made us puke. The thing ripped us apart like rag dolls. I was the last one standing. My rifle was empty and I had only half a mag left in my pistol. I'd accepted I was about to die."

Julie saw Cora's coffee cup trembling a bit and put a hand on her arm, "You can tell me the rest later if you want to, Cora."

"No, it's okay. I need to retell this story every now and then, especially after a mission, to remind myself of the importance of what we do," Cora replied.

"My back was against a tree, I was firing my last rounds at the thing's head. Suddenly there was a flood of light from above illuminating the whole area. That's when I saw him."

"Who?" asked Julie as the rest of The Watch team filed into the seating area and sat down to prepare for landing.

"Him," replied Cora nodding her head toward Ibutho, who had just taken a window seat across the aisle. "That man vaulted out of the jungle like a pouncing lion with a short spear in each hand and two more across his back wearing nothing but a pair of khaki shorts. Ibutho fought the beast hand-to-claw with inhuman speed and skill. He was always one step ahead of the creature's moves. It would swipe at him, miss, and he would slash it with his spears. The warrior knew what he was doing because each of his cuts drew a fresh spray of blood from the beast. I remember it took a big swing at him that he ducked under, and then he plunged one of the spears in deep under its armpit. The move apparently immobilized the clawed forearm on that side because it then took a swing at Ibutho with its other one and he plunged the second spear into that armpit. Up to that point the beast had been fighting on its hind legs, but those spear stabs caused it to fall forward – right in my direction. Ibutho leapt to one side and the thing's head fell onto the ground a meter in front of me. So I raised my pistol and put my last bullet into its eye. I think that killed it, but Ibutho made sure by jumping on its back and stabbing his last two spears into the base of its skull – several times. Then he was gone, the light from above disappeared, and I was left alone in the forest with the carcass of some mythological monster."

"Is that when The Watch recruited you?" asked Julie.

"Not right away. I stayed there motionless until dawn. The creature was dead but I was near a state of shock. Remains of my teammates were scattered all around me. I made my way back to the village as soon as it was light enough. There I discovered four more of my team dead and the other two unconscious, mortally wounded. There was no sign of the villagers other than the dozen or so dead that were strewn here and there. The survivors had already fled with whatever they could carry or drag. I radioed for medivac and backup in case there was more than one of those Mapinguari things in the area. Two helicopters arrived an hour later with medics and another tactical team. They said they found me alone, in shock, sitting cross-legged and rocking back and forth in the middle of the village square. And when they went to recover the remains of my team in the forest, the beast's body was gone."

"What happened after that?" asked Julie.

"I was taken to a military hospital near Lima and kept sedated. I can't tell you for how long," Cora replied. "When I finally came to, a couple of men arrived to see me – a white English fellow and a very large black man carrying a big bouquet of flowers. Both were dressed in expensive dark business suits with white shirts and blue ties. There was something familiar about the black man that I couldn't put my finger on at first, but then he thanked me for bravely saving him from a terrible monster in the rainforest. It was then I realized he was the man who had come to my rescue in the jungle. My visitors were Ibutho and Dr. Smythe. I was given the choice all potential new recruits are given and decided to spend the rest of my life avenging those villagers and the warrior sisters I lost that night. They were the closest thing I'd had to family. Ibutho took me under his wing to help upgrade my fighting skills, and now you know my story," Cora said as she put her coffee in a cup holder and buckled her seat harness. She nodded to a blinking light on the bulkhead above the cockpit door. "Time to strap in, Julie. The sea breeze sometimes makes landings a bit bumpy at Sanctum."

Julie did as Cora said and turned to the older woman. "I really appreciate you telling me what you did, Cora. You're a brave woman. And I also want to thank you for trusting me on this operation, especially in light of what happened before it with Simon."

"Forgiveness always begins with someone taking a risk, Julie. I took a big one believing I could trust you not to go after Simon again. Thanks for proving me right. But once we debrief, we are going to have a talk about you rushing that portal like you did. If it weren't for Simon, we might have lost you. And that would have given me the sads," said Cora, grinning for the first time since Julie had met her.

The Albatross decelerated rapidly as its swept wings fully extended outward and its wing-mounted engines pivoted to allow vertical landing. Four additional horizontal fan-like engines slid out from the fuselage, two on each side fore and aft, and the plane inched forward just a bit faster than a hover. A gust of wind off the ocean rocked the aircraft a bit before it gently touched down and taxied onto an elevator platform that lowered it into a subterranean hanger. Once the plane came to a halt and the seatbelt sign flicked off, everyone unstrapped and walked to the rear of the craft where the loading ramp was lowering. Dr. Jonathan Smythe stood waiting at the bottom.

"You've all had an eventful evening and little time to rest," Smythe began. "Everyone is now on mandatory recovery time for eight hours. Then we'll convene to debrief. I thank God you are all back safely and uninjured. The Yakwawi is no more. Well done. Now please eat, sleep and relax."

With that Smythe led everyone through the doors into Sanctum's familiar interior and team members dispersed to their quarters. Simon found the shaman waiting at the door of his newly assigned apartment.

"Wicasa!" Simon said with a smile. "I didn't know if you'd be here when I returned. It's good to see you. There is something I need to speak with you about. It concerns the Yakwawi and what happened on the mission. I don't think…"

"Neither do I, Simon Standing Elk, neither do I. But now you must rest if you're to be ready when the time comes. My room is next door. Come to me later if you need to, but you need sleep first."

"Thank you, Wicasa."

Simon entered his quarters, showered, donned a pair of green gym shorts from the dresser and fell onto the soft sheets of the bed. He was asleep in less than a minute. Then the visions came.

Chapter Twenty-Eight

Julie lay on her bed unable to sleep. She'd rested on the plane and couldn't quiet the thoughts racing through her mind since her talk with Cora. Rolling up to sit on the edge of the bed facing the screen door, she longed to go for a walk on the white sandy beach between her quarters and the clear, cyan-colored sea beyond it. The smell of the fresh ocean air and the calling of gulls only made her want to get outside more. She got up, reached for the latch handle and took a step back in surprise when the door opened a few inches. After staring at the opening for a moment, Julie slid the door all the way open and stepped onto the small faux-wood deck that extended out about six feet and ran the width of the door. The opportunity was too great for her to resist.

Julie ran back to her closet and yanked a navy blue one-piece swimsuit off its hanger. She'd assumed there was a pool at Sanctum and that she'd one day get to do some swimming for exercise as the reason it was in her room. Given the rather prudish vibes she'd picked up from some Sanctum residents, Julie figured it unlikely her bathroom activities were being watched so she stripped down next to the shower and slipped into the suit. On a hunch she'd been authorized to visit the beach at last, she checked the cabinet under her vanity and discovered a newly placed pair of sunglasses atop three beach towels next to a large tube of sunscreen, which she applied liberally. Grabbing a towel and semi-sheer, thigh-length cover-up she found under it, she ran barefoot out the door onto the fine sand.

It was actually a brief uphill climb until she crested the upper beach and stood atop the high-tide berm, clapping a hand over her mouth to keep from laughing aloud. Fifty yards to her right, Ibutho was swaying gently in a portable hammock wearing a pair of loud, bright, multicolored swim trunks. An oversized floppy straw hat covered his face. Water droplets were sliding down the sides of a tall glass containing a bright red drink on a small table next to him.

Jeff reclined in a lounge chair a bit farther down the beach, also wearing swim trunks. He was reading a big leather-bound book. Tops of several brown bottles protruded from a cooler next to him.

Julie decided it was time to get to know both men better. She walked over to Ibutho.

She was still several strides away from the big African when he unexpectedly spoke. "I hear the approach of Miss Julie," his deep voice resonated from beneath the hat. "Ibutho should teach you to be more stealthy," He said with a chuckle.

"I don't care about stealth right now," Julie replied as her shadow fell across the man. "I'm just grateful for what appears to be approval of my membership to The Watch's beach club."

"Please step aside, Miss Julie," Ibutho raised the hat to reveal a broad grin. "Ibutho is trying to work on his tan."

The pair laughed and Julie gave the hammock a shove to set the man swinging.

"I'll leave you to it then, big guy," Julie said with a smile and walked over to Jeff.

He closed his book and set it aside as she approached, "G'day sheila! Out for a bit of sun are we? Care for a cold root beer from my esky?" He offered using Australian slang and charm to its fullest.

"You bet," Julie replied. She grabbed a bottle from the cooler and popped the cap. Cold, sweet liquid rolled across her taste buds with a flavor unlike any she'd ever before enjoyed in a soft drink. "Wow, Jeff, that's fantastic! What brand is it?"

"My own, sheila. Make it myself right here during down time. Dr. Smythe let me have a wee corner in the wine cellar to keep it. Glad you like it. Tol says it's too sweet and Ibutho prefers his fruity juice blends. Nice to find someone here with appreciation for fine refreshments."

Julie took another long swig from the bottle. "What's the water like here? Warm enough for a swim?"

"It is, but be careful to stay in the swim zone," Jeff answered sitting up in his chair and pointing toward a series of round buoys bobbing beyond the breakers about 300 yards from shore.

"Why's that?"

"We've got some big sharks in these waters. There's an underwater barrier between the buoys that keeps them out a bit so we can enjoy the water closer in. Here. Take my swim goggles," Jeff prompted, removing a pair from a small beach bag. "There are some very colorful fish this side of the barrier that are pretty to look at."

"I'll take you up on that," said Julie as she accepted the goggles. "May I ask you something before I head out?"

"Sure thing."

"Last night, in the canyon, I saw you wearing a clerical collar and it looked like you were praying over some of the victims? Are you a priest of some kind?" Julie asked.

"Aren't we all to one extent or another, sheila? Priests and priestesses, I mean? But to be less philosophical, the straight answer's yes. Ordained Anglican years ago. Don't have a church of my own here at Sanctum, but sometimes we get in spots where people need a bit of hope and faith. Like last night. Some of those poor mates were dying and knew it. Seeing me in a collar and having me pray gave them a bit of comfort at the end. Let 'em know she'll be alright and all. Thank God I don't have to do that very often," Jeff answered.

Julie was glad she had sunglasses on to hide the doubt in her eyes. She knew it took at least six years of formal education and training to become a legitimate priest. A friend of hers in high school had gone that route and only recently been ordained. Jeff looked to be a fit, muscular man, in his mid-twenties. Attaining full ordination wasn't impossible for someone so young, but doing so would have left time for little else. She recalled similar doubts about Cora and decided to get direct with the Australian.

"Sorry, Jeff, but I'm not buying it. I'm guessing you're what, about twenty-five? That's just not old enough to be ordained for years and also been with The Watch a while. Either you look incredible for your age or you're pulling my leg. Which is it?"

"Well a priest isn't supposed to lie, Julie," replied Jeff, his face becoming more serious. "But everything you've just said is based on assumptions, and those can be misleading. Though I'm flattered you think I'm so young."

Not even sunglasses could hide Julie's shock. Jeff had dealt with the age question using words almost identical to those Cora had spoken, and it made her uneasy. She looked back over at Ibutho. His physique was impressive but she'd seen enough gray in his hair and wrinkles around his eyes for her to guess his age too. Julie had sensed that Jeff liked her so she decided to use that in an attempt to extract more information.

"Look, Jeff," she began as she dropped her towel on the sand and plopped down on top of it so he was looking slightly down at her. The swimsuit wasn't the most revealing she'd ever worn, but it did flatter her feminine form. She hoped putting on a cute smile and assuming a more submissive position where Jeff's gaze might occasionally wander to her chest might entice him to be more forthcoming. "If we're going to work together as a team, we have to develop some trust between us. Cora looks to be in her mid-thirties, Ibutho I'm guessing is close to 50 and you look 25, give or take. But when I do the math in my head, I can't believe what my eyes are telling me. How old are you, Jeff?"

"Age is just a number," Jeff replied as he removed his sunglasses so Julie could see his eyes. "Does it really matter as long as one can do the job and has the physical ability to succeed?"

Julie's smile disappeared and it was hard to hide her frustration. Again, Jeff had answered using nearly the same words Cora had. Why couldn't she get a straight answer from them? Jeff picked up on her displeasure and leaned forward, but not once did his eyes wander below her face.

"Listen, Julie," he began quietly. "I want to be your friend and yes, we do need to trust each other. Sanctum and The Watch have many secrets. You're new here. Trust is something we all must earn." Jeff did a quick look around to see if anyone other than Ibutho was nearby before continuing. "The longer you're with us, the more I and others will be able to share with you. You're smart. You know trust is built over time. Therein lies part of a secret I'll share with you because I think you've already figured it out." The Aussie leaned closer and continued in almost a whisper.

"What is time? It's a tool, that's all. Something we use to order things in the past, present and future, and all of those things relate to this moment right now in where they fall chronologically. So, time is relative, you see? And if time is relative, so is the passage of time because the frame of reference is constantly moving."

Julie was struggling to wrap her head around what Jeff was saying. "Are you telling me that time passes at different rates in different places?"

"For now, just think of time as a human-made construct we use to order events. Do you think those gulls overhead or those dolphins playing out there in the surf have any concept of time?" Jeff pointed upward and nodded his head toward a pod of dolphins jumping beyond the swimming area buoys. "And if they do, how is it measured? In minutes, hours, days or weeks?"

Julie was getting nothing but confused, but the mention of dolphins made her turn around and look. She'd always liked the creatures and never missed a chance to see them when she visited an aquarium. There was something about an animal that always seemed to be smiling she found impossibly cute, and she'd never seen one in the wild. Then it occurred to her that Jeff was right. Here she was on a tropical beach with beckoning clear water, a refreshing cold drink, a gentle ocean breeze, dolphins playing without a care and she was missing the moment by trying to investigate something that didn't really matter then and there.

"Thanks Jeff," she said as she rose and jogged toward the water with Jeff's goggles in hand.

"Don't mention it, sheila," Jeff called after her, relaxing his discipline, allowing his eyes to wander as he let out a quiet sigh. "Have fun and be careful!"

"'Tis you who must be careful, my holy friend," chided Ibutho with a chuckle from his hammock. "You're too old for her. Besides, her destiny lies with another."

"Aye, mate," replied Jeff. "But it didn't today... not today."

Julie Reed dove headlong into the breakers and marveled. Brightly colored tropical fish darted in and out of view once she'd cleared the silty backwash close to the beach. A strong swimmer, she worked her arms and legs for optimal propulsion through the clear water, taking in the splendid underwater scene unfolding around her. Its temperature was perfect. Movement caught her eye to her left, and then her right. Three dolphins had come alongside her to investigate the newcomer at the beach. She surmised they were able to jump over the barrier Jeff had mentioned. One of the creatures bumped against her gently as if to welcome her and then they all shot away into the blue ahead. Julie found herself smiling and feeling something she hadn't felt in a long time. She felt happiness.

Chapter Twenty-Nine

Dr. Sora Wu slid her chair back from the compact, yet powerful electron microscope and rubbed her eyes. There was no mistaking what she was seeing. Checking to be certain the recording equipment was capturing images in real time, the doctor turned her attention to the display on the screen and re-checked her notes. The sample of Yakwawi blood under examination revealed new and potentially disturbing information. She was about to pick up her phone when Dr. Jake Sanders entered the room.

"Dr. Sanders," Wu said with surprise in her tone. "I'd assumed you'd be sleeping after such an eventful night."

"Can't," replied Jake. "Too much on my mind. Thought I'd come down to the lab and take a look at the blood and hair samples we collected, if that's permitted of course."

"Indeed you may," Wu replied. "But look at you. You're exhausted. I can give you something to help you relax if you like. There's still time for a decent nap before the evening briefing."

"Thanks, but no," Jake responded, running a hand through his hair. "Simon and I had a pretty deep conversation on the flight back and things were said that...it's not important right now. Sometimes a science project can help me relax and take my mind off other things. Impressive images up on the screen, doctor. Amazing color and clarity. Are we looking at a blood sample?"

"Yes. Some Yakwawi blood collected from the scene of last night's battle," Wu answered. "It's the third such sample I've examined, all of which yielded the same results."

Jake pulled a chair up next to her and studied the images on the screen silently for about a minute, occasionally panning and zooming the image. "The same with the other samples?"

"Yes, but I've accelerated the process on this one by exposing it to ultraviolet light. The results are clear, Dr. Sanders. Damaged cells are healing and regenerating at an extraordinary rate."

"Please call me Jake, doctor."

"Only if you'll call me Sora."

"Done," said Jake perking up. "I think we may be onto something here, Sora. Based on the limited information we have, a hypothesis could be put forward that a Yakwawi may be able to heal from injuries at an accelerated rate in an environment where there are high levels of ultraviolet light. How much blood did we get from the samples?"

"Thanks to the battering you gave the beast, I have a few milliliters I've cleansed of environmental contaminants," answered Sora.

"Okay," Jake was getting notably excited, as was always the case when he thought he was on the brink of a significant discovery. "We know the thing ate red meat and had a preference for blood-rich organs. I assume you did a chemical analysis of the blood. What did the results show?"

"We have to consider that it had recently fed," Sora replied. "That may have altered the panel from a base state. Without anything to compare it to, I can tell you the Yakwawi blood collected has high concentrations of red and white blood cells, as well as platelets compared to humans. The plasma ratio is much lower than in known mammals, and the blood has very high iron content. And Julie was right, it was a male. Testosterone levels are off the charts."

"Interesting. The animal on this planet with the highest testosterone level we know of is the bull shark. It ranks third as a man-eater behind whites and tigers, but tends to be the most aggressive of the three. And it can adapt from saltwater to freshwater. Aggressive, high testosterone, adaptable, a taste for humans…sounds familiar," Jake noted. "What ultraviolet wavelength did you use to instigate the growth result?"

"Regeneration began at 380 nanometers and accelerated as I shortened them."

"That's starting point," said Jake. "It actually gives me some ideas about where to begin some more tests. Shall we Sora?"

"By all means," she replied. "What do you have in mind?"

◆ ◆ ◆

Simon Standing Elk woke with a start, his body drenched in sweat. He shot upright in bed.

"Tell me," said the shaman seated in a chair beside him, a bottle of water in his extended hand.

"A dream," replied the younger man with no apparent concern over the uninvited guest at his bedside. He accepted the water, took three big gulps and continued. "Perhaps a vision. It doesn't matter. The images are as real and clear as the paintings on the wall of this room."

"What did you see?"

"Yakwawiak."

"Mmmm. You used the plural form of their name. How many?" the shaman asked.

"I'm not sure," Simon answered. "Three or four maybe. More dog-men too. I can't be certain, but my guess would be close to a dozen."

"Shape-shifters," the shaman observed. "Ancient and evil. Far older than our people. The stories of them are all over the world. Tales of wicked beings able to change form between human and beast, often into upright-walking canines or felines."

"Skin-walkers," noted Simon.

"So the white man calls them. The Navajo refer to them as yee naaldlooshii, which loosely translates as *by means of it, they go on all fours*," the shaman replied. "And there are other names given them by many cultures as old as time itself. But the broader term is `therianthropy´, the ability to change appearance from animal to human and back again. The legends vary in some respects, but one thing they all hold in common. The shifters are evil and nothing good ever comes from their presence. Tell me what the shifters and Yakwawiak were doing in your vision."

"They were fighting us, Wicasa."

"By us, do you mean you and me?" queried the shaman.

"Not just us," answered Simon. "Cora's team, Julie and Jake were with us in an intense battle. Strange. Julie wielded a sword. The situation grew desperate. Then I saw flaming swords, rapid flashes of images and awoke to find you sitting here."

"Who wielded the swords of fire?" the shaman asked, failing to hide his concern.

"I don't know. That part of my vision was as if I was looking at events through the eyes of another person. A person with gold forearms."

"Who won?" the shaman wondered.

"I don't know," Simon answered.

"Did you see any members of The Watch die?"

"Hard to say. We all had blood on us, but I don't know if it was ours, that of our foes, or symbolic of something else," stated Simon.

"Do you recall anything of the other images you say flashed by in your vision?" the shaman persisted.

"I saw Dr. Smythe talking with a man wearing armor over a white robe or tunic of some kind. Portals opening and closing in space and time. A thick leather-bound book. A number flashing between the images," Simon replied.

"What number," the shaman asked with a sense of urgency.

"2122," said Simon. "What do you think it means?"

The shaman looked increasingly uncomfortable. "Could be a date, part of a lock combination or code to open a phone or computer. I just don't know."

"What disturbs you, Wicasa?"

"There is much you do not yet know or understand. Your gifting is advancing faster than my ability to instruct and properly train you," answered the shaman. "The Watch has survived nearly two millennia and has revealed its secrets slowly and selectively in order to do so."

"Am I to understand you and The Watch don't trust me fully?" asked Simon.

"It is not that, my young friend, but rather that trust is something built over time. You haven't been with us or interacted with a sufficient number of Watch personnel to have earned everyone's complete trust yet," the older man answered. "In time, complete trust will come. Until then, work with the others to show you're worthy of their trust."

"You didn't answer my question," Simon observed. "Do I have your complete trust?"

The shaman was silent for a moment, looked down and then returned his gaze to Simon. "I want to say yes, Simon. Do I have yours?"

"I also want to say yes," the younger man replied with agitation, noting his mentor had again given an answer that wasn't definitive. "But it would seem at The Watch, as it is everywhere else, we don't always get what we want do we, shaman?"

There was cold disappointment in Simon's tone and the shaman noticed he hadn't used the name of affection and respect given him in the reply.

"If you'll excuse me," Simon said with a nod toward the door of his room to indicate the older man should depart, "I'd like to shower and prepare for our debriefing."

"Of course," the shaman replied as he rose and put the chair back against the wall. "Please come to my room when you're ready and we'll go to the meeting together."

The shaman quickly walked through the door and into the hallway, pulling the door closed behind him. Simon stripped and stepped into the shower, inhaling the steam as his thoughts wandered back to the sweat lodge where the course of his life was changed.

Chapter Thirty

It had never known such agony. Colossal chains held it stretched between two massive pillars, unable to move. Strange creatures worked rapidly around it, moving from wound to wound. It growled when one of them probed deeply into a wound channel in search of a bullet to remove. As miserable as it was, it felt strength returning. It could feel the improvement building through its body more rapidly than usual. It was bathed in deep purple light and found the color to be the only pleasant thing about its circumstances.

The beings attending it were close to half its height. They smelled and looked like the pack hunters it had encountered in the forest it recently fed in, but walked upright like the two-leggers it preferred to eat. Such characteristics caused it to consider trying to kill one at the earliest opportunity to see what it tasted like, but for the moment they appeared to be allies trying to help. Whatever they were doing was working. One of them moved close with a long, sharp object protruding from a large cylinder. It sensed brief new pain as the being thrust it into a thigh. Soon the massive beast felt nothing and blackness replaced the violet light.

It awoke lying on its back in a large, wide pit with high walls that looked smooth, like polished stone. Taking several moments to assess its surroundings, the creature rose with difficulty and fought the urge to roar as new waves of pain coursed through its body when it moved. Though severe, the discomfort and stiffness was nothing like what it had experienced when it was brought to this place with the sensation of its existence ebbing away. It lumbered toward a wall.

They were three times its height and slick to the touch. It saw nothing to grab onto that could help it climb. At the top were occasional bright flashes of energy like it had seen during noisy and wet storms where it had recently hunted. Instinct told it to avoid the energy flashes. The area around the beast was illuminated by intense deep-purple light. Though it didn't understand how or why, the creature sensed the light was playing a part in the healing it felt. But the light did nothing to lessen the growing pangs in its stomach and an intensifying urge to get meat in its jaws.

As if its benefactors could sense its needs, a panel on one of the walls opened and a pair of wriggling bags slid out onto the dirt floor of the pit. The top of each opened and a pair of two-leggers emerged, both female. One was nearly naked and bound. The other wore a flowing red and black robe with something around her neck that dangled an inverted gold five-point star on her chest. She saw the beast and held the large pendant out toward the creature, defiantly shouting something in a commanding tone. It didn't care. Both were quickly dispatched and the creature became more invigorated with each bite of fresh human flesh.

◆ ◆ ◆

Julie felt refreshed after her swim and a shower. With just more than an hour before the planned debriefing, she left her room and headed toward the cafeteria. She'd just rounded a corner when she saw Tol stepping out of a room with a heavy steel door.

"Greetings comrade Tol," Julie said with a smile.

"Hello Julie," the beefy Russian responded with a heavy accent. "And please. The comrade stuff went away with Gorbachev. I think perhaps you have seen too many movies with Russian bad guys, no?"

"Sorry Tol. Didn't mean to offend. I actually know more about China than I do Russia. I'm on my way to get some food. Care to join me and enlighten this cowgirl about the Motherland?"

"I was also going to eat," Tol replied. "I'm just locking up here."

"What's behind the armored door?" Julie asked.

"This is one of The Watch armories," Tol answered.

"Do we have time for me to take a peek?" Julie asked, flashing as cute a smile as she could muster.

"I see no harm so long as I am with you," Tol replied as he swung the big door open again and motioned for Julie to enter.

"Holy shi...take mushrooms!" Julie exclaimed after motion and sound sensors flicked the lights back on to illuminate multiple rows of every

175

conceivable kind of small arms from tiny handguns to shoulder-launched air-to-air and antitank weapons.

Tol slid into the armory behind her and secured the door as Julie slowly walked among the weapons awestruck.

"You said this was one of the armories?" Julie asked. "How many are there?"

"Da," Tol replied. "And there are...enough."

"Enough to repel an invading army, I'd say. Do you know how to operate and maintain all of these?"

"Da. I am proficient with all and train others," the Russian replied.

Julie rounded a corner and both hands shot up to her mouth, eyes wide with excitement. One wall of the armory, which was a large room she guessed to be about 30 feet wide and 70 deep, had an enormous display of knives, swords and edged martial arts weapons. Like a child in a new toy store, Julie hurried to an impressive selection of swords and pointed toward some katanas.

"Don't tell me that's a Yoshindo Yoshihara katana!" Julie said excitedly. "It sure looks like one. I can tell from the blade's Jihada."

"I will honor your request and not tell you," Tol replied with a bit of sarcasm and a smile.

"C'mon, Tol. I mean seriously? The Watch has Yoshiharas? They're the finest Japanese swords in the world. Thousands of dollars each. I got to hold one once when I was in Japan."

"Hold one of ours," prompted Tol.

Julie carefully removed a katana from the display. She instantly could tell it wasn't what she'd expected. The grip conformed to her hands like it was custom-made for her. The balance was without equal. She gingerly touched the edge with a finger and instantly pulled it away as mere contact produced a small cut.

"Careful," urged Tol. "Our edged weapons are beyond sharp. You can almost be cut by just looking at them. The blades are stronger than steel but lighter than titanium, possessing the best features of both."

"How is that even possible?" Julie asked.

"I'm a soldier and tactician," Tol replied. "I just use them. Others make them for us."

"Who?"

"The Watch is highly compartmentalized," Tol explained. "In the interests of security, none of us knows more than we need to, and only a handful know everything or close to it. I'm glad to have the best of the best, and some equipment that is better than the best of its kind anywhere. Even the inner workings of some firearms you see in this room differ from standard production models. That makes our guns the most accurate and reliable in the world."

His comment triggered Julie's recollection of what Simon had told her about the bullets in her gun, so she decided to follow up on Tol's remark. "Does the Watch makes its own ammo too?"

"Da," Tol answered, "Though we do use readily available commercial ammunition as well. It all depends on the assignment."

"The bullets in my Glocks during the mission weren't lead, were they?"

"No. Not just lead."

"What were they made of?" Julie pressed for more information.

"A special blend of metals we use on missions involving certain kinds of entities. Those in your guns were made of lead, silver, gold, depleted uranium and traces of mercury," explained Tol. "Dr. Jake was correct when he said some creatures have a highly allergic response to certain elements. Bullets on our most recent assignment were constructed using materials we've found most likely to cause such targets to react negatively. Did you see how quickly the wolf-like creatures dropped when one of your slugs hit vital areas?"

"Yes," Julie answered.

"They were reacting to the silver in the bullets."

"Tol, you can't mean those were werewolves," Julie chided. "That's just a bunch of Hollywood bull. Werewolves aren't real."

"I did not say they were," Tol asserted. "I merely pointed out the presence of silver in the bullets you fired seemed to have an immediate effect on the creatures you hit."

Julie had him where she wanted and pressed on with her questioning. "Okay Tol. How could you know which was the secret ingredient in my bullets that took those things down? Unless, of course, that wasn't the first time you did battle with those particular beasts."

Tol realized he'd erred by sharing more than he should have. He glanced at his watch and noted, "We best get to the cafeteria and grab some food to go on our way to the briefing. It begins shortly."

Julie knew better than to press the Russian for more. She planned to leverage what she'd been told at a future time but didn't want to make Tol so uncomfortable as to cause him to avoid talking with her again. She carefully returned the katana to the display and moved toward the door. "You're right. Let's go big guy."

Tol visibly relaxed a bit. He'd been ready for confrontation if Julie persisted with her questions but was relieved when no more were asked. He let Julie out the door, pulled it closed and entered a security code on the keypad next to the frame. A green light indicated the door was locked and he turned to follow Julie to the cafeteria.

Chapter Thirty-One

The conference room was full for the debriefing. In addition to those directly involved on the mission to take down the Yakwawi, Dr. Smythe, Moses, Dr. Wu and The Watch personnel from R&D, research, aviation, surveillance and logistics were in attendance.

For the newest members of The Watch, the initial presentation summaries offered by heads of various departments and Cora were eye-opening and concerning. The team's entire encounter with the beast had been captured in high-definition video and audio by a swarm of tiny stealth drones released and retrieved by the Skyray. Every move made and syllable uttered by team members was replayed for the assembly, including Jeff's prayers for the dying and the private conversation between Simon and Julie. Jake was seated between the pair and could sense the discomfort of both when their talk as the team started gathering evidence was replayed on the room's large viewing screen for all to see and hear. He felt humiliated when the screen showed video of him vomiting after he'd gone to look for evidence at the base of the cliff and came upon the partially disemboweled corpse of a young EMT. That was something he'd been unprepared for and had hoped to keep from the others. When all the video clips had played, Dr. Smythe stepped into the center of the U-shape made by the table and chairs.

"First, I congratulate everyone on the successful completion of a most difficult operation," he began. "This was an assignment complicated by tremendous tragedy in that so many lives were lost. Yet we happily welcome back all who took part in the mission, some of whom were on their first sortie with us, to Sanctum safely. Having reviewed summaries from our leadership team, we will now engage in open discussion in order to share any new information and answer questions anyone may have."

Jake and Dr. Wu stood almost immediately and were recognized by Smythe, who motioned for them to step into the U so all could see and hear what they had to say.

"Dr. Sanders and I ran a series of experiments on blood and tissue samples we identified as coming from the Yakwawi," Wu began. "In doing so, we made discoveries that may be able to help us if The Watch ever has to deal with such a creature in the future. I'll let Dr. Sanders explain."

"Thank you, Dr. Wu," said Jake as he used a remote to display an image of Yakwawi blood taken with the powerful microscope. "What we're looking at is a blood sample from the scene. I won't get too technical but will point out a number of cells that appear damaged or distressed."

Jake used a laser pointer to indicate the cells he was talking about and then set a time lapse of images in motion.

"You can see as we move through images of the sample over time that those same cells are somehow able to repair themselves and, in some cases, appear to die and then re-form into healthy cells again. This, in itself, is not unique. Most species on Earth, including humans, possess some regenerative capabilities and scientific breakthroughs are being made regularly to enhance them. What's special about the Yakwawi is the amazing speed of regeneration. A healing process that would take many days or weeks in other creatures appears to occur in hours with Yakwawiak."

"Dr. Sanders," one of the lab technicians spoke up. "We see the evidence of regeneration in blood cells you've provided. What leads you to believe such self-healing extends beyond blood cells?"

"Good observation," noted Jake. "What I have up on the screen now is a tissue sample of what we believe is Yakwawi muscle found in a larger pool of blood. As I roll the time lapse through, please notice the cellular repair and regeneration taking place in it as well. This is fascinating because it is occurring on a piece separated from the host organism."

"Surely you aren't suggesting that a piece of a Yakwawi will grow into a clone of the original," Moses interjected.

"Not at all sir," Jake responded. "In the samples we examined, regeneration was limited to the original boundaries of the sample. It is not beyond the realm of possibility, however, that a damaged internal organ could regenerate back into a healthy version of itself provided no mitigating circumstances are involved. Let me show you what I mean by circumstances."

Jake pressed the remote and a split-screen image of blood samples appeared behind him. "I'm slowing down the time lapse now to show something that could be of importance. Dr. Wu, if you'd be so kind as this discovery was yours."

"Initially we see both samples moving through what we assume to be a cellular repair process," Wu explained. "Now watch what happens when we expose the one on the left to concentrated ultraviolet light and the one on the left to intense infrared wavelengths."

There were audible gasps followed by murmuring. The sample exposed to UV radiation suddenly began to grow at an alarming rate. In seconds all damaged cells were repaired. In contrast, the sample hit with IR radiation quickly degenerated until all the damaged cells in the sample were dead. Dr. Wu replayed the lapse three times before nodding to Jake.

"As you see," Jake stated. "Exposure to UV radiation increases the rate of healing almost exponentially, while the opposite is true when IR radiation is introduced. We don't know why this is, but its reality was verified by subsequent repeat tests without exception."

"This is fascinating, doctors," commented Smythe. "So let me ask the question that is doubtlessly on the minds of several present. What would happen if a badly wounded Yakwawi was withdrawn from danger and placed in an environment with abundant UV light?"

"While we can't be certain," Wu answered, "It is quite possible that the beast would experience accelerated healing with potential for full recovery."

Again there was murmuring among the attendees but it was Julie who spoke up. "What are the chances the one we supposedly took out can find its way back from wherever it went?"

"It will return," Simon boldly proclaimed as all eyes fixed on him. "And I fear it will not be alone when it does."

The shaman was sitting next to Simon and put a hand on his arm, a cautionary expression on his face, but Simon continued in spite of the warning. "I had a powerful vision this afternoon. One in which members of The Watch were in a desperate battle with more than one Yakwawi. I did not see how many. And wolf-human shape shifters were with them.

Simon had again expected mockery and derision. Instead the room was quiet. Smythe rose and motioned for the doctors to return to their seats. Tense silence filled the room as everyone's gaze shifted to the tall Brit standing before them wearing, as always, in a fine tailored suit. Hands in his pockets, Smythe walked deeper into the U to stand across the table from Simon.

"When and where, Simon Standing Elk?"

"I do not know for certain," the Lakota answered. "What I can say is that the battle in my vision took place in a forest clearing on grass that was almost lawn-like. A man and woman not in this room were also there." Simon left out the part about a flashing sword and the brief third-person perspective in his vision.

Smythe stared into Simon's eyes for several moments before backing away and addressing the group. "That will be all everyone. You are dismissed. The Watch thanks you for your courage, skill and devotion to our cause."

Everyone stood and began to file out of the room. Simon felt a hand on his shoulder and turned.

"A word with you privately," said Smythe in a tone conveying it was not a request.

"Of course," Simon responded, and he was soon alone in the room with the Brit.

Chapter Thirty-Two

The scent made its pulse race. Drool dripped from its jaws as a grimace that passed for the closest thing it had to a smile fixed upon its snout. Lascivious desire coursed through its veins. Much time had passed since it had last smelled its own kind, let alone a female in her breeding cycle. But excitement and anticipation turned to caution when its sensitive nose detected yet another scent close by. That of another male, perhaps a rival for the female's attention.

Two large panels opened on the sides of the pen in which it had been feeding and recovering. The head and upper torso of a female Yakwawi cautiously peeked through one opening, staring at it tentatively. Suddenly, a male bounded through the other doorway into the pen but halted the charge when it saw a larger, more powerfully built version of itself standing in the middle of the arena it had entered. The smaller male was younger than the dominant creature before it and was just reaching sexual maturity. It had been aroused by the scent of a female in season as well, but kept its distance from the larger male for the moment. Contests for the chance to breed were often fought to the death, and it was unaware that its prospective opponent was recovering from serious wounds. The smaller male incorrectly assumed the battle-scarred monster looking at it had received the injuries from battles with other males. Though it stood more than nine feet tall and was in perfect health, it decided to take more time to study its rival before engaging in anything more serious than a bluff charge.

The female had entered the circular enclosure while the two males were sizing one another up. She rose from all fours to stand more than 10 feet tall. Her form was far lither and movements more graceful than the males in the pen. In spite of her appearance, the female's strength, speed and agility would present a challenge to either of her potential suitors if she chose to rebuff any advance. But instinct told her the time for breeding was coming to a close and she would have to choose a male to sire her offspring soon or lose the opportunity.

A number of demonic-looking canine entities were assembled behind the electronically charged parapets ringing the arena below, eager to see the anticipated result of their experiment. Their presence had not gone unnoticed by the Yakwawiak below, the biggest of which bellowed out a deafening roar when it saw them assemble. The larger of the watching entities, broad shouldered with silver fur and glowing yellow eyes, let out a long howl in response that began low and deep with a building crescendo as the pitch rose. Yips, howls and snarls emanated from the other beings ringing the pen at the sound of their leader's vocalization.

The female Yakwawi chose the larger of the males, sniffing heavily as she circled closer. The big male pretended to ignore her, fixing a menacing gaze on the other male. Spectators hooted and howled at the initial coupling, which lasted a few minutes. Some jeered and threw refuse down at the smaller male as it sulked off to one side while the mating took place. It was hoping the female would allow it to have her when the large male was finished. But the leader of the demonic host watching just stared with its fiery yellow eyes, lips curled upward at the ends in a smile of grotesque satisfaction. Soon, they would make their move.

♦ ♦ ♦

"When you're asked to share information, I expect you to share all of it," Smythe told Simon in a voice that was both quiet and assertive. "You're here because you have been blessed with an uncommon gift. One that I suspect is manifesting itself more frequently as you grow in spiritual strength and insight."

"It is true that the dreams and visions are becoming more frequent," Simon admitted. "But what makes you think I am not forthcoming?"

"You didn't share your out-of-body experience in the most recent dream," answered Smythe. "Or the part about the flashing sword."

Simon was dumbfounded. How could the man know his thoughts and dreams? Did he have access to some strange new technology that somehow allowed the reading of minds?

"Your revelation of this information is most concerning," said Simon a bit more sternly than he'd intended. "The invasion of another person's dreams is something I wish to have no part in. Nor do I want to be near those possessing such ability."

"Be at ease, my newfound friend," Smythe replied gently with a smile that seemed genuine. He gestured to four padded chairs around a small round table in front corner of the conference room. "Please, sit and let me explain."

Simon held Smythe in his gaze for a few seconds before tentatively moving toward one of the chairs and seating himself. Smythe grabbed a bottled soft drink and a can of ginger ale from the refreshment table as he went by on his way to the chairs. He placed the can on the table in front of Simon and sat down across from him, twisting the top off the dark bottle in his hand before taking a long drink.

"Ahhh. You must someday try one of Jeff's root beers, Simon," said Smythe with unnerving relaxation. "I do believe the fellow has his own special gift for brewing refreshment. I understand you've developed a taste for ginger ale recently. Please. Enjoy. And let's talk honestly with one another."

Simon seemed hesitant as he reached for the can. He kept his eyes on Smythe as he popped the tab and took a drink himself before speaking.

"You talk of honesty while probing the thoughts of others. For all I know, you can listen in on prayers to The Great Spirit as well," said Simon.

"Please Simon, I know how it looks," Smythe began. "But something you'll get accustomed to here is that looks can be deceiving and things aren't always as they seem. Because I knew the content of your recent dream, you assumed someone was able to read your mind. I assure you that is not the case. The Watch does possess highly advanced technology, but mind reading and telepathy are things we have not, and will not, get into."

"So you say," Simon remarked. "Yet you know parts of my dream known only to me."

"Only you?" prompted Smythe.

Simon was perplexed for a moment, and then the recollection hit him, "The shaman. He shared my dream with you! It was wrong of him to do so without first asking me. He spoke to you about it when I was showering."

"He did not," stated Smythe. "I did not speak with him about you at all prior to the meeting."

"Yet you knew the dream," Simon noted.

"Have you read the Bible, Simon Standing Elk?" asked Smythe.

Simon was taken aback momentarily by the question. "Do not change the subject, Dr. Smythe."

"Humor me for a moment," the Brit replied.

"When I was encouraged to embrace a Higher Power as part of my 12-step program, I did read significant portions of the white man's Bible," Simon answered. "I think doing so helped me reconnect with The Great Spirit in a way. I still read it occasionally. Why do you ask?"

"Do you remember reading stories about men such as Joseph and Daniel in the Old Testament?" asked Smythe.

"Was not Joseph the man who got in trouble but was later hailed by kings because he could uncover the meaning of men's dreams? And, correct me if I'm wrong, could not Daniel even tell people what they dreamed before interpreting them?" Simon queried.

"Something along those lines," answered Smythe. "Those men, and a few others throughout history, were gifted with the ability to see the dreams of others and interpret their meanings. Such is not precisely the case here at Sanctum, but close. I occasionally have vivid dreams that are not my own. I can't always know whose dreams they are, nor does this happen often. But today I took an afternoon nap in my study before the meeting. You see, Simon, I know what your dream showed you because I had the identical dream."

Simon stared at the man with surprise. He didn't seem to be lying and spoke with sincerity of tone and demeanor. The explanation offered a less nefarious means by which Smythe could have known what he dreamt, and he wanted to believe the Brit because the alternative was too frightening.

"How can this be?" asked Simon. "Perhaps of equal importance is why can this be?"

"Dreams are mysterious things," replied Smythe wistfully after taking another long pull of root beer. "Instances in which they have guided the affairs of humanity, for good or ill over the centuries, are common in almost every culture. But to share dreams with others in this way? That is not as common. In fact, it is rare."

"Even if what you say is true, and I do want to believe you, I still find the concept disturbing on many levels," stated Simon. "That you can see my dreams is disquieting."

"Simon," Smythe said gently as he put his bottle down on the table and stared intently into the Lakota man's eyes. "Are you absolutely certain I was seeing your dream?"

"What do you mean?" Simon asked.

"Have you considered it may have been you seeing my dream?"

Shame, fear and revelation hit Simon simultaneously. It had not occurred to him that it was he who was the invader of another's thoughts, and the possibility horrified him.

"I…I may owe you an apology, Dr. Smythe. Please forgive my accusatory tone earlier. So many things are happening so very fast inside of me that it seems I could be making rash judgements prematurely," said Simon.

Smythe leaned forward and spoke with sincere compassion. "There is nothing to forgive, Simon. In fact, you remind me of someone I knew long ago who shared your name. The conflict between rapid spiritual growth and past traits, such as an impulsive personality and tendency to think oneself superior to those thought less enlightened, is one that is bound to result in occasional blunders."

"It seems I've misjudged you, Dr. Smythe. You speak with the wisdom and grace of The Great Spirit upon you. Again, I am sorry."

"I believe this is where Miss Reed would say something along the lines of, not my first rodeo," replied Smythe and both men laughed. "I really do believe The Great Spirit, as you say, has brought you here with a purpose for a time such as this. Great things will be done by you if you follow His lead."

"I'm humbled and will do my best, Dr. Smythe," Simon replied.

"I know, and I'm here to help you Simon," said Smythe. "And as a small token of my friendship, when we're in private conversation such as this, you may call me Jon."

Chapter Thirty-Three

Zach Everley gave his wife, Linda, a parting kiss on the cheek before climbing into his old 1984 Dodge Prospector pickup. He waved goodbye to his son and daughter, who were playing with other neighborhood children in the yard. Cautiously, he checked all the mirrors for any other youngsters behind him and glanced back at his wife on the front porch for clearance to safely back out of the driveway. He put the truck in reverse and rolled slowly backward when she gave him a thumbs-up and a warm smile. He drove a short distance through the Cumberland, Kentucky, neighborhood before taking a left onto Highway 119 toward Putney.

It was a beautiful autumn morning and the trees were alive with vibrant fall color. Everley hummed along as country music played on the radio. The lovingly maintained 318 V8 engine purred under the hood. A short, wiry man of 48 with combed-back black hair streaked with tinges of gray, Everley had returned to his small hometown after three tours with the Army in Iraq. His build made him ideally suited to drive an M1 Abrams tank, and a natural aptitude for fixing just about anything made him popular in his platoon. Though the economy in the coal-producing region he called home was depressed, he made enough as a versatile handyman to live comfortably and provide for his family. His first appointment of the day was at Mrs. Adelman's trailer house where he was to make sure the heat tape on her pipes was ready for the coming winter so they wouldn't freeze up. The elderly woman often called Everley for odd jobs around her place and always sent some fresh sweet cornbread home with him to share with his family when the job was done. He took a right off 119 just past Laden and headed north on a winding road toward Daniel Boone National Forest. Though the toolbox across the front of his pickup bed was stocked with a collection of parts and tools that prepared Everley for almost any repair task, nothing could have prepared him for events that morning.

♦ ♦ ♦

It sat with its back against the smooth wall of the enclosure, the female asleep and snuggled against its legs. The other male chewed on a femur from a large ox-like creature the trio had fed on following the mating. Bones were nearly all that remained of the beast it had easily dispatched with a powerful blow to the neck. As was the custom in Yakwawiak tribes, the alpha male and its mate ate first. Subordinate creatures in the hierarchy fought over what was left. It and the female had consumed all of the blood-rich organs inside the animal, along with the choicest meat. The lone remaining male had eaten what remained and picked through the bones more out of boredom than a need for more food.

A panel in one of the walls slid open. The big male rose cautiously. More food was not needed so soon. Curiosity prevailed and it walked slowly toward the opening. It stopped when one of the two-legged canine things stepped into the pen without hesitation. It recognized the newcomer as the apparent leader of the beings that had been caring for and feeding it, the one he'd seen in an apparent position of authority above the wall. All the more reason to kill it.

The Yakwawi rushed at the visitor, which effortlessly sidestepped the assault. Angered, the big male attacked again with the same result. The female was wakened by the noise and immediately moved to help her mate. She pounced at the entity between her and the male, but it eluded her and momentum sent her crashing into the big male. The third Yakwawi entered the fray but no matter how they coordinated or tried to anticipate the canine-human, it avoided the attacks with uncanny speed and agility. It was as if the being was, if only for a millisecond, in two places at once. In time, the Yakwawiak tired. Their efforts became clumsy, their breathing labored. Eventually, all three sat down panting and staring at the strange creature in their midst, a creature that seemed to be smirking at them with a self-satisfied look.

The entity walked over to the big male Yakwawi and locked eyes with the massive predator. Its form began to shimmer and the big male took a half-hearted swat at the elusive being, but it had leapt upward higher than the walls. At the apex of its jump, the entity let out a blood-curdling howl that morphed into a shriek as it transformed into something that resembled a large prehistoric bird that started flapping around the arena just below the tops of the walls.

All three Yakwawiak were instantly on their feet, unsure if the flying creature meant to attack. The thing evaded all attempts to jump up and catch it. Then the bird swooped low, curled up and rolled along the ground only to pop upright in a different form, this time that of a large, very black humanoid with a feline face, glowing yellow eyes and bat-like wings. At the sight of the new creature, the Yakwawiak drew closer together and stepped back in fear. Their kind instinctively knew the power shape-shifters possessed. The entity started walking toward the Yakwawiak, growing in size with each step until it stood taller than the large male. It morphed again and took the shape of a huge male Yakwawi looking down on the others. After several seconds, during which it communicated through intense glowing eyes that it wasn't to be trifled with, it turned and walked toward the still open door in the pen's wall. The shifter changed again, getting smaller with each step until its transition to a new form was complete. It was the form of a very attractive blonde woman in her twenties with an athletic build and wearing a Crook County deputy's uniform. It turned to look back at the Yakwawiak, focusing on the big male, and gave a sly smile before making an obscene gesture and gliding through the open door. The largest Yakwawi roared in rage and charged the opening, only to skid to a halt just as the smooth door slammed closed. It roared again up at the purple sky, chest heaving in anger. It would kill that two-legger female, it promised itself, by taking its time eating her alive.

Chapter Thirty-Four

Dr. Jake Sanders sat under a palm tree scrolling through an article in "The International Journal of Zoology and Applied Biosciences" on a laptop. The rugged computer was a gift from Dr. Smythe shortly after the Yakwawi incident and it was a welcome one. Covered with rubberized armor and sporting a 17-inch vivid color touchscreen, it was deemed waterproof, shockproof and guaranteed to be among the fastest and most powerful portable units in the world, excluding others at Sanctum. Simon and Julie had also been provided with similar laptops, though Jake's nerdy and introverted nature meant he made far more use of his.

Nearly two weeks had passed since the event in the Black Hills and life at Sanctum was settling into a routine. Jake had learned many of the Sanctum staff regularly attended religious services at the chapel mornings or evenings, though there was no pressure on anyone to do so. Those with regular duties were typically at work by eight but Sanctum didn't punch clocks, leaving time for physical training, recreation and personal enrichment.

Since discovering Sanctum's library, Jake had spent his free time doing little else until Dr. Wu prescribed at least two hours of sunshine a day. The number of original volumes and book material in the library was so vast that elevators were needed to travel between sections. Though Jake couldn't be certain, he thought Sanctum's collection of writings exceeded that of the Library of Congress and Smithsonian Institute combined. He'd spent more time outdoors since Dr. Wu informed him he could access any material in the library from his laptop, a concept Jake found mind-blowing when he contemplated the memory requirements but, sure enough, anything in the library he wanted could be carried in his arms.

Jake desired a measure of structure in his life. He typically rose at six each morning to visit the gym and work out. Then he'd shower, dress, and be in the cafeteria by seven. Not being good at making friends, he ate alone more often than not. Occasionally other Sanctum personnel would ask to join him and he'd learn a bit more about the place.

By eight Jake was usually in the library. He partitioned his mornings into reading at least an hour each on history, zoology and cryptozoology before allowing a break for lunch. One of the treasures Jake had uncovered in the library was a special archive of The Watch's operations going back several centuries. Though portions were redacted, he gained insight into how vast, secretive, efficient and, at times, ruthless the organization was. His excitement grew when he found detailed notes about each of the creatures in Dr. Smythe's taxidermy collection and was dumbfounded by how rapidly The Watch's technology had advanced ahead of the rest of the planet. He spent the first half of each afternoon reading The Watch's archived reports and then, per Dr. Wu, finally ventured outside.

"Heads up!" called Cora as a volleyball hit the tree trunk above Jake's head.

Tol, Dom and Cora were engaged in a game of beach volleyball against Julie, Jeff and Ibutho a short distance away. It was a pretty even match, apart from the big African's tendency to occasionally send a spiked ball flying in any direction with tremendous force.

"Hey, book boy," called Julie as she ran up to retrieve the ball. "Come join us. I bet under that substantial brain is a fit fellow who knows his way around a volleyball court. Besides, I'm beginning to think you don't like me anymore."

"Oh, I like you," Jake replied and then caught himself. "I mean, I like you…no, I don't…wait, no…I'm sorry, I just…Aw fudge it."

Julie laughed as Jake turned so red it looked like he'd been badly sunburned. "No seriously, Jake, please join us. It's good to have fun once in a while."

Jake balked until Julie gently took the laptop, set it aside and helped him up. "Let's go, Einstein, the local militia has the upper hand on the scoreboard."

The game resumed and Jake managed to acquit himself well by blocking a couple of Tol's spikes and scoring with a few of his own. It didn't take long before he found himself laughing and joking with the rest of the players. He realized it was the first time since his wife's death that he was actually having fun with others, and it felt good. But then he started feeling guilty about feeling good so soon after Gail's passing. That's when Dom's spike hit him in the face.

"Jake! You okay, mate?" Jeff's face came into focus and Julie pulled off her bandana, pressing it to Jake's bloody nose.

"Ow!" Jake protested.

"Need to keep the pressure on until it stops bleeding," remarked Cora. "Do you think it's broken?"

"No."

"How can you tell?" asked Julie.

"Because your hair smells really nice," Jake replied before thinking. He immediately blushed again when the others started laughing.

"He will be fine," declared Ibutho. "Let us help him up and take him to get cleaned up."

Jake took over applying pressure and headed back inside toward his room. Julie and Cora tagged along. When they arrived at his door, Julie told Cora she could handle things and ushered Jake inside, seating him on the bed. She then retrieved an ice tray from the small refrigerator/freezer in the room, tossed a couple of ice cubes in a washcloth and replaced the blood-soaked bandana with it.

"I liked that bandana," Julie remarked. "Hope it comes clean."

"Really, Julie, I'll be fine. Thank you."

"Dom really smacked you, Jake. I don't mind. Besides, you and I haven't spent much quality time together lately."

"If you want some alone-time, you can just ask instead of having someone print Wilson on my forehead," Jake remarked.

"Great! It's a date then. Dinner at six. Will I be meeting you in the cafeteria or will you be coming by my room with flowers to escort me?" Julie responded.

"Wait, what?" Jake lowered the washcloth and Julie promptly put it back under his nose. "Careful now. Don't spoil the mood. We'll have plenty of time to talk this evening. Just keep the pressure on for another five minutes and you should be fine. Then get cleaned up and I'll see you at six. Oh, and don't wear something nerdy," said Julie with a grin and she was out the door.

Jake sat there with the bloody washcloth under his nose wondering what had just happened. He stood after a few minutes and was about to get showered and cleaned up when there was a knock on his door. Upon opening it, he saw Dom standing in the hallway, hands behind his back.

"I'm sorry I hit you in the face," Dom apologized with sincerity. He produced a small bouquet of flowers. "Got you these as a peace offering. Or you can share them with someone else," he said with a wink.

"Wait," said Jake. "Have I just been set up?"

"I've no idea what you're talking about," Dom replied. "But if the answer is yes, and flowers are involved, it sounds like it could be fun."

Dom smiled, gave a casual salute and headed off down the hall. Jake shut the door and leaned his back against it. He stared at the fresh-cut bundle of wildflowers in his hand for several minutes, conflict welling up inside him. He'd been a happily married man just a few weeks earlier. Presenting another woman with flowers so soon after his wife's death seemed wrong. He did find Julie attractive, but she was so different from Gail. Or was she?

Jake made his decision, pulled his bloody shirt off and headed toward the shower.

Chapter Thirty-Five

The shaman stood silently in the shade of one of the garden's many trees, his eyes fixed on his fellow Lakota. Simon Standing Elk sat cross-legged on a patch of green grass surrounded by a splendid array of flowering tropical plants, head bowed in apparent prayer. The older man had mentored many young Native Americans over the years but never had he seen anyone grow in knowledge, wisdom and spirit as quickly as Simon had, and he was concerned. Too much growth in too short a period could clear a path to pride and overconfidence, both of which the shaman had seen lead to tragedy in the past.

"How long will you lurk in the shadows, Wicasa?" Simon called without moving. "Come. Please sit with me."

"Your powers of perception may exceed my own," the shaman replied as he approached Simon. "If you continue to progress at the rate you have, soon I shall have nothing more to teach you."

"He who can no longer learn is dead," said Simon. "He who chooses to no longer learn is a danger to himself and others."

"Profound, Simon," the shaman observed. "Where did you hear that?"

"In my prayers," Simon replied. "Actually, in the silence between my prayers. I find it to my benefit to listen as much as I speak when praying to The Great Spirit. Don't you agree, Wicasa?"

"To listen more than speaking is beneficial in all conversation, Simon. Whether conversing with The Great Spirit or anyone else," the older man answered.

"You're concerned, Wicasa," Simon noted. "You are worried that The Great Spirit is teaching me too quickly and that my rapid growth will result in the downfall that pride brings."

"I'm pleased with your progress, Simon," said the shaman.

"Yet you evade my observation."

"Was it observation or speculation?" the shaman asked. "One is a statement of fact, the other is an assumption."

Simon turned to the shaman at last and gestured for the man to sit with him. "Why have our conversations become more antagonistic, Wicasa? Have I behaved wrongly or with disrespect? Lately you seem to challenge everything I say," said Simon.

"Are not all worthy things born of some measure of conflict?" the shaman asked.

"Questions to answer questions," Simon noted. "No. Not all worthy things are born of conflict, Wicasa. Some are born of love, others of revelation or inspiration. Still others are the result of intentional personal challenge. Please stop me if I do not speak truth."

"And what is truth, Simon?" the shaman inquired.

"Truth is," Simon replied.

"Truth is what?" asked the shaman.

"Truth simply is, Wicasa," Simon answered. "It is a rock, a foundation, the cornerstone atop which all of humanity and reality rests. Truth is timeless, unchanging, the flagpole on which fly all the banners we call facts. Truth was in the beginning and will be long after we are gone. It is self-existent and eternal, independent of anyone or anything here or elsewhere."

"Be careful, Simon," said the shaman. "You speak as though truth is The Great Spirit himself."

"No, my friend," Simon replied with a hint of eagerness in his voice. "The Great Spirit is Truth."

The Shaman tried to hide his awe at the younger man's proclamation. It often took years for someone to arrive at the kind of definitive conclusion Simon had.

"What of wisdom?" the shaman asked to test the younger man.

"Wisdom, to be considered such, must be recognized as a product of Truth."

"What of love?"

"Can love be pure unless it is true?"

"What of those who say they have their own truth?

"They lie. For Truth to be what is true, it cannot be fluid or subject to differing interpretation. Anything that is, is not Truth."

"What of the Yakwawi?" the shaman blurted out leaning forward, his face inches from Simons, their eyes locked. His intent was to gauge how Simon reacted to the shock of a triggering question that had nothing to do with the subject being discussed.

"They come," Simon answered without hesitation or even batting an eye, his expression neutral.

The younger Lakota rose quickly, the shaman a moment later. Simon closed his eyes and tilted his head back to face the blue sky overhead. He spread his arms and raised them, mumbling something the shaman couldn't make out. Then Simon brought both arms down quickly to grasp each of the shaman's shoulders as he looked into the older man's eyes. The shaman squinted from the glare of Simon's brightly shining eyes. The intensity of the look and otherworldly glow made the shaman wonder for a moment if Simon had been possessed by a spirit.

"They come again to the land of dark and bloody ground!" Simon exclaimed. "A portal opens soon!" He turned to look away from the shaman. "AVADSA! Show me a map of Kentucky!"

The Watch's ever present A.I. interface responded by projecting a holographic 3-D map of the state beside the two Lakota men. Simon closed his eyes for a moment before manipulating the image to zoom in on the southeast corner near the border with Virginia.

"Here," said Simon poking a finger through the projection at Black Mountain, the highest point in Kentucky. "They come in the morning shadow of the mountain."

The shaman considered what was happening with amazement, but then looked hard at the map. "This time of year the rising sun will cause the shadow of Black Mountain to fall in a west-northwest direction. When, Simon? When do you see this happening?"

"We must go to the operations center now. There is no time to waste. I can't pinpoint an exact time but I know if we do not get there soon, it will be too late."

Simon took off at a run, the shaman followed as quickly as his older legs could move.

◆ ◆ ◆

No food had been provided since they'd fed on the bovine beast, and it was hungry. Pacing around the enclosure accomplished nothing other than to offer momentary release of energy. The other two with it were fidgeting nervously.

A panel on the side of the arena creaked as it slid upward to open and the Yakwawiak stopped in their tracks, anticipating a new creature to feed on. Instead, a dozen of the wolf-human creatures entered. Each wore chain mail armor and a bowl-shaped helmet with flared sides and a sharpened crest. They grasped long-handled axes that ended in spear points on the ends opposite the blades. The warrior shifters formed two parallel lines either side of the opening. Then the shape-shifter leader appeared, this time as the bat-winged, feline-faced humanoid.

It began to change, edges of its being became increasingly indistinct to create a phantom-like apparition floating in place. It held that form and raised its arms toward the open door. A dark disc materialized over the door and began to grow. When it was roughly 15 feet across, four of the warrior entities moved behind the Yakwawiak and began to prod them forward toward the portal with the spear-point ends of their long axe handles. The female took a swing at one of the prodding warriors but it deftly dodged and poked her again. It never saw the massive paw of the big male that came at it from another direction, swatting it like a line drive into the far wall of the enclosure. It disintegrated into a cloud of dark-colored dust on impact. Other warriors stepped back but continued to motion for the Yakwawiak to enter the portal.

Tiring of the game, the big male roared, put its head down and charged through the opening. The other two Yakwawiak followed close behind. Then the remaining eleven demonic warriors formed a line and marched into the portal after them.

Chapter Thirty-Six

"We hope the new bolts will promote tissue degeneration at the cellular level inside the wound channel," explained Cora as she showed the rest of the team the new design of the bolt guns used in their previous encounter with the Yakwawi. "When an internal sensor detects the bolt's forward motion has stopped, a small power source activates the infrared laser inside the shaft to cast an intense but cool beam out the back into the wound behind it for several minutes. Bolt length has been changed to 15 inches to allow the beam to project rearward through more of the creature. And the developers kept the beam as cool as possible to avoid cauterizing the wound."

"And," interjected Tol, "Capacity per cylinder is now nine shots. Thanks to R&D, we were able to accomplish this and still reduce the overall size and weight of the weapon. Dom, Cora, Jeff and I will have one bolt gun and two spare cylinders each in addition to whatever other weapons we choose to carry. If there are no questions, we'll take turns outfitting in the armory in pairs. Ladies first."

Cora and Julie stood and headed to the armory inside the big Albatross supersonic stealth transport plane. The rest of the team was seated in a conference room aft of the sleeping berths with one of the new bolt guns on the table. The team had scrambled quickly after Simon had alerted Dr. Smythe, but this time the shaman accompanied them. He sat with Simon to his right and Jake on his left.

"Tell me Dr. Sanders," the older man said turning his seat to face Jake. "Why do you think infrared light inhibits Yakwawi regenerating abilities?"

"I can only speculate," Jake began. "We know that UV radiation is harmful to humans when we're exposed to too much. It's what causes sunburn and can damage eyesight. Apparently the reverse is true with the Yakwawi. Infrared light degrades it while UV light heals. Our atmosphere protects us to some extent from solar UV radiation, but there are other sources. It's possible that the Yakwawi is susceptible to certain wavelengths of the spectrum because those wavelengths are less intense, rare or don't exist where it comes from. We also know that certain animal species can actually see infrared light that we can't. Snakes, frogs, blood-sucking insects and fish, for example, use that special sense to help them find prey in low-light conditions. Perhaps UV radiation enhances Yakwawi's eyesight and IR degrades it."

"Then why can we not use a strong IR laser as a weapon against it?" the shaman asked.

"I can answer that," replied Dom. "It's a logistics problem. The Watch has done well in developing directed-energy technology but still faces the two big problems of power and portability. A laser weapon capable of being effective on a beast like that would be too heavy and large for us to carry into a fight. Even if we could, the beam might zap only two or three small holes through the creature without causing a fatal wound before the power source is depleted."

"And," Jake added, "The wound would be cauterized instantly, resulting in no shock trauma or blood loss. I suspect we're still years away from a ray gun with settings ranging from stun to disintegrate."

"We still have that other idea you came up with," noted Tol.

"It was actually Dr. Wu's idea, but yes. We'll see if it works. I sure hope it does," Jake replied.

"It's not that you aren't welcome, shaman," said Dom to the older Lakota. "But I'm not clear exactly why you came along on this op."

"I don't know about you, mate," interjected Jeff, "But I'm grateful for all the spiritual support we can get on this mission."

"Appearances can be deceptive," the shaman replied. "Don't assume that my presence here is just to lend spiritual and moral support. Need I remind everyone that I was on ops such as this long before any of you were born?"

"I should very much like to hear about some of those," said Jake.

"Another time boys," Cora interrupted, her face peeking around the doorframe. "Time for you guys to suit up. We're about an hour out."

The men rose and filed out of the room toward the cargo hold. Dom and Tol peeled off into the armory as the group passed the door. Julie was waiting for the group in the staging area.

"Should we review our attack plan?" suggested Julie as the team entered. Jake and Jeff stopped and stared when they saw her. Julie was clad from neck to boots in what appeared to be a seamless form-fitting ultra-black outfit. A large samurai sword was slung across her back. A gun belt just above her hips held holstered pistols on her thighs. Her blonde hair was pulled back into a single ponytail stuck through the back of a black baseball cap, a pair of tactical goggles rested above the bill. Black vambraces covered her forearms and each had three throwing knives in integrated sheaths. Impact-resistant polymer greaves covered her shins above a pair of lightweight tactical boots.

Cora, who was wearing a similar outfit, walked in front of the two men. Though by no means an unattractive woman herself, she doubted any male with a drop of testosterone in his blood could ignore the striking goddess-of-war image Julie was projecting. "I believe Julie asked us a question, gentlemen," she noted, and both gawking men were immediately embarrassed to realize they'd been staring. "We should review our tactical objective. If you would please, Dr. Sanders."

Jake reluctantly took his eyes off Julie, who had not let his attention go unnoticed, and began the discussion just as Tol and Dom rejoined the team in full tactical gear. "If Simon is correct, we'll be up against a foe that has fought us before. It's also going to be morning where we're headed with a sunny day forecast. That means our disorienting strobe light will likely be ineffective in broad daylight. The area is relatively remote and rural. It was a hub of activity when coal mining was at its peak, but has struggled economically ever since. Population centers are spread out with plenty of dense forest nearby."

"Not unlike the northern Black Hills," noted Dom. "Why do you think this area was chosen for its return?"

"I'm going out on a limb with a theory here," Jake replied. "We know the Yakwawi was taken through a portal by presumed hostile entities. Why? What would anyone want with a nearly dead Yakwawi? The shaman and Simon identify these new entities as shape-shifters. As a scientist, I find that concept really hard to grasp, but I've seen so much other stuff that's hard to get my mind around in recent weeks that I'm pretty open to possibilities right now. Anyway, Native American lore has nothing good to say about shape-shifters from what I'm told. So, bad guys take a Yakwawi and somehow restore it to health. If they've got it out for humans, the shape-shifters might try releasing it back into our world or dimension or whatever we call it. If the ultimate goal is to basically use monstrous beasts as instruments of terror to further an agenda, a Yakwawi is a good candidate if it can be controlled. My hunch is that this is a test run for something bigger they have in mind."

"Like what?" Julie asked.

"Like opening a portal under the bleachers at a Little League game, a school playground, a church picnic. Some place or event with a lot of innocent potential targets and a low probability of effective resistance. Think of the physical and psychological trauma a series of such hit-and-run attacks could have, let alone the rippling impact into political and economic areas if such attacks were coordinated over time to appear random, yet common. It's like a new form of bio-weapon. Terrorism by monster," answered Jake.

The distinctive sound of slow clapping from one set of hands echoed across the cargo hold. Dr. Smythe emerged from a previously unseen door in the rear of the armory walking toward the group. Those who'd been with The Watch for some time were not alarmed but Jake, Julie and Simon couldn't conceal their astonishment.

"Bravo, Dr. Sanders, bravo indeed!" commended Smythe. "You have brilliantly delivered a concise summation for the very reason The Watch exists. I congratulate you."

"What are you doing here, Dr. Smythe?" asked Julie.

"Am I not welcome, Miss Reed?"

"No. I mean yes…well…things are about to get a bit crazy, and seeing you in a British SAS battle uniform instead of a suit is a sight we're not used to," Julie answered.

"I assure you, dear girl, the uniform was earned and I am no stranger to tactical field operations. But don't worry. I'll be careful not to get in your way."

Julie bristled at Smythe's reference to her as a girl, but let it slide for the moment.

"Welcome aboard, sir," said Cora. "It's an honor to have you with us."

"Spoken like a true soldier, Cora. Thank you. I realize a few of you still need to get ready, so let me explain the situation as concisely as I'm able to our newer team members," said Smythe. "Creation is divided into two warring but unequal factions. Let's call them light and darkness for now. The Watch and its members are allied with the good guys on the light side."

"Figures," interrupted Julie. "I saw a T-shirt back home calling on people to join the dark side because they have cookies."

This time Julie's attempt at humor bombed. No one laughed and Smythe shot her a withering look before continuing. "You are likely about to meet a new set of bad guys. Think of them as demons. The ones Dr. Sanders has aptly called shape-shifters if you prefer another name. They despise humans and have employed various methods to destroy as many of us as possible throughout most of history. There are different kinds of demons, and a hierarchy that they adhere to, but you'll be going up against mid-level entities. I'm here to brief you on them."

"Dr. Smythe," Jake protested. "You know I'm a man of science. Are you seriously asking us to embrace mythological beings as reality?"

"Fail to do so at your own peril, doctor," Smythe replied. "We can debate this all you like after the mission. For now, I need to share what you might encounter."

Smythe spoke for a few minutes, explaining the strengths and perceived weaknesses of the beings the team could encounter in addition to the Yakwawi. When he finished, Jake bowed his head and shook it slightly trying to grasp what they'd just been told. Simon nodded thoughtfully. Julie just stared at Smythe with eyes the size of golf balls.

Chapter Thirty-Seven

Zach Everley sensed something was amiss as soon as he turned onto Mrs. Adelman's long driveway. The elderly woman loved her flowers, and the walkway to the front door of her trailer home was lined with planters made from old whisky barrels cut in half. Each contained a colorful variety of plants. She watered and tended her flowers religiously every morning without fail, usually clad in an old sun dress and wide-brimmed straw hat. Everley grew concerned when he didn't see her outside on such a beautiful morning. His concern grew to worry when he saw the trailer's screen door far out in the lawn and noticed one end of the home itself was off of the foundation blocks on which it usually rested. There had been no severe weather in the area the night before and no earth tremors he knew of, though they weren't unknown in coal-mining country.

Everley parked a bit farther down the driveway than usual to assess the situation. His tank unit had thought him psychic for the number of times the man's uncanny ability to sense danger saved them from ambush and IEDs. He scanned the lawn area for signs of the woman and reached for the pickup's glovebox. When it popped open he withdrew a holstered Colt Python .357 Magnum revolver. Reaching under the seat, Everley found a small bag containing four speed loaders for the gun, each holding six cartridges. The hills of eastern Kentucky are beautiful, but also home to bears, wild boars, copperheads, rattlesnakes and occasional troublemakers of the two-legged variety, so Everley always traveled prepared.

The handyman exited the truck and approached the trailer home with his head on a swivel, scanning the area for trouble. The closer he got, the more damage he noticed. Windows were broken, siding was damaged, and the home was set back from the front steps, leaving a gap.

Everley jumped back as the ground in front of his feet exploded, spraying his shins with dirt and sod. He dove behind the nearest planter just before another blast hit right where he'd been standing. Popping his head up for a moment, he saw Mrs. Adelman standing in her front doorway reloading a double-barrel shotgun.

"Mrs. Adelman!" he shouted. "It's Zach Everley! Don't shoot!"

The woman looked confused and raised her gun again, "Y'all best show yerself or I'll put ya under them flowers 'sted of behind 'em!"

"Okay, Mrs. Adelman! Like I said, it's Zach Everley here to check your pipes. Remember? Please just lower your shotgun so I can stand up and show myself, okay?"

The old woman took her cheek off the gunstock and lowered the barrel slightly. Zach put his empty hands high in the air. His revolver was holstered on his right hip and the reloads were in a front pocket. As soon as he was fully standing, the woman brought her gun up again and leveled it at him.

"Why are ya armed?" yelled Mrs. Adelman.

"Why are you, ma'am?" Everley replied cautiously stepping forward. He'd been shot at more times than he could count and thought himself a pretty good judge of intent. If Mrs. Adelman had meant to kill him, she'd have done so. Or so he thought. "I was pulling up and it looked like you'd been robbed or something. Being an Army man sworn to defend folks and all, I figured best I get my revolver on before coming to check and see if you're okay?"

Everley was a pro at defusing situations and had done so many times overseas. He knew the woman's late husband had served in Vietnam and both her sons did tours in the military. One was a helicopter pilot in Desert Storm and the other a career Army officer soon to be a colonel, if he recalled correctly. Reminding her of his service worked. Mrs. Adelman broke open the shotgun's action to cradle it in her arm.

"Best be getting yer skinny rumps in here then," Mrs. Adelman advised, beckoning him to come with no small sense of urgency. "C'mon, hurry up in case they come back!"

Everley broke into a trot as he closed the last 40 feet to the front stoop. The woman backed into the home so he could jump the gap from the wooden steps to the inside. He tried to shut the door behind him but the doorjamb was askew and it wouldn't close all the way.

"Good morning, Mrs. Adelman."

"Mornin' Mr. Everley. Apologies for nearly ventilatin' ya, but I is a bit jumpy with all the goings on hereabouts."

"Why don't you put the gun down and tell me just what happened here," said Everley gesturing toward a couch in the nearby living room, the floor of which was littered with spent shotgun shells and shattered glass from windows, picture frames and broken knick-knacks. It was then he noticed her beagle, Buster, cowering in a corner. He thought that very strange as Buster was usually glad to see him. Something had obviously shaken both dog and owner.

Everley also caught a whiff of alcohol on Mrs. Adelman. Though known to enjoy a finger or two of Kentucky's finest on occasion, the woman was a regular church-goer and far from an alcoholic so far as he knew.

"I'll be keepin' my shotgun handy, thank you," Mrs. Adelman replied tensing up. "Along with extra shells in my apron 'til them things are killed."

"What things?"

"Werewolves and Bigfoots! Look at what they went an' did to my house!" the woman exclaimed as she broke down and began to cry. "Poor little Buster and me was scared to death!"

Everley began to have serious doubts about Mrs. Adelman but didn't immediately respond. She was frightened. The cowering dog began to whimper when he saw her crying but the beagle couldn't bring itself to stop shaking in the corner. Glass cracked beneath the handyman's shoes as he made his way over to the dog and crouched in front of it, extending a hand. Buster sniffed his fingers and looked up at him with sad eyes. Everley took care to move slowly as he gathered the pup up in his arms before heading back to Mrs. Adelman. He stroked the dog's head gently and chose his words with care.

"Werewolves, you say? And Bigfoots? Was it this morning or last night they came by?"

"Aw, now don't go patronizin' me, Mr. Everley. I know how it sounds. Heck, I'd be thinking someone crazy if they'd told me the same thing. But as sure as you're here, they was. A bunch of 'em."

"Mrs. Adelman, I wasn't here. It's not my place to judge. But if you don't mind me asking, might that be a bit of Wild Turkey I smell on your breath?"

"Ya know yer bourbon son. I makes no apology, even though sun's not to midday yet. After what Buster and I been through, I needed somethin' to calm my nerves. I may have had a shot or two, but that was after them monsters was here. And I ain't by no means drunk, Mr. Everley."

"Never said ya was, ma'am."

There's a difference between drinking and being drunk. Everley knew that line and believed Mrs. Adelman hadn't crossed it. He handed Buster to her, a move that forced the woman to lay her gun on the kitchen counter so she could comfort her dog.

"Mrs. Adelman, I think I'd better have a look around outside," said Everley. "Now no more whiskey until I get back, okay? And I will announce myself before I come back in so you don't shoot me."

"Okay," the woman replied as Everley turned back toward the door. "Oh and Mr. Everley? Please be careful out there."

The handyman turned and nodded before walking out into the yard.

◆ ◆ ◆

"I'm not sure they were ready for that," the shaman remarked.

"It was a bit like drinking from a firehose, wasn't it old friend?" Smythe replied. The two men sat alone on jump seats against the fuselage wall as Cora's team loaded the last of the equipment into the Skyray docked in the cargo hold.

"Simon can accept such things, though I'm concerned his rapid progress may be fostering hubris that he'll come to regret," the shaman replied. "But Dr. Sanders is highly conflicted. He's a scientist whose agnostic worldview is challenged by that which cannot be quantified, measured, observed and tested. And Julie? She has no idea who or what she is yet."

"Dr. Sanders will come around," Smythe predicted. "His thirst for knowledge and insatiable curiosity will sustain him until he has no other choice but to accept the reality of what he now finds unacceptable. As for Julie, she will either be The Watch's salvation or its downfall."

"You're taking quite a risk with them, Jon."

"And what of you?" asked Smythe. "You didn't have to come on this mission."

"Nor did you," the Lakota noted. "We have three other teams in the field right now. What if you're needed at Sanctum?"

"One team is containing a new virus in Bolivia. They're undercover with the World Health Organization and it's under control. Another team is monitoring yet another live mammoth that's turned up in Siberia. What's that make now, four in the last three years there? Anyway, the cover of Russians trying to resurrect the species via cloning is great fodder for the tabloids. And the crew of our submersible *Galilee* is still tracking something massive, we don't know what yet, in The Horizon Deep. That's been going on for two weeks and I see nothing urgent happening there anytime soon. Besides, we have worldwide coms if I should be needed for something," Smythe concluded.

"It's still risky. I don't like it when you leave Sanctum," the shaman confessed.

"Yet you come and go all the time," noted Smythe. "If we gave out frequent flyer miles, you'd have paid for a trip to Alpha Centauri and back … perhaps twice."

Both men chuckled before the shaman gave Smythe a serious look. "Jon, sooner or later one of us won't be coming back from one of these forays."

Smythe turned to look at his friend solemnly. "Have you sensed something? Had a vision or dream concerning the demise of one of us? Even with my gifts, I have not. Nor has He revealed anything to me."

"We have both lived a very long time, Jon," the shaman said wistfully. "We have seen many wonderful and terrible things. Much more than men were meant to see in one lifetime."

"Why so melancholy? I'm concerned," Smythe confessed.

"Alright everyone, we're almost to the drop zone!" Cora shouted. "Team members, all-board the Skyray now!"

Her team gathered at the walkway to the smaller craft and started boarding. The shaman rose and walked toward the Skyray as well.

"Where are you going?" Smythe called after him. "You're staying here with me!"

"I am not, Jon," the shaman replied, grabbing the lone small backpack remaining on the deck of the cargo hold before resuming his walk to the Skyray.

"You can't go into battle! I forbid it!" Smythe was up and trotting after the Lakota.

The shaman was at the bottom of the walkway when Smythe caught up and grabbed his arm. "I said, I forbid you to go!"

Smythe released the man's arm when he stared into a face projecting intensity and resolve. The two men had never clashed in front of others in all the years they'd known one another. Smythe saw more than determination in the shaman's eyes. He saw a warning.

"*You* forbid *me* to go?" Then the shaman laughed. It was a loud laugh filled with joy, and he kept laughing as he went up the walkway to where Cora was waiting for him. He handed her his pack, turned to look at Smythe below and called out, "Here, there or in the air, my friend."

Smythe raised his right arm in a half-hearted wave. "Be the wise man I know you are. See you again soon."

With that, the shaman headed down the hatch into the Skyray and Cora followed. Once they were aboard, Smythe made an executive decision about where he'd be during the anticipated confrontation. He turned and strode toward a ladder that led straight up into the Skyray cockpit's bottom hatch.

Chapter Thirty-Eight

They'd arrived on the mountain before dawn and headed northwest not really knowing why. Hunger drove them. The urge to feed was strong. Shortly after crossing a rural road, they found a creek where a whitetail doe and two fawns were drinking. The deer were dispatched quickly and eaten in their entirety. Though still shadowed by the strange warrior creatures that had come through the portal with them, no attempt was made by them to join in the feeding. Those creatures kept their distance, though their intent remained unclear. As long as they didn't interfere with hunting or feeding, the Yakwawiak were content to let them be. The meat and blood nourished them but it wasn't enough.

Many of the mountains in the area bore the scars of aggressive coal mining and the amount of cover for wildlife varied. There was a distant familiarity about the place that appealed to the Yakwawiak. Though they couldn't have known about the gore-filled clashes between their ancestors and native human warriors that had done battle in the same hills centuries earlier, the blood shed by Yakwawiak of the past seemed to call for vengeance from deep within the soil as the beasts headed for what they perceived to be more favorable habitat in the forests on the northwest horizon.

The eastern sky transitioned from purple to pink with brightening patches of orange as dawn reluctantly surrendered to splendid fall day. The monsters timed carefully their crossing of what looked like a main trail for the wheeled machines the big male had encountered on a previous journey through the new land. It had learned the presence of many of the machines was not favorable, nor was getting hit by one.

The scent of a lone female two-legger with one canine nearby came to the nostrils of the younger male first. Forgetting stealth, it blundered into the yard recklessly as the woman was just beginning to tend her flowers. A shotgun was leaning against the planter nearest her because she'd seen a large copperhead snake near her plants the previous two mornings and had a strong desire to end those encounters. Buster was first to sense them and barked ferociously at the Yakwawi, which startled the creature momentarily because it was confused by how such loud noises could come from such a small animal. Then Mrs. Adelman's screams added to the commotion just as the big male and the female emerged from the tree line flanked by the shape-shifters.

Shotgun blasts rang out as the woman and Buster ran up the steps into the trailer home, hitting the young male with little effect other than a rage-inducing sting. It charged the home, ramming into it with a shoulder hard enough to move it a couple of feet and send breaking glass flying. Shots came through the broken front window to deliver more sharp stings to the Yakwawi's torso. It swung a massive forearm to land a blow on the home, breaking off siding and bending a wall inward. The big male and female started circling around the rear of the trailer but stopped when one of the shape-shifters yipped. Turning, they saw it extend an axe toward the road where a distant cloud of dust and rumbling sound signaled the approach of something or someone. As a precaution, the big male grunted and gestured with its head toward the tree line. All of the otherworldly invaders retreated to the trees to wait for what was coming up the road.

They'd watched Everley arrive from their cover in the trees. The young male wanted to attack as soon as the male two-legger emerged from his wheeled metal shell but the larger male bared its fangs in warning. The monsters were in no hurry and the big male wanted to see what would unfold. All three Yakwawiak stepped back farther into the trees when shots were fired again, unsure if they were the targets. They watched the exchange between the two-leggers and waited several minutes. The big male wondered if there were more than just two of the tasty creatures inside the box and, if so, what kind of defensive weapons they might have. Its last encounter with armed two-leggers had introduced a new measure of caution to the way it hunted them.

Zach Everley emerged from the home a few minutes after going in and jumped onto the small deck atop the front steps. He wrinkled his nose in disgust. A fowl stench floated across the yard from the direction of the trees to the southwest. Being a hunter, he noticed the wind had shifted since his arrival and something ranker than a family of skunks was in those trees. He knew it.

Drawing his revolver and slowly descending the steps, Everley kept his eyes locked on the tree line. Every fiber of his being screamed danger but it was hard to see very far into the dense foliage. The only thing he could think of that could possibly smell that bad was a drift of wild hogs. Though his handgun was powerful enough to take down a boar at close range, he was not equipped to handle a group of them if they decided to attack.

Keeping his revolver at the low-ready position, Everley moved sideways toward the truck in the driveway without taking his eyes off the trees. He fully expected a dozen wild pigs to come running at him at any moment. When he reached his truck, the handyman slipped over to the passenger side to put the vehicle was between him and the trees. He carefully opened the door and reached behind the seat. A wave of assurance came over him when his hand closed around the grip of the Mossberg 500 tactical shotgun he kept there. Its magazine was loaded with eight Pit Bull shells. Each contained six large buckshot pellets in addition to a lead slug. Everley felt he was then equipped to repel an attack from the most formidable of foes, be they animal or human. He was mistaken.

The sound of someone whistling a merry tune carried up the driveway. Everley turned to see a tall mail carrier coming toward him from the direction of the road. The big Yakwawi male was angered by the sight of the musical interloper but didn't immediately attack. It decided to see how things would progress.

"Good morning!" Everley called to the approaching man. He knew most of the local postal workers and figured the stranger to be a new hire. "Sorry for the smell. I think there's a drift of wild hogs over in those trees. Best watch yourself around here today."

The handyman was perplexed. The mail carrier just smiled broadly and waved as he came closer. Everley thought the fellow might have earbuds in, listening to tunes or a podcast on his route. He yelled a bit louder to warn of the potential danger. "Hello! I said I think there may be boars in those trees!"

The mailman was less than 20 feet away. He smiled at Everley and then looked at the trees as he continued toward the truck. Everley was getting nervous. Something wasn't right about the guy. The smile was too fixed and, as he got even closer, there was something about his eyes when he looked at Everley again. The handyman had seen his share of evil in war and, in spite of the flawless broad smile, the eyes of the approaching postal worker broadcast evil intent.

"Hey, what's the matter with…?"

Everley didn't finish the sentence before the man's mailbag morphed into a battle axe and his face grew a fanged snout. Momentarily stunned by what he was seeing, Everley's response was just a hair too slow as the wolf-human raised the axe to strike.

In a blur of motion, the attacker's right arm separated at the shoulder and it let out a grotesque howl as a black figure catapulted off the truck. A flash of steel, the whoosh of a blade through air, and the wolf-human severed head followed its arm toward the ground. The headless, disarmed thing remained upright a bit more than a second before disintegrating into a dark, ash-like substance that disappeared into the ground as if sucked in by a vacuum cleaner. The air cleared to reveal a stunning, well-armed woman in black tactical gear with a drawn katana sword standing just behind where the monster had been a moment before.

"Hi! I'm Julie. You should run away now."

Chapter Thirty-Nine

"DUCK!!"

Julie caught motion in the pickup's passenger side mirror just as Everley shouted. She went low in a fast pivot, swinging her sword hard in an arc behind her as the handyman let off a blast from his shotgun over her back. Another of the canine-human demons had rushed up on them when its comrade disintegrated. The force of the shotgun shell's payload struck hard on its armored torso, stopping the entity's forward momentum just in time. Its extended arms twirled to recover balance when Julie's sword connected a split-second later, literally cutting it off at the knees. Everley had the sense to stand clear of Julie's swing as she continued around in a complete circle, hoping for a second clean decapitation. Instead, the shape-shifter's axe deflected her blow as it fell backwards. Lack of follow-through momentum sent Julie staggering back off-balance for a second, so Everley stepped forward to deliver another blast beneath the demon's chin. He couldn't have known that his shells, though powerful, lacked the special metal content to which the demon was allergic. As a result, the force of impact sent the shape-shifter scooting along the ground on its back a few feet as Julie flipped the sword in her hands and plunged it vertically into the demon's gut. It wasn't an immediately mortal blow. The resulting shriek caused the tree line to erupt with noise and movement as the remaining shape-shifters and the Yakwawiak charged the pickup.

"Julie, get the civilians out of here!" shouted Cora as she and the rest of the team rushed forward from various hiding places to provide cover for the handyman and their teammate.

Julie tried to respond but the entity at her feet grabbed one of her ankles to send her tumbling backward. Everley drew his revolver and fired all six shots into the demon's face at point-blank range. It thrashed about but still wouldn't die.

"One side please!" shouted Ibutho above the noise of gunfire, roars and howls as he shoved Everley against the truck and stabbed a short spear's special metal blade into the demon's chest. It immediately dissolved to black ash that was pulled into the earth. Everley didn't let his displeasure at being manhandled show but used the momentum to spin and start firing his shotgun across the hood of his truck at the oncoming Yakwawiak.

Julie sprang to her feet and assessed the situation. Tol was on the roof of the mobile home in a prone position, firing at targets in the yard when he had a clear shot. The chaos of battle with multiple combatants attacking one another at close quarters prevented the kind of sustained fire he'd been able to pour into the Yakwawi at Roughlock Falls. He had to choose his shots carefully to avoid hitting team members.

Dom and Cora stood back to back, P90s empty at their sides. Shape-shifters rushed them from every side only to be repelled at the last moment by pistol fire. The handgun bullets were having trouble getting through the demons' armor and the sudden rush deprived them of precious seconds to reload their submachine guns with armor-piercing rounds.

Jake and Jeff had just come around the far side of the home and engaged the enemy from the flank. Julie saw another of the shape-shifters tumble to one side and disintegrate, felled by a shot from Jake's powerful lever-action rifle that found a gap in its armor. Jeff was firing bolt after bolt into the Yakwawi closest to him, the female. Simon and the shaman crouched in bushes next to the trailer home, medic bags ready at their sides.

And Ibutho — he was everywhere. Leaping, stabbing, hitting, kicking and running with the speed and agility of an angry leopard. The demonic host was always a second late in reacting to the warrior's blows but there were so many of them.

The big male Yakwawi was almost to the truck, filled with rage and bloodlust, when it stumbled. Its eagerness for a kill made it misjudge and it tripped over one of Mrs. Adelman's barrel planters, which shattered to send dirt and flowers flying. The stumbling beast smacked face-first into the truck, knocking both Everley and Julie into the lawn on the opposite side of the vehicle. For the first time, the monster got a good look at Julie and let out a deafening roar of hateful recognition as it rose up to attack. Then its head jerked to one side as if slapped in the face.

"Look at what y'all went an' done now!" shouted Mrs. Adelman from her front stoop, trusty double-barrel shotgun leveled at the monster's head. "It ain't enough ya trash a woman's home?! Ya gotta kill 'er flowers too?! Take this ya dern Bigfoot!" Her next shot struck the end of the Yakwawi's snout to deliver a jolt of electrifying pain. She broke the gun open and reloaded with surprising speed using shells from her apron. She fired again, giving the beast both barrels.

"Mrs. Adelman!" screamed Everley.

He started running for the front door only to be tackled by Julie just as the big Yakwawi's powerful forearm swept over both of them to send the pickup tumbling end-over-end down the driveway. They rolled to one side, narrowly missing a crushing blow from the beast's other arm. Everley jerked his shotgun up, propped its stock on the ground and started pumping more shots into the monster as fast as he could cycle the gun's action. To his surprise, the creature began to stagger backward. The handyman couldn't have known it was shots from Tol on the roof helping drive the monster back. A flash of metal and Everley's shotgun went flying, knocked from his hands by a demon's battle axe. A second blow buried in the ground between Julie and Everley as they rolled in opposite directions, but the shape-shifter recovered fast. Axe raised and about to deliver a fatal blow to Julie, its chest started shooting a dark-colored fluid outward. Bolts from Jeff perforated the entity's torso as the Aussie ran forward shouting. The demon exploded into dark dust that blanketed the handyman and woman on the ground before disappearing. They both sat up just in time to see a massive limb strike Jeff and send him flying into the side of the home with a gut-churning thud.

"JEFF!" cried Julie, rocketing to her feet and turning to face the young male Yakwawi bearing down on her. She drew both her pistols and fired into the charging monster.

The beast reared violently back shrieking as a pair of short spears plunged into its upper shoulders. It clawed furiously at the warrior on its back clinging to the spears. Ibutho had come out of nowhere to strike the charging creature only to find himself hanging on for dear life. The Yakwawi stumbled. Concentrated fire from a pair of P90s streamed into its lower legs as Cora and Dom stepped around Everley and Julie pouring penetrating projectiles into the creature. They'd escaped the rush of shape-shifters when Cora went dual-wielding with the Glocks and kept them back long enough for Dom to reload and get his submachine gun back in the fight.

The big male tried to intervene but was unable. Tol and Jake kept pummeling it with the mixed-metal bullets from their big rifles. The female strode forward and attempted to grab Ibutho when she staggered sideways. It was the shaman with the bolt gun dropped by Jeff. The medicine man was not in a healing mood as he advanced on her, his bolts penetrating deep into her torso and their rear-firing internal lasers keeping the wounds open. Then his bolt gun was empty.

Chapter Forty

The female reached for the shaman only to snatch her clawed hand back again, like a child touching a hot stove.

"Ya married chief?" yelled Mrs. Adelman over the noise as she stepped up beside the shaman to deliver a second shotgun blast to the female monster's stinging hand. She gave the shaman a flirtatious smile.

The gray-haired Indian looked at the old woman with a mixture of gratitude, admiration and horror. In that moment he wasn't certain which of the females in close proximity frightened him more. All he could manage to utter was, "No! I am not!"

Ibutho rode the young male to the ground, tumbling in a roll over its head when its face impacted sod. The warrior whirled and hurled one of his short spears, piercing the young male through an eye socket as it struggled to rise. Julie let one of her throwing knives fly. It pierced the creature's other eye. The beast collapsed and was still. Thunderous howls and roars erupted from the remaining demons and Yakwawiak at the sight of the fallen monster.

The battle scene darkened as thick, clouds obscured the sun. Bewildered eyes looked up. Simon stood on the roof of the mobile home, his arms extended upward as if summoning the clouds and darkness. A shape-shifter leapt up to take down the shaman's apprentice. It swung its axe only to see it break in half before hitting Simon, the axe head spinning off into the forest. The demon took two steps back, a look of horror on its face.

The tall sentinel materialized next to Simon, who was in a trance-like state softly chanting and glowing brightly in the thickening gloom. The new arrival's drawn sword shone like the sun, his own brightness matching that of his gold armor and white tunic. Piercing blue eyes assessed the situation, his long blonde hair dancing in the wind. Demons recoiled, Yakwawiak snarled, humans gasped but all were transfixed. Then his sword swung with speed that made its arc look solid for a millisecond and the rooftop shape-shifter exploded into ash.

One of the remaining demons attempted to summon a portal to create an escape route. The dark disc opened behind the monsters, between them and the woods. But with a *WHOOSH* a second portal opened in front of the first, this one radiant. From it leapt two more sentinels differing from the first only in the color of their skin and hair, and, like their companion on the roof, this time they were visible to all. One had distinctly Native American features and the other appeared Asian. They crossed their swords and lowered them. Both portals closed behind them top to bottom like windows, following the motion of the swords. However the fight would end, it would do so in the realm of humans.

The new arrivals engaged the shape-shifters in fierce fighting. Swords flashed and clashed, axes delivered blow after blow. The combat had its desired effect by taking some pressure off the outnumbered and hard-pressed humans.

The female Yakwawi's blow came down hard and fast with a roar, her talons stopping millimeters from the shaman's face. In confusion, she looked down to see a spear all but completely buried in her abdomen, thrust there by Ibutho. The shaman threw an arm around Mrs. Adelman and whisked her toward the home's front door, taking advantage of precious seconds bought by Ibutho's courage. The warrior was unable to dodge the female's second swing. A sickening *SMACK* was heard above the din of renewed battle and Ibutho flew like a rag doll over the driveway, skidding along the grass on the other side.

Jake advanced on the wounded female working the lever action of his rifle between head shots placed with perfect precision. She staggered back with each impact, struggling to remain upright. Then the male came out of nowhere to step between Jake and his target, hoisting one of the planters to crush the scientist.

The planter fell and smashed harmlessly on the walkway. Yakwawiak screamed and tried to shield their eyes. Deep, intense, reddish light engulfed the monsters. The Skyray materialized hovering overhead with Dr. Smythe visible at the controls through the cockpit windows. Spotlights beneath the craft were bathing both beasts with intense infrared light, most of which wasn't visible to the humans below as anything other than a projected blood-red glow. Jake's idea was having the desired effect on the monsters. They were disoriented and seemed to physically weaken. Julie didn't hesitate.

Her strong legs propelled her from a planter to a railing along the home's front steps and from there to the roof. She crouched just for a moment, like a panther ready to pounce. In that moment the rooftop sentinel rushed forward and merged his form with Julie. Only Simon saw what was happening as two beings became one. Julie was only aware of an instantaneous surge of incredible strength, courage and an acute awareness of the battle before her. A new light source appeared. Julie's eyes shone like bright sapphire-blue stars on a moonless night. She pushed off the roof, summersaulted in the air and drew her sword to strike as she flew at the big male.

The monster's head snapped back. Its jaws opened to receive the woman, the silhouette of her form growing larger as it blocked out more and more of the red spotlight. It felt a surge of grotesque delight in anticipation of the taste of Julie's blood. Then it saw her eyes — bright, intense, sapphire blue eyes projecting supreme confidence, power and vengeance, her face broadcasting a look of righteous judgement and ... a smirk?

The beast reacted fast. The woman was faster. She struck, her sword momentarily inscribing a brilliant arc of silver-blue fire on the reddish gloom cast over the battle. She kicked off the massive chest and landed on the grass in a three-point stance, one arm extended out to her side, sword in hand. A large grotesque head landed beside her with a squishy thump, a look of alarm and abject terror on its face. The colossal headless corpse crashed to the ground behind Julie a second later and she snapped her piercing gaze toward the female.

Cora and Dom were pouring bullets from their P90s into the backs of her ankles. Tol was unloading a bolt gun into her torso. He'd come down from the roof and was steadily advancing on the big carnivore. Jake was nearest and closing in with his rifle.

CLANG!

The rifle flew from Jake's hands, sent flying by an uppercut from a shape-shifter's battle axe. Without missing a beat, Jake grabbed the demon's weapon and kicked the wolf-human hard in the gut. It staggered backwards and then slammed forward hard into the ground to reveal Julie looking down on it in a Wing Chun ready stance. She twirled her sword into a vertical hold for a finishing stab into the demon.

"Julie wait!" shouted Jake extending a palm toward her. Axe in hand, he pivoted just as the female started to fall forward. Jake bolted under her, turned, and planted the axe end of the weapon into the ground before jumping aside just as the monster's lower jaw hit the spear point. He ran up a forearm of the impaled, quivering beast, drew a Bowie knife from his belt and plunged it into the base of the shaking skull. The quivering stopped. Jake nodded at Julie, and the last demon disintegrated instantly when her blade pinned it. Jake lurched on the creature's back when the weapon through its head turned to ash a moment later, and he rolled off it into Julie's arms.

Glowing sapphire eyes returned to normal as the sentinel detached itself from Julie. She and Jake exchanged a look. A nod. Then they ran.

The shaman was already kneeling at Jeff's side when Julie got there. The Aussie's eyes were open and seemed to brighten at the sight of Julie but he wasn't able to move, his spine shattered. She glanced up at the medicine man. He somberly shook his head slightly.

"Hey, hero," said Julie as tears began to well up in her eyes. "Who asked you to save the damsel in distress?"

Jeff's lips quivered as he tried to speak. He coughed up blood. There was a low, ominous rumble as he tried to breath. "P-p-lease p-p-pray," was all he could manage, his eyes held Julie's in a pleading gaze.

Julie looked up at the shaman with an uncharacteristic look of helplessness. "I...what...I don't... how?"

The shaman extended a hand and gently touched her shoulder. "He's held on for you. Whatever you say will bring comfort."

Julie turned back to look into Jeff's pleading eyes and couldn't contain a sob. Tears flowed down her cheeks as she stammered saying the only prayer she knew. "Our Father...who art in heaven..."

Jeff tried a smile as she finished but it was difficult. His dimming eyes turned to the shaman who put his ear close to the dying man's face. "She'll... be... alright."

The old man gave Jeff a reassuring smile and the Aussie was gone.

Cora cradled Ibutho's head in her lap. The warrior winced in pain as Simon probed his chest and side.

"That's three broken ribs, my brave friend," he noted. "And a compound leg fracture in addition to a certain concussion. You don't do anything small, do you?"

"I think he'll make it but we need to get him back to Sanctum," Cora observed with concern.

"This will help," said Simon as he injected Ibutho with a potent pain reliever from a medical kit.

"I'll get us a stretcher from the Skyray as soon as it lands," announced Jake. He and Tol stood over the big African watching Cora and Simon tend to him.

"It has," said Smythe arriving on the scene with a folding stretcher under his arm. "I'll leave this with you as I'll have a good deal of explaining to do when the sheriff and his deputies arrive in a few minutes. Best not delay. Let's get Ibutho out of here."

"And Jeff?" asked Jake looking over toward the home.

Smythe hung his head for a moment. "He will be sorely missed."

The news hit the team members hard. They hurried in solemn silence to finish preparing Ibutho as best they could. Cora, Tol, Jake and Simon each took a handle on the corners of the stretcher and carried the wounded warrior to the stealth aircraft parked on the lawn near the forest's edge.

"C'mon, son, ya gotta try my sweet cornbread," Mrs. Adelman pleaded extending a plate with one hand toward Dom. "And wash it down with some of Kentucky's finest right here." She held out the whisky bottle in the other. He was in the mobile home with Everley and the old woman awaiting instructions on what to do with them.

"I'm not ungrateful, ma'am, but I am on duty," Dom replied.

"Nonsense," the woman chided. "We just gave them werewolves and Bigfoots a spankin' that even got the attention of angels above. Merciful Lord I done seen it myself! They was dern handsome what with the shiny armor and short skirts an' all."

"I believe those were tunics, ma'am," corrected Dom.

"Toooon-icks?" the woman replied. "Don't change nuthin'. There ain't been that much action in these parts since Prohibition."

"Sir," interrupted Everley. "I'm former U.S. Army and know a soldier when I see one. I'm also pretty sure you can't let us leave here for fear we'll talk about what just happened. Let's cut to the chase. What will you do with us? Kill us?"

"No," answered Dom. "In these situations there are usually two options. A drug that will erase all memory of what you've experienced in the last few hours is one."

"What's the other 'un?" asked Mrs. Adelman, the whisky beginning to have effect.

Dom took Everley aside and left the old woman giggling in her kitchen. "Mr. Everley, I don't think there's a second option for her," he said tilting his head toward the kitchen. "But you showed some real skill and a can-do, cool-under-fire composure out there we don't often see. I suspect you'll be getting a visit from a tall British gentleman either shortly or in the near future. He may have an offer for you. But for now, being ex-military, I need you to understand what happened here cannot get out."

"Understood, sir," Everley affirmed. "I don't claim to be the brightest man in the world but I know a threat to national security when I see one. Can I ask you something?"

"You can ask," Dom replied.

"Just what were we dealing with out there? Aliens? Mutants? A government science program gone terribly wrong?"

"I'm sorry, Mr. Everley, but the less you know at this stage the better. And let me assure you that very soon it either won't matter because you'll have no recollection of it, or you'll be looking at the universe in a whole new way."

"And her?" Everley nodded toward the kitchen where Mrs. Adelman had started singing to her dog. "Memory wipe?"

Dom chuckled when he looked at the woman. "Seems like she's well on her way to that all by herself."

Chapter Forty-One

Two deputies in a county patrol vehicle were racing down a gravel road in response to a "shots fired" call that identified Mrs. Adelman's place as the location. Such calls typically didn't alarm them as gunfire in rural southeast Kentucky isn't uncommon in the fall. It's a prime destination for hunters and some seasons were open. But the two men were on high alert as they approached that morning because the complaint had mentioned the possibility of machine guns, and that likely meant something drug-related.

They'd just rounded the last bend in the road before the turn up the driveway when the driver slammed on the brakes. Standing in the middle of the road before them was a pair of large, well-built men wearing short tunics and what appeared to be armor. Once certain the deputies had a good look at them, the two sentinels took off running down the road past the turnoff into the Adelman place. The deputies gave chase, marveling at how their suspects managed to stay just ahead of their SUV, even at speeds higher than 40 mph on the curvy road through the forested hills.

"You have my gratitude, Jehoel," Smythe turned from watching the deputies pass by on the road below to look at the large blonde sentinel standing next to him halfway up the driveway to Mrs. Adelman's home. "May I ask what brought about your welcome intervention on our behalf?"

"We were ordered to do so," the sentinel replied, gazing off into the distance as if Smythe was a distraction from something more important that needed to be done.

"Did He personally send you?" Smythe asked.

"No. Not personally."

Smythe chose his next words carefully. "I know there is interest in at least one of our new arrivals. You were watching Simon at the lodge?"

"I was not the only one doing so."

"Why? Why Simon? Why now?"

"Simon has a role to play," the sentinel replied as he finally turned to look at the Brit. "But he is not the only reason we gave assistance today."

"Why then? Was it concern for the battle's outcome?" Smythe probed.

"No."

"Was it the girl?"

There was no reply. Smythe changed the subject to try another approach. "We lost Jeff today, and Ibutho is in pretty rough shape. But I suppose you know that already," Smythe noted.

"Yes. Ibutho will heal. He always has. There was rejoicing when Jeff arrived. He fought bravely and well, as he has for a long time."

"You saw him after...?" Smythe went too far.

"Enough, Jon. I've likely told you too much already. My role is that of messenger and, when it needs to be, warrior. Compassion moved me to share what I just did. Now I must go."

"Before you do, Jehoel," Smythe persisted. "You merged with a member of my team. You saw her soul and her mind while you were united?"

"Yes."

"And?"

"My commander summons," the sentinel replied curtly turning his gaze again to the distant horizon. "Goodbye for now, Jon."

The sentinel's two companions appeared as if teleported behind Smythe. They'd drawn the deputies to where the road ended in a trailhead and led them into the woods on foot before leaving that area abruptly to rejoin their fellow warrior. The three of them then strode off into the woods together and vanished, leaving Smythe to contemplate the sentinel's words alone as he walked up the driveway deep in thought. He approached Cora, who was speaking with Everley at the base of the Skyray's loading ramp.

"We're loaded and ready to go, Dr. Smythe," Cora reported.

"Thank you, Cora. A word please Mr. Everley?"

Cora boarded the craft leaving the two men alone. They spoke for a couple of minutes after which Everley came to attention and saluted Smythe. The Brit smiled and acknowledged the gesture before boarding.

The Skyray cloaked as it rose and disappeared into the late-morning sky. Two furniture delivery trucks rolled up the driveway a moment later, along with a big glass and siding repair van. The vehicles disgorged teams of professional-looking men and women clad in coveralls sporting logos that identified which vehicle they were associated with. One team went to work loading Yakwawi carcasses into one of the furniture trucks. Another set about removing damaged furnishings from Mrs. Adelman's home and replacing them with exact copies from the other truck. Her dog, Buster, watched from the lap of the old woman as she slept soundly in an old recliner, oblivious to the work going on around her. It took a little more than an hour for the skilled workers to return the home to the state it had been in before the morning's events.

Just before noon, the trucks pulled away down the driveway and passed the sheriff's deputies who were pulling in. Everley stood in the yard next to a beautifully restored 1987 Dodge Prospector pickup, installing a cross-bed toolbox in the back. Smythe had offered him the truck, which he was to explain had been a surprise gift of gratitude from Mrs. Adelman for his many projects at her place, in exchange for the wreck that was his old truck along with some guarantees. The deputies got out and approached the handyman.

"G'morning Mr. Everley. Nice truck you got there," one of the lawmen began.

"Thanks Deputy Williams. Good morning Carson." The second deputy had gone to high school with Everley so they were on a first-name basis.

"Howdy, Zack," Carson greeted. "We've had quite the morning. Chased us some wannabe hippie streakers down the road into the woods on our way here to check on someone supposedly shooting a machine gun. You wouldn't know anything about that, would you?"

"Sure enough do," Everley wiped his hands and faced the deputies. "I got here early this morning to help Mrs. Adelman fix some siding and take delivery of some new furniture. When I drove up there was a drift of wild hogs passing through her yard. Had my revolver and some speed loaders so I put a bunch of rounds downrange at 'em. Think I hit a couple but they didn't go down. No machine gun but I was shooting pretty fast and can see how echoes off the hills might have made me sound like one. That Colt Python of mine is quite loud."

"Where's the gun now, Mr. Everley?" asked Deputy Williams following protocol.

"Put away in the glove box. Take a look if you like. And you'll recall I do have a permit."

"That won't be necessary," Williams replied. "House looks nice, truck looks nice and it's a right fine day. We'll let you get back to work."

"See you in church Sunday?" asked Carson.

"Oh, you can count on that," Everley replied a bit too emphatically before catching himself. "I mean I dropped a hutch on my toe and cussed up some mighty un-Christian phrases so I feel like I need a good soul-cleansing."

Both lawmen chuckled and got back into their vehicle. Carson gave a wave as they went down the driveway. Everley waved back and smiled. As soon as they were gone, the handyman dropped to his knees and vomited.

When he'd finished, he rolled to rest his back against a truck tire and stared at the sky, tears streaming down his cheeks. The intensity of the morning had finally caught up with him and he let them flow for several minutes in a needed release of post-combat stress. He thought it would take considerable time for his brain and emotions to link up again. He felt moisture on his hand. Buster was licking him. A folding camp chair plopped down beside him.

"Good day, Mr. Everley," said Mrs. Adelman. She sat down on the chair and handed him a cold can of soda before popping the top on one of her own. "You been busy. The house looks real nice, like ya painted it or some-thin'. And ya must've cleaned for me while I overslept cuz everything looks all nice and shiny, almost like new. Anyhow, let me tell ya 'bout this weird dream I had. Seems there was these Bigfoots after my flowers..."

Everley tuned the woman out, returned his gaze to the sky and took a long drink of soda. The sweet bubbly fluid tasted better than he could have imagined in that moment. He looked at the can. Ginger ale. Somehow he thought that both strange and appropriate but didn't know why.

Chapter Forty-Two

The mood aboard the Albatross was somber. Jeff's body lay covered by a blanket on a table in the cargo bay. Ibutho was on a cot a few feet away resting, an IV dripping needed pain medication and antibiotics into the warrior's body. Cora sat on the floor beside him tenderly holding and stroking his hand. Dom and Tol watched from jump seats still clad in their tactical gear, weapons beside them.

"This was not to be," said the shaman. He and Dr. Smythe stood together at the front of the cargo bay taking in the sight of the battered and broken team dealing with grief and concern. "It was to have been me."

"It would seem He who is the arbiter of such things disagrees," replied Smythe, his face expressionless. "I won't say he was too young. I will say he had much untapped potential and his departure leaves a certain…emptiness. He will be missed."

"I was ready," the shaman remarked. "I was certain it was my turn to journey to the realm of spirits at the Sky Road's end. It seems I am not yet worthy."

"You are wrong, old friend," said Smythe turning to the medicine man, putting a hand on his shoulder. "Surely you know better. That none of us are or ever will be worthy in and of ourselves. All have transgressed. After all we've seen and been through together, I am certain He's prepared a special place for you. But it seems that Jeff's place was completed first. Why, we'll never know in this plain."

"You speak truth, Jon. Yet stating what is already known does not quickly comfort mourning hearts. How many times have we looked upon the fallen and wounded? Frequency doesn't make it easier."

"No it does not," the Brit replied. "The Watch hasn't lost a team member in years. Today brings back so many memories. Images of sorrow and valor, horror and hope. Our work is so vital, yet it is also so…lonely."

"It was not always so," the shaman noted. "We had wives, families and dear friends. We've known joy in the midst of sadness. Would that such feelings from the past were eternal in this realm."

"He told us we'd have trials and sorrows here," said Smythe. "And that surely has been the case."

"But must it always be so, Jon? You and I have had the fullness of what this life offers. What of these and others of The Watch? Some among us have not had the opportunity to know the joy and sorrow of true love and companionship. That is something we need to address."

"Perhaps," said Smythe. "Now is not the time. I must prepare to bury our dead and ensure the recovery of our wounded. Please excuse me. I want to be sure Sanctum is making all the necessary preparations for our arrival."

Smythe walked first to Jeff's body. He put a hand on the head under the blanket and bowed in silent prayer. After a few minutes, he knelt beside Ibutho opposite Cora. Smythe spoke to her briefly and then whispered something into the wounded man's ear. He then went over to Dom and Tol. The two soldiers rose as he approached. The three spoke softly for a while. Smythe put his hands on a shoulder of each man before motioning with his head for them to sit and rest again. Then the Brit disappeared into a door at the front of the cargo area to leave the solemn vigil behind.

Julie scrubbed as hard as she could between sobs. No matter how many times she washed and rinsed herself, the shower and soap couldn't clean away her sense of guilt over Jeff's death. Over and over she replayed the battle in her mind, each time trying to come up with something she could have done, a move she could have anticipated, anything at all that could have resulted in a different outcome. She couldn't. There were too many variables, too many moving parts, too many opponents for her to see an outcome other than the one that occurred. She'd been in many fights. Some with multiple adversaries. She'd been hurt, bruised and cut. But she'd never lost a partner on duty. Until the Yakwawi fatally swatted Jeff like some insignificant insect.

Turning off the water, Julie dried herself and wrapped the towel around her body. The tears stopped as she dug deep inside for the resolve she was convinced made her strong. Jeff had died saving her as she tried to save a civilian. Ibutho was hurt saving the shaman as the shaman tried to save a civilian. When it came down to it in her mind, the whole operation was about The Watch saving people, the same thing cops put it all on the line to do every day. Somehow, putting what had happened in that context took some of the edge off Julie's sorrow and sense of remorse.

She took a small blow-dryer off a mount on the wall beside the sink and turned it on. Then she turned it off, staring at her reflection in a mirror as a new line of thought took over. She'd jumped off a roof with a sword and decapitated a monster. What had happened was clear in her mind. But for the first time since the fight she allowed herself to wonder how it had happened.

Getting up on the roof wasn't that hard. Off the planter, off the railing and up. But the monster was a good 20 feet away when she'd pushed off from a crouch with enough height and momentum to follow through with a sword swing. She wasn't certain, but thought she remembered from her time on the track team in high school that the world-record long jump without a running start was around 12 feet. That realization bothered her.

And though she'd loved her training with swords and felt confident using one, reflection on the power and precision required to slice completely through a heavily muscled, almost non-existent neck with a single stroke while flying through the air gave her pause. Facing the mirror she asked herself, *"Am I that good? Or just that lucky?"* She gasped and dropped the hair dryer, clutching her towel close with one hand, the other over her mouth. For a moment, and only for a moment, as she'd been staring at her reflection, her eyes had gone from their usual deep blue to a pair intense sapphire-colored lights and back again. Had it been her imagination? A hallucination brought on by a physically and emotionally taxing day? Yes, she decided. That was it. It had to be. She hurriedly put on her underwear, leggings and a polo shirt before heading down the hall to the forward passenger area.

Dr. Jake Sanders sat in the aircraft's conference room alone with his laptop computer. Though exhausted, he couldn't rest. The coffee onboard was exceptionally good. He poured a third cup from the carafe a member of the crew had brought him.

The screen before him displayed four open windows, each showing video of the incident in Kentucky from a different angle. One view was footage taken by the Skyray, and the others were from small camera drones launched from the aircraft when they'd first arrived on the scene. Jake was going over them a sixth time, pausing occasionally to take notes on a legal pad. The imagery was exceptionally clear and graphic.

Jake used the computer to measure and catalog everything he could about the creatures they'd encountered. He was driven by intense desire to find vulnerabilities in the Yakwawiak and what Smythe had called "demons" so The Watch would have an advantage if such monsters were encountered again. Each time he ran through the footage he came to the same conclusion. As bravely as the team had fought, they'd likely have lost had it not been for the intervention of those he called "super-humans" in his notes. It was their intervention against the "demons" that gave the team the ability to concentrate on taking down the Yakwawiak. Of the eleven wolf-human beasts that charged from the trees, Julie had killed two. He, Ibutho and Jeff each killed one. The other six were dispatched in savage fighting with the super-humans after Jeff and Ibutho had been taken out of the fight. Though the team's special metal bullets knocked them down and seemed to weaken them, they were not very efficient when it came to killing them. Julie's sword and Ibutho's spears worked better but necessitated getting dangerously close. Jeff had gotten his with multiple torso hits from a bolt gun but that was the exception. Edged weapons seemed to be key. And it wasn't lost on him that the super-humans also fought with swords. And just who…or what…were those big warriors that could apparently open and close portals at will? Jake needed time to think. He closed the laptop, tucked it under his arm, grabbed his coffee and exited the conference room.

"I wondered when you would want to talk," said Simon Standing Elk. He sat in one of two generously padded lounge chairs looking out the window at a carpet of high clouds passing below, a ginger ale can on the small round table between them. He'd sensed the shaman enter the room but did not turn to face him.

"To say you helped today would be an understatement," the shaman noted as he slipped into the chair across the table from Simon. "When did you learn to summon clouds and darkness in the middle of the day?"

"To learn means to acquire a skill or knowledge, Wicasa. I did neither."

"Please help me understand, Simon. What made you decide to climb up on the roof, strike a pose like Moses parting the Red Sea, and beseech The Great Spirit to blot out the sun for our IR spotlights?"

231

"The blonde spirit warrior. If that's what he is. He called to me from the roof and I obeyed."

The shaman paused for a moment to consider where the conversation should go. "You can see the sentinels even when they choose not to reveal themselves to the rest of us?"

"Whether or not and when others can see them I do not know, Wicasa. But I can. Are you also able to see them?"

"Yes. If they so choose," the shaman answered. "How long have you had this gift?"

"Since Julie pointed a gun in my face."

"In the plane? Before the Black Hills mission?"

"Yes."

"What did you see then?"

"A woman," replied Simon. "A beautiful woman. She stood very close to Julie and whispered prayers of forgiveness in her ear."

"Simon, please think carefully before you answer this. Did the female sentinel on the plane know you could see her when others did not?"

"Yes. And though I can't be certain, I think it surprised her."

"Hmmm," was all the shaman managed in response.

"This concerns you, Wicasa?"

"I do not know how to answer that, Simon. We call these beings sentinels. They are watchers, guardians and messengers. They serve The Great Spirit."

"So do we, Wicasa. But we are not angels. Are they?"

"To call them such would be... incomplete."

"What do they want with us?"

"Nothing, Simon. Nothing at all."

"Yet they have been my helpers and allies since I first saw one," noted Simon.

"Perhaps longer, my friend. Longer than you realize."

Simon swiveled his chair to face the shaman. "You've had past dealings with them?"

"On many occasions."

"What do they want with me?" asked Simon. "What is their interest in helping me?"

"Are you asking me for help, Simon?"

"Yes, Wicasa."

"Then perhaps there is hope for you yet."

Chapter Forty-Three

Two weeks later...

"You're late. A couple of weeks late," Julie chided playfully having opened the door of her room to find Jake standing there awkwardly with a small bouquet of wildflowers in his hand. "Aw, flowers. How sweet."

Jake thrust the flowers toward her more quickly than he'd have liked. He'd been so stunned by Julie's appearance he'd forgotten them in his hand.

"I'll just put these in some water and we can be on our way," said Julie as she accepted the gift and twirled away toward a vase on her nightstand, the hem of her light blue sundress rising to her thighs and falling back into place.

Jake couldn't take his eyes off her. The dress, her long blonde hair in a ponytail tied with a matching ribbon and a pair of red cowgirl boots triggered shades of Dorothy's visit to Oz in his mind for a moment. Then a pang of guilt stabbed him when memories of Gail flashed in his mind.

"It's okay, Jake," said Julie taking his arm and bringing him back to the present and seeming to know his thoughts. "We're just a couple of friends enjoying an evening together. Let's have some fun."

Sanctum's so-called "personal" dining area consisted of several booths in a room adjacent to the cafeteria. The lighting was low, but not overly so, and the motif was nautical. Walls were adorned with paintings of sailing ships from bygone generations interspersed with artifacts that included navigation tools, fishing and whaling equipment, clothing items and smaller items a sailor might bring aboard.

Julie ordered baked swordfish with rice pilaf and buttered asparagus. Jake opted for lightly breaded sirloin tips, a baked potato with butter and sour cream, and grilled green beans with bacon bits. By mutual agreement, conversation steered away from Sanctum and The Watch. Jake listened with interest as Julie spoke of her studies and training in the Far East. They learned they'd been in China at the same time when Jake related a story about working with the government to establish new protocols for protecting that country's nearly extinct tiger population.

Following dinner, the pair went for a stroll in Sanctum's botanical garden. Among the tropical plants and flowers were some that had been saved from extinction or were unknown prior to discovery by The Watch. Here and there along the path were sitting areas for people to read, chat, meditate or pray. Though Jake and Julie weren't alone in the garden, it was quiet and far from crowded. They opted to sit on a long, sofa-like piece of furniture across from an array of fragrant flowers displaying a rainbow of color. The pair's mood became somber.

"I recognize several of those flowers from Jeff's funeral," Julie remarked.

"As do I," confirmed Jake. "It was an impressive service. And I had no idea Sanctum had that many personnel. There must have been a couple thousand people there. Jeff was well-liked."

"The music was amazing with so many singing," Julie reflected. "And Dr. Smythe's eulogy was inspiring. It's incredible that someone so young could have crammed so much life into so short a time."

"It would be, if I could believe it were true," noted Jake turning to Julie beside him. "But call it a gut instinct or educated guess. I think some of the people here at Sanctum are much older than they let on. Don't ask me how it's possible, but I feel it."

"You're right, Jake. In fact, I'm certain of it. Has Cora told you the story of how she and Ibutho met?"

"No. Not yet."

Julie recounted the conversation she and Cora had on the Albatross coming back from the Black Hills. Then she related the conversation she'd had with Jeff on the beach as Jake listened intently. She'd just finished when Simon Standing Elk rounded a bend on the walking path and approached them.

"May I sit with you a while?" he asked.

Jake motioned to a chair to their left at the edge of the small sitting area. The trio was engaged in friendly conversation when Cora came down the path pushing Ibutho in a wheelchair. He wore a loud flowered shirt that rivaled the garden's blooms in bright colors and his floppy straw hat sat atop his head. The big African's leg was in a cast jutting out in front of them like a battering ram. A large leather-bound book was in his lap.

"Looks like this is a popular place this evening," said Cora with a smile. "I try to get here a few times a week. It's good for my soul. And it's also a chance to get this guy out of physical therapy and into a more calming environment. Moses said we might find you here, Julie. Ibutho has something for you."

Julie and Jake exchanged knowing glances confirming their suspicions that The Watch was still keeping track of them. When Cora pushed the wheelchair close to Julie, the woman rose and put a hand on Ibutho's arm.

"It's great to see you out and about, Ibutho," said Julie. "How is your recovery going?"

"Miss Julie, you look lovely this evening. Your beauty rivals that of my shirt," Ibutho answered with a grin and Julie bobbed a curtsy with a smile of her own. "The spirit is willing, but the flesh is too slow I am sad to say," Ibutho continued. "Dr. Wu says I have a few more weeks before we'll be sparring again in the gym. I brought you this." He extended the big book with both hands.

"What is it?" asked Julie, momentarily struggling with the weight of the massive book. "Whoa! Definitely not light reading."

"It's Jeff's Bible," answered Cora. "He had only a few possessions but indicated in his will what he'd like done with them if something happened. Strangely, he submitted a new will and testament three days before his last mission. It stipulated that his Bible was to go to you, Julie. That book meant a lot to him. And he left you these, Jake."

Cora reached into a pouch on the back of the wheelchair and withdrew a box made of fine polished hardwood, handing it to Jake. He undid the brass latches and opened the top to reveal an interior lined with purple felt and pair of authentic Australian boomerangs. They were flawless and painted with elaborate aboriginal designs.

"I don't know what to say," Jake remarked. "They're beautiful."

"And they really do fly and come back," noted Ibutho. "He made those himself and practiced often. A man of many skills, Jeff was."

"Well we won't disrupt your evening any more than we have," said Cora. "Besides. It's getting close to bedtime for Ibutho."

"Why do you not let me have fun, Cora?" the warrior complained. "I miss spending time with our friends."

"Because Dr. Wu will certainly let me know if I keep you out too late," explained Cora in a motherly tone. "And she says you must rest to let your bones heal properly."

"Here my large friend," said Simon with a smile as he extended a small pouch toward Ibutho. "Ginger chews. The shaman says they're good for everything. It helps that they're tasty."

Ibutho eagerly accepted the pouch, took out a candy and popped it into his mouth. Moments later he took off his big hat and fanned it in front of his face.

"OOOOO," the man cooed. "Sweet and zingy. I like. You must bring me more tomorrow."

"I will stop by with a whole box as soon as the shaman shares his secret about how to make them," said Simon. "Rest well."

Cora smiled and wheeled Ibutho away down the path as he waved goodbye with his hat and continued to make sounds of satisfaction with each bite of candy.

"Guys, look at this," said Julie as soon as they were gone. Jeff's Bible was an old one. Julie had it open on her lap and pointed out to the others that it was a family Bible edition published by C. Cooke in London in the 1760s. The three admired the book's beautiful illustrations as Julie carefully turned over pages. There were voluminous notes in the margins, presumably written by Jeff. It was clear he spent a great deal of time studying the writings.

The trio spent several minutes with the book. As Julie paged through the Gospel of John, it seemed to naturally fall open on the twenty-first chapter. Notations on the page were even more than what they'd seen on others.

"Notice," said Simon. "Discoloration of the parchment around those verses there. As though someone ran a finger across them many times. What does it say?"

Julie read the verses to them.

"Peter seeing him saith to Jesus, Lord, and what shall this man do? Jesus saith unto him, If I will that he tarry till I come, what is that to thee? Follow thou me. Then went this saying abroad among the brethren, that that disciple should not die: yet Jesus said not unto him, He shall not die; but, If I will that he tarry till I come, what is that to thee? This is the disciple which testifieth of these things, and wrote these things: and we know that his testimony is true."

"The apostle John wrote these words?" asked Simon.

"I was told in the Jesuit schools I attended that he authored the gospel," affirmed Jake.

"And that's what I learned as a child in Sunday school," confirmed Julie. Simon's brow furrowed as if deep in thought. "Is something wrong?" asked Julie.

"The twenty-first chapter, verse twenty-two," replied Simon. "The number 2122 kept flashing in my mind during the vision I had before our last confrontation with the Yakwawiak. The passage seems to be a discussion between Jesus and his followers about how some of them were to die. How did the apostle John die?"

"I'll have to look it up," answered Jake. "I seem to recall most of the original twelve disciples met gruesome ends. All but one that is. Keep in mind it's been years since I had to study such things, but I think John was the only one said to have died of natural causes."

"Natural causes?" asked Julie with a hint of suspicion. "Tell me there's a grave somewhere."

"I think there's a church in Asia supposedly built on his grave," said Jake with uncertainty in his voice.

"Supposedly?" asked Julie.

"Why the interest in such things, Julie?" asked Simon.

"Well," she answered, "Jake and I were talking before you joined us. We think there's a possibility people here, at least some of them, may be a lot older than they let on. Probably a wacky notion, but humor me for a minute. What if the John we're reading about here somehow didn't die?"

"C'mon, Julie, that's a big stretch with not a lot to go on," said Jake.

"Agreed," she replied. "But think about it for a moment. How much knowledge, wisdom, insight, wealth and, yes, power, could a person acquire over a period of, say, two thousand years? It sounds like a crazy movie plot, but imagine traveling around the world visiting and learning from different cultures over several centuries. Think of the technological insights a person could glean from blending advances discovered in disparate people groups."

"Julie, I…" Jake began before Simon interrupted.

"Wait, Jake," he said. "Just consider for a moment what she says. And, though I'll admit it sounds insane at the moment, consider the first name of the person in charge at this place."

"Jonathan. Jonathan Smythe. But c'mon you two, he's British," Jake protested. "The name's a coincidence. And someone living hundreds of years?"

"Gentlemen." said Julie holding up a yellowed piece of folded parchment up for them to see. "You might want to take a look at this. It was tucked between the leather and the spine of the Bible. I don't think anyone knew it was there."

Jake carefully took the delicate paper from Julie, gently opened it, and read a note bearing the marks of having been written with a quill and ink. A moment later he dropped it on the ground. "No. No. I can't accept the implications," he said wagging his head.

Simon stooped to retrieve the note and read it aloud.

My dearest young Geoffrey,

Accept these sacred writings as a gift of deepest gratitude for your uncommon valor in vanquishing the yahoo devil creature that has so long vexed the farmers of our colony. May Our Heavenly Father guide and protect you along life's path.

With great affection and thanks,
Richard Johnson, Chaplain
Sydney Cove, New South Wales
June 6, 1789

"Oh," said Simon. "This seems to open a doorway to new questions and possibilities, doesn't it?"

The sound of one person slowly clapping echoed in the office of Dr. Jonathan Smythe as the man watched the trio in the garden on a live video feed from a security camera.

"Indeed it does, Simon Standing Elk. Indeed it does."

About the author

Dan Carlson's journey has taken him down many paths. Meteorologist, business owner, journalist, teacher, pastor, author and writer, threat analyst and futurist, he lives with his wife of more than 30 years on a farm in western Nebraska. In addition to writing, Dan's many interests include fishing, hunting, military aviation and military history, geopolitical analysis, cryptozoology and storm chasing. Follow him on Facebook at www.facebook.com/danqcarlson, and visit his websites at www.dancarlsonwrites.com and www.dancarlson.net.

Made in the USA
Middletown, DE
15 December 2020

27785774R00149